THE TREE OF LIFE

AND OTHER TALES OF THE BIOTECH REVOLUTION

by

Brian Stableford

The Borgo Press
An Imprint of Wildside Press

MMVII

Copyright © 1991, 1993, 1994, 1995, 1999, 2001, 2002,
2007 by Brian Stableford

All rights reserved.
No part of this book may be reproduced in any
form without the expressed written consent of the
publisher. Printed in the United States of America.

FIRST EDITION

CONTENTS

Introduction 5
The Tree of Life 7
The Skin Trade 35
Out of Touch 50
Skin Deep 74
Carriers 96
Rogue Terminator 115
The Home Front 136
Hidden Agendas 154

About the Author 199

INTRODUCTION

The eight stories in this collection belong to a loosely-knit series tracking the potential effects of possible developments in biotechnology on the evolution of global society. Most involve relatively moderate variations of the future history sketched out in a series of novels comprising *Inherit the Earth* (1998), *Architects of Emortality* (1999), *The Fountains of Youth* (2000), *The Cassandra Complex* (2001), *Dark Ararat* (2002) and *The Omega Expedition* (2002), all published by Tor, which was itself a modified version of a future history mapped in *The Third Millennium: A History of the World 200-3000 A.D.* (Sidgwick & Jackson 1985, written in collaboration with David Langford).

The broad sweep of this future history envisages a large-scale economic and ecological collapse in the twenty-first century brought about by global warming and other factors, followed by the emergence of a global society designed to accommodate human longevity (although that is not necessarily obvious in stories set in advance of the Crash). Other stories of a similar stripe can be found in two earlier collections, *Sexual Chemistry: Sardonic Tales of the Genetic Revolution* (Simon & Schuster U.K. 1991) and *Designer Genes: Tales of the Biotech Revolution* (Five Star, 2004), and in two companion collection from Borgo/Wildside, *The Cure for Love and Other Tales of the Biotech Revolution* and *In the Flesh and Other Tales of the Biotech Revolution*.

Six of the stories included here first appeared in *Asimov's Science Fiction*, "Carriers" in the July 1993 issue, "The Tree of Life" in the September 1994 issue, "Out of Touch" in the October 1995 issue, "The Skin Trade" in the November 1995 issue, "Hidden Agendas" in the September

1999 issue, and "Rogue Terminator" in the April 2001 issue. "Skin Deep" first appeared in the October 1991 issue of *Amazing Stories*, and "The Home Front" in *The DAW 30th Anniversary Anthology: Science Fiction* (DAW, 2002), edited by Elizabeth R. Wollheim and Shelia E. Gilbert.

THE TREE OF LIFE

The clamor of the wind in the trees kept me awake all night, although I was calm enough in myself. It must have been nearly dawn—the darkest hour, according to rumor—when I finally drifted off. I slept for a long time and my dreams were pleasant; when I woke up the storm had blown itself out and the sky was blue again. After the strident night the gentle afternoon seemed preternaturally quiet.

I went out to inspect the damage to the house, confident that it would be trivial. Grandfather was no architect, but he had been fully aware of the dangers of tropical storms when he had erected the windowed façade to mask, protect and let a little light into the living-quarters and workplaces burrowed into the hillside. I was more worried about the trees, many of which hadn't the benefit of millions of years of adaptive natural selection to brace them against the raking fingers of hurricanes, but very few of those near to the house had actually fallen and the debris of loose branches and palm fronds wasn't too bad.

The only tree that really mattered, situated deep in the island's heartland, was too well-protected to have come to any harm.

Later, I went down to the beach to check the boat. That *had* taken a battering; a big wave had snatched it up and hurled it against the palms that fringed the beach, and the timbers in the port side near the bow were badly splintered. I knew that it would take me at least a week to fix it unless the fishermen from Bahu condescended to lend a hand next time they came over. I wasn't optimistic about that but I wasn't unduly troubled by the prospect of the boat being out of commission for a while. I had no plans to go fishing, and no desire to go anywhere else.

It wasn't until I went around the boat to check the starboard side that the blob of Day-Glo orange in the distance caught my eye. I knew immediately what it was: a self-inflating podsuit like the ones issued to passengers by the masters of the tourist boats that carried gawkers through the archipelago from one petty Eden to another. The trade had boomed in the last thirty or forty years, while the once-green continental landmasses had gradually turned black, and there must have been fifteen or twenty boats on tour when the storm hit. It was difficult to believe that any of them had gone down, but not so difficult to believe—tourists being tourists—that someone relishing the experience of the hurricane might have gone over the side. One of the many mental attributes that have atrophied in the rigorously-ordered modern world is a sense of danger.

The podsuit was in bad shape, given that it had supposedly been designed to survive *anything*. The faceplate hadn't shattered but it was badly scratched and scarred, and the electronic beacon had been reduced to shards. Its occupant was unconscious, and when I had excavated several layers of foamy plastic to get to her underclothing and the skin beneath I was horrified by the extent of the bruising. It was obvious that she had been bounced against the reef at least a dozen times before a big wave finally carried her over.

A quick check revealed that she had at least one major fracture, of the left tibia, and three less nasty breaks, but her internal technology was already hard at work. She had that tell-tale all-over warmth which repair nanotech generates when it gets down to serious business, and I figured that she'd be perfectly okay, provided that her brain had managed to withstand the hammering without sustaining a major hemorrhage.

In my usual paranoid fashion I immediately began to wonder whether there really had been an accident, or whether this was some clever ploy to sneak an agent into my camp. It was difficult to believe that any multinational agency—let alone a UN organization—could have planned to subject one of its operatives to that kind of punishment in the interests of chasing a myth, but perhaps they hadn't realized how dangerous it was to cast someone adrift in an "infallible lifesaver" during a full-scale storm. The balance of probability, however, seemed to favor the hypothesis that it really had been an accident, or a case of reckless misadventure.

Whatever the truth of the matter, I could hardly leave the injured woman on the beach. When I had all the wrapping off I carried her as gently as I could up to the house, and put her to bed. Then I went back—hurriedly, because the sun was setting—in order to get rid of every vestige of the Day-Glo orange. I searched the wreckage of the podsuit for bugs, just as I had earlier searched her body and belt, but there was nothing in the least suspicious.

I took the debris into the forest and buried it where no one would ever find it. If she did turn out to be a spy, and I had to do something about it, I didn't want anyone to have incontrovertible evidence that she'd reached the island. While the hypersensitive guardians of the stabilized world couldn't be sure that Grandfather's island harbored anything dangerous they were content to turn a blind eye to its anomalous status, but anything that provided legal grounds for an invasion might start a snowball effect.

I must confess, though, that there was another side of me, which wasn't entirely displeased by the fact of the woman's arrival, even though the timing could have been more convenient. If it really were an accident of fate, there might be a certain propriety about it. An Eden with only an Adam and a forbidden tree—and, of course, an absent Creator—is two characters short of a myth. However unappealing the thought was that I might have been landed with a treacherous serpent, the idea that I might have been gifted an Eve had a certain charm.

I'd been alone for a long time, and I was well used to it, but everyone has dreams and fantasies, just as everyone has secrets to keep.

* * * * * * *

THE TREE OF LIFE, BY BRIAN STABLEFORD

The woman slept right around the clock while her inbuilt Medicare kit worked on her bones and her bruises. Her nanotech was more nearly state-of-the-art than mine, but in this day and age that didn't necessarily signify that she was rich. Preservative nanomachines were one of the key elements of the great stabilization: a foundation stone of the kind of equality enshrined in the New Rights of Man.

It was impossible to tell how old she might be; overt indications of aging were way out of fashion and almost all the modern signatories to the treaty went to their voluntary deaths looking as fresh as the day they became old enough to sign.

I went to look at the tree while she was still comatose, but most of the fruits were still a day or two away from full ripeness, and I thought it best to leave the gathering until I had a clearer idea of what the woman's arrival might portend.

I cleaned myself up in honor of her anticipated reawakening, trimming my hair and beard. All my supposedly self-repairing suits had suffered more than somewhat from the ravages of Grandfather's thorns, but I found one whose scars were reasonably discreet.

I watched the woman's reaction very closely when she first opened her eyes and saw me. Doubtless she'd have been well schooled in the art of astonishment if she were a fake, but there was always a possibility that she might give herself away. Her eyes grew wide with alarm, but the alarm died what seemed to be a natural death as it was overtaken by the grateful recognition that she was, after all, still alive, and by the reassuring knowledge that whoever I might be—even if I were a primitive or a green zealot—I was unlikely to mean her any harm.

"Where am I?" she asked, sticking to the time-honored script.

"On today's maps the island's called Moro," I told her. "One of Grandfather's little jokes. It's not on any of the tour routes, but they tell tall tales about it on some of the islands that are, so you might have heard of me. I'm John Drummond."

The Tree of Life, by Brian Stableford

She didn't seem to recognize the name. She was supposed to respond in kind by telling me her own name, but she didn't. "The boat...," she said, and stopped. I couldn't tell whether she'd been halted by uncertainty or whether she'd paused for melodramatic effect. "I couldn't hold on...did it go down?"

"No idea," I told her, dryly. "I doubt it—they're difficult to sink even when they're crewed by idiots. You turned up on the beach in one of those fancy lifesaving suits, fully inflated for total protection against any and all eventualities. You didn't have an easy time getting past the reef, but your molecular machinery seems to have patched you up as good as new."

She was still looking at me as if I were an alien—which, in a way, I was. I was probably taller and more solid than she was used to, Height wasn't as far beyond the pale of fashion as wrinkles, but there weren't too many two-meter men abroad in the brave new world, even in its remoter outposts, and I was a full thirty centimeters taller than she was. Even without the wrinkles, I must have looked uncommonly old in her eyes. Did she, I wondered, know how old I actually was?

"What's your name?" I asked, when she still didn't offer it.

"Haven't you checked my smartcard?" she countered, lifting the sheet to look down at her lightly-clad body. Her belt was still in place, with all its fixtures and fittings. "Surely you've reported finding me."

"I haven't got the machinery to interrogate a smartcard," I told her, "nor the means to report your presence here."

"You're a primitive?" she said, jumping to the natural conclusion—or perhaps following a carefully-rehearsed script.

"Not exactly," I said. "I'm a sort of betwixt and between. I have good internal technology, but not much in the way of externals. No cable to the Net, no virtual reality suit, no artificial photosynthetics. I'm not a citizen of the new world order. This island still qualifies as property under the pre-crash rules. It was willed to me by my grandfather, and the UN hasn't got around to annexing it yet, even though I won't play ball with the tourist trade. I like to think of it as one of the last independent nations on the face of the earth, and of myself as its once and future king, but you'd be perfectly entitled to think of me as a victim of delusions of grandeur. Are you going to tell me your name or not?"

"Hilda," she said, absent-mindedly, while she furrowed her brow as if to struggle with the implications of what I'd told her. "Hilda March. You mean you're not a signatory to the treaty?" It was a nice, suitably innocuous name—and a predictable question.

"No I'm not," I said. "I took the other option. I'm content to live as long as I can and die in my own good time, bravely sustaining whatever mental degeneration Mother Nature cares to inflict. I'm a hundred and eighty years old and completely *compos mentis*, at least in my own estimation. By way of compensation for my insistence of saying the course, I've fathered no heir and don't intend to. I honestly don't know whether Grandfather would approve, and I honestly don't care."

Three mentions of the word *grandfather* were enough; she either caught on, or figured it was safe enough to pretend to have caught on. "Drummond," she repeated, with an echo of recognition. "Are you...?"

"Samuel Morgan Drummond's grandson," I finished for her. "Contrary to anthropological speculation, not all the makers of the world before yours were mere myth-figures. Some of them actually existed." She knew it was some sort of joke—there was no doubt whatsoever of the actual existence of all the heroes and villains of the Second Industrial Revolution, although some of their creations had been relegated to the status of mere legends—but she couldn't quite see the irony of it. I was almost convinced by her attitude that she was exactly what she seemed to be, and nothing more, but I couldn't afford to relax completely. At any other time, I could have let it go, but the fruiting of the Haeckel tree—which didn't happen every year—always filled me with a suspenseful sense of hopeful anticipation, attended by a corollary shadow of dark anxiety.

"You'd better come and have something to eat," I said. "You've been unconscious for rather a long time, and I couldn't rig up any kind of drip-feed to help your nanomachines along. You probably won't like the food, but it's all reasonably nutritious."

She nodded slowly. "I'm terribly thirsty," she said, as she sat up for the first time. "I could do with a drink—water, that is."

"Water and goats' milk are all I have," I told her, helping her to get up from the bed. She was able to stand without too much discomfort—the fractured tibia had been very efficiently patched up—but she was a little unsteady as I led her to the door and I kept my hand on her arm in case she stumbled.

The physical contact was not unwelcome. I liked her. I wanted her to be what she seemed to be and I wanted the accident of fate which had brought her to the island to turn out to be a happy one.

Unfortunately, wanting things to turn out right is rarely enough to make certain that they do.

* * * * * * *

While Hilda March drank her water and made what was to her an extremely unsatisfactory meal I explained why I couldn't summon anyone to pick her up. I told her—truthfully—that I'd once kept a radio for emergencies but hadn't bothered to repair it when it broke down because I didn't want people bothering me. I also told her about the damage to my boat, and explained that it might be a week or more before a boat from one of the other islands came to call. If they were searching for her, a copter might arrive before then, but not necessarily.

"I must admit," I said, smoothly, "that most visitors are unwelcome here, tourists especially. I value my privacy, and find it difficult to tolerate its violation. I make no claims on the myriad bureaucratic institutions that have taken it upon themselves to regulate and automate the affairs of modern man, and so long as they tolerate my refusal to allow them to make claims on me I'll continue to refuse. I hope you won't mind too much if I leave you to your own devices while you're here—I have plenty of work to do."

It was an awkward speech, which struck me after I'd made it as being slightly stupid and not really what I meant to say. It got the response it deserved.

"I won't presume too much upon your hospitality," she told me, in a faintly wounded manner, as she pushed her plate away across the table-top and sat back, trying to find a comfortable way of sitting in a chair which was far harder than the ones she was used to. "You might have no radio of your own, but there was a signaling device attached to the podsuit. That will summon someone to pick me up."

"I'm afraid not," I told her. "The device was pulverized, apparently as a result of one of your several collisions with the reef. It might, of course, have provided an indication of your whereabouts before it ceased to function, but I wouldn't bank on it. A boat from Bahu will arrive eventually—the islanders here come to exchange fish for fruit and vegetables that they don't cultivate themselves. Their politics are at the far end of the grey-green spectrum but they do have emergency communication equipment. A copter will come out from Palau to pick you up."

"Thanks," she said, in a lukewarm tone. "I dare say I'll survive, in spite of the food."

"In the meantime," I said, "feel free to look around. You might enjoy it—this really is an unspoiled demi-paradise, unlike the tourist traps where the cruise ships go. On the other hand, it hasn't been sanitized the way the tourist islands have, so you'll have to be careful. The beach is safe, and so is the forest on this side of the ridge, but the interior is virtually impenetrable because of the swamps and thickets of poisonous thorn-bushes. Your internal technology will make sure the thorns can't hurt you badly, but any scratches you sustain will sting horribly."

"Are there snakes too?" she asked. I couldn't tell whether it was an honest question or a subtle joke.

"No. There are less than fifty vertebrate species on the island. The vast majority are birds and bats. Grandfather didn't get around to introducing any mammal species except the goats he kept for meat and milk. He was a purist tree-man at heart, and he wasn't much concerned with adding animal species to decorate his forest. My guinea-fowl were his, too, although I don't bother to keep them penned up any more, but the other species winged their own way here from the other islands. I've often thought of establishing a colony of monkeys, but one has to be careful; a major upset to the island's ecology could be disastrous. A small group of cats or mice could turn into a devastating plague within half a dozen generations."

"If the local ecology was so well-designed," she said, "how come the interior is full of bushes with poisonous thorns?" It was a good question, but it might have been entirely innocent. The real answer was that they were there to keep inquisitive intruders at bay without advertising too loudly the fact that there was something very specific that Grandfather had wanted them kept away from, but I wasn't about to tell her that.

"They did get out of hand," I said, "but they aren't a problem so far as I'm concerned. I'm used to them, and over the years I've become immune to their stings in much the same way that beekeepers become immune to bee-stings. As I said, your repair nanotech will easily fix up any damage you sustain, but it's best to be careful.

"I will be," she promised, ambiguously.

* * * * * * *

She was careful. She didn't go far into the forest, and she trod very carefully.

If she were a spy from the UN or one of the corps she'd have known already what a thankless task it was trying to get into the interior. Several people had tried, and although no one had died, they'd had a profoundly uncomfortable time. None had got to within a hundred meters of the Haeckel tree. You might think that it wouldn't be too hard searching an island less than four kilometers across, but when the island is as rugged as Moro, and as comprehensively decked in hostile shrubbery it isn't easy at all—and when every tree is unique and you haven't a clue what the particular one you might be interested in actually looks like, the task of tracking it down becomes genuinely impossible.

As the old proverb says, if you want to hide a tree you only have to put it in a forest. It's all the more effectively hidden, of course, if no one can be sure that it really exists.

The UN inspectorate had once tried parachuting men directly into the interior so they wouldn't have to run the thorny gauntlet, and had more than once tried depositing clever bugs to keep tabs on me, but the parachutists and the bugs had found the island environment equally uncongenial. I was determined that if they had changed tactics and sent a seductress in, she'd find the going just as hard, and the task just as frustrating—but I was equally determined that she shouldn't suffer unduly from my suspicions if she were genuine, so I didn't keep too close a watch on her and I tried to be a good host. I didn't make any advances to her—I couldn't be sure how she'd react, given that her normal sex-life was probably restricted to the idiosyncratic deployment of intimate technology, and it seemed only polite to wait for some sign of encouragement.

She went with me a couple of times when my daily routines took me into the forest, but she wasn't sneaky about it. I didn't go anywhere near the heart of the maze during the next couple of days, even though I was curious to know how the new crop was faring.

"I'm glad I was washed up here," she said, on the evening of the second day after her awakening. "It really is a marvelous place. Now that I can get things in perspective, this is the kind of experience that makes a holiday into something more, something special. I'm glad that happened."

Flattery can get you almost anywhere, I thought, *but sometimes your target needs to know where it is that you want to go.*

"It must make a change from all that orderly black and white," I conceded, "But I suppose you'll be glad to get back to less garish surroundings when the chance comes."

"Continental cities aren't studies in monochrome," she informed me, slightly stiffly, as if she feared that her lifestyle and worldview were about to come under attack. "They dress in all the colors of the rainbow, including green. They have a beauty of their own—as do the fields. It's silly to be prejudiced against black because of all the unfortunate connotations the color used to have in olden times. Artificial photosynthetics are only black because they soak up all the visible wavelengths in sunlight rather than just a few—it has nothing to do with aesthetics."

As she pronounced the last word she looked around distastefully at the dingy walls and the dreadful furniture, which seemed unusually ugly even to me in the yellow glow of the lamplight.

"It has everything to do with aesthetics," I said, as mildly as I could, given that it was a sore point. "Aesthetic discrimination is what makes us fully human—it's the foundation-stone of art and morality alike. Without aesthetic judgments, life is robotic, a mere matter of survival. It isn't an accident of choice that black is the color of evil and grief; black *is* darkness and negation. The new photosynthetic systems that have turned the planet black have dressed it in mourning for our sense of beauty, our sense of dignity and our sense of shame. The blackness of the fields that feed modern cities is the funeral of everything natural, everything truly alive, everything that was murdered by mankind in the name of stability and comfort. The blackness of the continents is the shadow cast by mechanical civilization."

I was quite sincere in saying all this. My particular greenness might be a very peculiar shade, but it was wholly authentic. I liked to think of it as Lincoln green: Robin Hood's color. I was proud to be an outlaw, after my own trivial fashion, because I considered my side to be the side of light and life.

"If I remember my history rightly, your grandfather was no green zealot," she said, perhaps getting to the real point of her visit at long last, or perhaps just trying to hold her own in a debate which had turned unexpectedly fervent. "The Creationists were technophiles through and through. Their biotechnology might have preserved Mother Nature's favorite color, but it was revolutionary in every other sense."

"What do you do for a living, Miss March?" I asked. "How do you earn your daily bread and your preservative nanotech?"

"I'm a robotics engineer," she said. "Hardware rather than soft—I deal with the motion rather than the motivation.

Macromachines aren't fashionable, but all the heavy work that smart molecules can't do still has to be done."

"And it pays well enough for you to take holidays beyond the boundaries of your over-organized world," I observed, cynically. "Little ventures into the beyond, away from all that blackness and all that bleakness...and a chance to stare at all the madmen and malcontents who live in exile from your well-ordered society."

"We don't send our malcontents into exile," she told me, "and we don't have any madmen. Madness is the prerogative of those cowards who insist on growing old." That was cant, but she seemed to believe it, and she seemed to think that what I'd said was sharp enough to warrant that kind of reprisal.

"I shouldn't have said *exile*," I agreed. "I suppose the islands are more of a refuge, for all those who don't want to die on time. But you civilized people do need a refuge, don't you? You do need an alternative to the lifetime treaty, so that its signatories feel that they have a choice."

"Everyone has a choice, Mr. Drummond," she said, quietly. "I'd rather die with dignity, at the end of an agreed span, knowing that I'll be creating the space for my children to exist, than cling to life knowing that although my body is effectively immortal my mind is bound to deteriorate." She said it with considerable feeling. I took it for granted that she was maligning me.

"Do you really think my mind has deteriorated?" I asked, in a gentle tone that was meant to dress my iron resentment in a velvet glove. "Do I really seem senile, or mad, to you?"

She wasn't in a mind to bother with polite denials. "I've seen a lot of primitives who do," she told me, quietly. "Men and women much younger than you. It's not an eventuality I'd like to gamble with. Maybe some people can stay sane for two hundred years, but many can't—and no one can hold on to his marbles indefinitely. Until we figure out how to keep our minds in good trim, physical immortality is a limited blessing, and we must take responsibility for its limitation. Necessity as well as politeness demands that we make room for new generations eventually—better that it should be a planned and disciplined process than a ragged patchwork of little wars of succession fought by men whose memories and thought-processes have sclerotized."

"Unlike you," I said, "I relish a gamble with destiny. So did my grandfather. This whole island was a gamble with destiny to him—but you probably know that already, from your history lessons."

"No," she said. "All I know is his name. To me, you see, Samuel Morgan Drummond is ancient history, like Noah's Ark."

"More like the Garden of Eden," I reminded her. "Perhaps you suspect it of being complete—unlike all the other Edens hereabouts—with its own fabulous and forbidden tree."

"I don't know what you mean," she said, perhaps truthfully.

"It's only a myth," I told her, lightly. "The last of the Creationist legends. You know, of course, that there were two special trees in the original Eden, according to *Genesis*: the tree of life and the tree of knowledge of good and evil. It was the second one whose fruit God forbade Adam to eat—and because they ate the fruit of that one, they never got to taste the fruit of the other. After the Fall, of course, they lost their chance—but not forever. There came a day when men could create trees of their own...trees to bear all kind of wondrous fruit. Some people, of course, think there was a second Fall soon after the time when men first began to make their own trees, but others don't."

"I still don't know what you're talking about," she said. She said it in a faintly aggrieved tone, as if I'd changed the subject that she had wanted to discuss.

It occurred to me, belatedly and embarrassingly, that what I'd taken as an attack on me might actually have been a shoring-up of her own wavering conviction.

"How old are you?" I asked, far too bluntly.

"Ninety-one," she told me, without hesitation.

"And when...?"

"Ninety-two," she said, without waiting for me to spell it out. "The contract I signed with the new world order is due to end in a matter of months—but I'm not about to defect,

THE TREE OF LIFE, BY BRIAN STABLEFORD

Mr. Drummond, not even to the Garden of Eden. It's a place everyone ought to visit once in a lifetime, but it's not where I belong. In my opinion, it's not where any truly human being belongs, in the twenty-eighth century."

* * * * * * *

I left the house early the next morning, while Hilda March was still asleep. She was fully recovered now, but the internal repair work had soaked up almost all of her energy reserves and left her rather weak. She was active enough while she was awake but she slept long hours and she had a ravenous appetite. The kind of food I lived on seemed to her to be coarse and unedifying, but once she'd overcome her initial apprehension she'd begun to swallow it down with some enthusiasm. She often asked what she was eating, and listened to my explanations with bewildered fascination; to someone reared on artificially-textured and synthetically-flavored manna and tissue-culture meat the contents of my larder were all new and quite unrecognizable.

I went warily into the maze, as was my habit, but I didn't keep looking back. Even if Hilda March had been a spy and an expert tracker it would have been almost impossible for her to follow, given the awkwardness of the terrain and the many natural pitfalls lying in wait for the unprepared. I was more afraid of the possibility that she might not have to follow me in person; after all, she only needed to locate the Haeckel tree, and secure a sample of its fruit for analysis. I'd checked my clothes and boots for bugs as best I could, just to be on the safe side, and I'd found nothing, but I couldn't entirely shake off my unease.

I stopped to rest at the top of the ridge, letting the sun dry the sweat from my shirt and brow. It would be sticky in the interior, and I'd be screened from direct sunlight by the thick canopy. The sea was calm, deep blue out beyond the reef and greener within, flecked with foam where it broke over the jagged edges of the dead coral. There wasn't a sail in sight; I was monarch of all I surveyed, unchallengeable lord of the world that my grandfather had made.

THE TREE OF LIFE, BY BRIAN STABLEFORD

When I went on I collected my customary ration of scratches, but my acquired immunity to the toxins with which the thorns were dressed enabled me to ignore them. I was proud to think that I didn't need any mechanical aid to withstand the chemical effects: that I could do it myself, like some modern Mithridates.

I came, in the fullness of time, to stand before the tree.

It was a giant, but it was surrounded by other giants, so it didn't stand out. It was more than four hundred years old now, and it had never stopped growing. It was thirty meters tall and its trunk was eight meters in diameter; how extensive its roots might be I had no way of guessing, but it was easy enough for me to imagine them spreading out beneath the entire island, exploring depths that even the cleverest moleminers had yet to plumb. Like me, it looked old but not decrepit; it was gnarled but there was no evidence of decay in its outer tissues. No creeper grew upon it, neither rust nor lichen streaked its bark, no caterpillar fed upon its leaves. The Haeckel tree welcomed parasites, but it did not tolerate them; it sucked them in and devoured them. Birds could perch safely on its branches, and fruit-bats might have roosted in its crown had they been so inclined, but anything that sought more intimate acquaintance with the giant found the tables turned and the biter bit.

So far as I could tell, the vast majority of birds and bats that had made their home on the island scrupulously avoided the fruits hanging on the tree. I presumed that it was the same with the insects. That was inconvenient, but not entirely surprising. Natural selection inevitably worked to produce that effect. In any animal population, however, there are experimenters. Had life no intrinsic inquisitiveness or inherent boldness no new ecological niche would ever be found. Had it been left to its own devices, without my assiduous aid, the tree would still have been able to do its work, tempting the rash and the reckless to collaborate in its endeavors.

All progress depends on the rash and the reckless.

Perhaps the tree would have been able to do its work more quickly, I thought, as I stared up into the rich foliage, if the island were subjected to a plague or two, whether of rats or mice or snails—the enrichment of the island's ecology by winged visitors had not yet resulted in any population explosions, perhaps because the fertility of the various decolonizing species was still somewhat impaired by the legacy of the third nuclear war.

The fruit was ripe, as I had expected it to be. The picking was no mere matter of reaching up to pluck it, or using some implement to shake the branches; I had to climb. The lowest branches were a good five meters from the ground but the gnarled trunk offered footholds enough for a nimble man, and I was well-used to their provision. It was easy enough to clamber into the crown, and disappear into the magical microcosm of its foliage. I never contented myself with the closest and easiest fruits; I always took the time to search for the best and most luscious.

The new fruits were all big, the best of them not quite as large as a football, and much the same shape. The last crop had been much smaller, few of the fruits being substantially larger than a tennis ball and most of them being shaped like oblate and slightly irregular spheres. That had been two years before—sometimes, for reasons quite unfathomable, the tree skipped an entire growing season.

There had never been such a marked difference between two successive crops before, and it reinforced my conviction that the tree's progress was gathering pace. At first, I was assured by grandfather's careful records, the tree had fruited every year, but its fruits had been very tiny and varied hardly at all from crop to crop. They were, according to Grandfather's notes, "like bedraggled prunes." The goats to which those early fruits had been fed had often been able to break them down and absorb them like any other food; that never happened nowadays.

My grandfather had gone reluctantly to his grave—reluctantly even by the standards of his own day—without ever seeing anything more than the most trivial effects of what he called "the food of the gods," but his analytical machinery had shown him enough drama at the sub-cellular level to reassure him that the task was in hand, and would proceed to its culmination if only the tree were given time. I felt privileged to have seen wonders of a kind, even though they were only modest ones, and every new thing delighted me more because I knew how Grandfather would have delighted in it too.

Grandfather appointed me to be the custodian of the Haeckel tree before I was even born; the seed of my dead father was taken from the banks for that purpose alone. He never told me who my mother was, and I never cared enough to try to trace the history of the donor of the egg. From Samuel Morgan Drummond's point of view, as from mine, I was *his* heir, and his alone—but not, of course, his only heir. I buried him beneath the tree, giving his flesh to its roots; in a way, the tree was a truer inheritor of his genius than I was.

I took seven of the fruits. I had come intending to take ten, but their bulk was such that seven was all I could manage—and more than enough for the various purposes I had in mind. I was already certain, of course, that I ought to include Hilda March in my plans. If she were a lying spy, there would be a kind of poetic justice in treating her thus, and if she were not....

However firm her own views on the matter might be, I thought that she deserved better than the fate to which she had agreed seventy-some years before, in recognition of the supposed necessities of the new world order.

One fruit, I knew, would be more than sufficient for the meal that I intended to offer my visitor. For my own plate I picked the fruit of another tree that grew nearby, equally exotic in its way but utterly bland in all its attributes. The fruits were not similar in form, but once sliced and seasoned with something sweeter the difference would not be noticeable under the kind of uninformed examination to which Hilda March habitually subjected the food I offered her.

I was pricked a dozen times on the way home, although I was more careful than I had been on the way out, but the wounds hardly bled at all and my mood transformed their trivial itching into a thrill of triumph and expectation. For the rest of the day, I busied myself with very ordinary and very uninteresting work, even condescending to spend a few hours repairing the boat, allowing Hilda to assist me in the work of cutting and shaping the new timbers, so as to lull any suspicions she might have had. Nothing untoward happened; no ship appeared on the horizon, nothing glinted in her eye. My fantasies notwithstanding, her interest in me clearly did not extend so far as lust.

At dinner, she ate the first course that was set before her without any evidence of real enjoyment. I could hardly blame her, given that the meat was poor and the potatoes sour, and that the whole looked like lumpy grey-brown mud. I had taken some trouble to make the dessert much more appealing to the eye and the nose.

"I hope you aren't too full," I said. "I had hoped to tempt you with some of this."

"Not at all," she said.

* * * * * * *

"Are you certain that you've never heard rumor of the Haeckel tree?" I asked, when we had finished our meal and our plates were clean. "It was a common tale at one time—and exactly the kind of fantasy to amuse bored tourists."

"I don't believe so," she said. "Perhaps it would have surfaced later in our itinerary."

"Perhaps," I agreed. "But it would have been a garbled version. I'm the only one who can give you a truly coherent account. I don't mean to imply, of course, that it's any more than a story—a mere legend or flight of fancy—but you might find it intriguing as well as amusing. Do you know who Ernst Haeckel was, by any chance?"

"No," she said.

"In the early days of evolutionary theory, not long after Darwin's death and some time before the first synthesis of the theory of natural selection with the wisdom of biochemical genetics, Haeckel proposed a law whose sole virtue was its succinctness: *ontogeny recapitulates phylogeny*. He had observed that mammalian embryos, in the course of their development, go through a series of stages which seem to echo the evolution of their species. In particular, he was struck by the fact that a mammalian embryo briefly displays gill-like structures, which quickly disappear, and which seemed to him to be a structural memory of the ancestral fish from which all other vertebrates are descended.

The Tree of Life, by Brian Stableford

"The law was, of course, false; an individual does not, in growing from a single cell to a mature adult, recapitulate the entire evolutionary history of its species. The fact that it commanded belief even for a while has far more to do with its aesthetic appeal than its fidelity to actual observation. And yet, it retained some force as a kind of metaphor, because the adult body of a mammal is an eclectic patchwork, in which systems evolved by many of its ancestor-species have been selectively conserved, refined and recombined. The pinnacle of evolutionary achievement, the human brain, is really several systems in one, piled atop one another in a hierarchy of command. There's the stem and spinal column, which regulates a system of autonomic reflexes; then the hind-brain, which is the seat of whatever vestigial instincts remain to us; then a layer which is capable of accommodating sub-conscious learning; and finally the cerebral lobes, which are the seed-bed of consciousness and reason. There's a loose sense, therefore, in which the brain does recapitulate, in its growth and eventual structure, the pattern of progress which produced it. Are you following me so far?"

"I think so," she said. If she was a spy who'd been properly briefed all this would be mere ABC, but she gave no evidence of impatience to get on.

"In the heyday of the Second Industrial—or First Biotechnic—Revolution," I told her, "Many genetic engineers became intoxicated with the idea that they had usurped godlike powers. There was an attitude abroad which said that natural selection had brought the pattern of progress to its own terminus, and that men must now carry it forward, creating by clever and careful design rather than by haphazard mutation and trial by fire. But there were some among them—and Samuel Morgan Drummond was of that company—who took the view that the creativity of the human imagination, constrained as it was by utilitarian notions of need and purpose, was a poor replacement for the exuberance of natural selection. According to these men, a world whose future was to be planned, however ingeniously, was bound to turn into a mere Utopia, full of comfortable and contented people but guarded and insulated against the fury and fever of change. History has, of course, proved them right."

"I don't think so," Hilda March retorted, evidently feeling that her way of life was under attack again, and still being unreasonably sensitive about the possibility. "We're comfortable enough, and contented enough, if you set the standard by people like yourself and the other inhabitants of these wild islands, but a certain restlessness is intrinsic to human nature, and we're no strangers to ambition and the desire for further discovery. Our world is by no means static, and no one regards it as finished. It's full of novelty, still evolving."

"That depends on what you mean by *evolving*," I pointed out. "In my grandfather's opinion, the novelty of your world is mere cultural and genetic drift, not true progress. It's the kind of world in which true progress couldn't be entertained, because true progress would make humankind redundant."

"We've adapted men for life in low-gravity environments" she said, quickly. "In time, we'll adapt them to live on the surfaces of other worlds. We've made some progress in the enhancement of intelligence as well as in the conquest of physical aging. I think we're doing a better job than natural selection could, and we're certainly making *true progress*."

I noticed that she wasn't reluctant to say *we*, although she had already signed away her future.

"Perhaps you're right," I said, mildly. "I'm merely telling you what Samuel Morgan Drummond thought—because that's why, according to legend, he set out to grow a Haeckel tree."

"A tree that would recapitulate its own evolutionary ancestry?" she said, plainly bewildered by the notion.

"No," I said. "A tree that could and might recapitulate, after its own fashion, the entire evolutionary ancestry of life on earth...and carry that evolution further."

"I don't understand how a tree could possibly do that," she said.

"The crude version of the legend says that my grandfather designed a tree whose buds produced animals," I said.

THE TREE OF LIFE, BY BRIAN STABLEFORD

"According to that account, the early crops were simple invertebrate creatures like nematodes and mollusks—worms, slugs, snails, and suchlike—which grew to maturity hanging from stalks and then struggled free, dropping down to the ground and dispersing. Later crops produced more extravagant wormlike creatures, then fish, then frogs and salamanders, then reptiles and birds...what a wonderful sight it would be, don't you think, to see birds growing on the branches like feathered pine-cones, finally breaking free and taking flight? But that, of course, is a layman's understanding of a Haeckel tree, a phantom of the uneducated imagination....

"Have you ever heard the saying *you are what you eat*?"

The abrupt sidestep startled her, but she nodded her head.

"In the common way of thinking, of course, what you eat becomes *you*, in a very crude sense. Your body breaks down your food into elementary chemical building-blocks—amino-acids and so on—and subsequently reassembles these blocks into structures designed by its own genes. My grandfather devoted the greater part of his life to the development of artificial assimilative systems which could do rather more than that: systems that could appropriate the DNA of consumed material without breaking it down. He developed very simple artificial organisms, which were capable of rapid evolution within a single lifetime by virtue of their capacity for genetic predation. He produced entities that started life as tiny microscopic worms, but enjoyed spectacular metamorphic careers as they were fed on the flesh of other creatures. Not exactly Haeckel-creatures, but creatures whose ontogeny was phylogenetically promiscuous.

"Grandfather's creatures became what they ate in a very different sense—not a simple and straightforward sense, because they retained the capacity for further change, but a sense that was nevertheless very interesting. They acquired many of the characteristics of the species they consumed, and the best of them—the vast majority either perished or became permanently set in one particular form, according to the logic of natural selection, but a few did remain viable—gradually built up a spectacular repertoire of forms and functions. He called them *DeVriesian chimeras*. De Vries was another early evolutionist, who proposed a version of mutation theory."

"I've think I've heard of them," Hilda March admitted. "They were banned, weren't they? They were considered dangerous, because some of them were capable of reproduction even though no two were ever alike."

"A few were capable of vegetative reproduction," I confirmed. "Parthenogenetic self-cloning. In fact they were far less dangerous than people feared; even the cleverest of them didn't live for long. They were too unstable, you see; they wasted themselves recklessly in their metamorphic fervor. Grandfather always thought the problem might be overcome, but when his main lines of research were proscribed he had to divert his efforts into other lines of work. He was strictly forbidden to continue working on his plan to create an artificial organism that would combine the longevity and essential stability of a tree with the experimental fervor of his chimeras: a Haeckel tree, as he elected to call it. His dream was the creation of an organism that could take up the DNA of any and all species, pouring the entire legacy of earthly evolution into a crucible from which anything at all might be eventually brought forth, to be tried and tested on the great battlefield of existence—but the dream was sufficiently disturbing to be outlawed.

"All the great genetic engineers of the Second Industrial Revolution were, in the end, restricted by statute and regulation; their godlike ambitions were mummified in bandages of red tape. Their fellow men came to them with commandments written in stone, saying: *thou shalt not make the tree of life*. They were permitted and encouraged to devise many other fruits for men to gorge themselves, but the ultimate fruit they were forbidden to make or to eat. Their fellow men, you see, had already overeaten of the tree of the knowledge of good and evil, and had become bitterly dyspeptic."

Wisely, she chose to ignore my sarcastic commentary on the state of the world. "If the layman's image of the Haeckel tree is false," she said, coming instead to the heart of the matter, "what would it actually have been like?"

"It wouldn't produce actual creatures instead of fruit," I said. "It would produce fruits of a special kind. You might like to think of them as chimera-fruit, except that they were to apply the logic of *you are what you eat* in reverse. Most fruits, of course, exist in order to be eaten—they're bribes offered to the creatures they feed, so that those creatures will also carry away the seeds of the tree in their bellies, distributing them far and wide. The fruits of the Haeckel tree are—would be—the ultimate fruits. They too would exist only to be eaten, but the seeds they contained, provided that they resisted digestion, would themselves become consumers, gifting metamorphic potential to their unsuspecting hosts—or, if you prefer, exercising their own metamorphic potential through the flesh of their hosts. The vast majority of the hosts would derive little benefit, and most would die, at least in the early days of the tree's career...but if the most successful could be programmed with an instinct to return to the tree after a suitably testing interval, and give back whatever they had created, whatever they had learned and whatever they had proved, then each generation of fruit might be cleverer and more adventurous than the last...and so, *ad infinitum.* Evolution unlimited, Miss March: the tree of life itself."

Her expression was suddenly bleak, and I knew that she understood at least a little better than she pretended—and now understood what it was that she hadn't understood before. Perhaps she had even begun to suspect what I'd done, but her voice was still level, still calm.

"If something like that existed," she opined, "it would be a terrible thing. It would be a threat to all life on earth."

"Hardly," I said. "Birds, bats, and insects would soon learn to avoid its fruit, because any members of their species that didn't would automatically be eliminated from the breeding population. The vast majority of its own progeny would perish, and those which didn't would return to its bosom. It wouldn't launch a plague of ravenous chimeras upon an unsuspecting world."

"It could reproduce itself, vegetatively," she pointed out.

"Trees live on a more relaxed timetable than human beings," I reminded her. "They're slow to grow, slow to spread. Forests aren't easy to replace once they've been cut down, as the human race once found to its cost. To grow a forest from a single tree would be the work of millennia. No,

THE TREE OF LIFE, BY BRIAN STABLEFORD

Miss March, you're quite wrong about the danger posed by such a hypothetical tree, just as your ancestors were about the danger posed by my grandfather's chimeras. Men could live alongside it quite safely and happily, untroubled by its nearness, observing and wondering at its produce. In time, of course—and I'm talking about tens of thousands of years now, or hundreds of thousands—it would produce new species better by far in unimaginable ways than *Homo sapiens*, but even that's an eventuality no one need fear. After all, the evolution of *Homo sapiens* didn't require the cockroach and the rat to give up their ways of life and become extinct. Contrary to vulgar Darwinian belief, the competition involved in the ceaseless struggle for existence has a great many winners; its variety is potentially infinite, provided only that we don't limit that variety by blind and wicked legislation. Mankind needn't fear supersession, and ought not to murder a Haeckel tree—if any such thing existed—out of horror or fear."

"There are very few people in the world who would agree with you," she said, truthfully.

"That's why I'm here in my private Eden," I reminded her. "A lonely Adam, devoid of Eve and serpent alike, honoring the memory of my grandfather."

"If any such thing were proven to exist," she went on, doggedly, "the people of the world would probably demand its destruction. If they had grounds to believe that one such tree existed in a whole vast forest, and couldn't tell which one it was, they might well burn the forest."

"If even one such thing were known to exist," I told her, coldly, "no one could ever know for sure that it had been killed, even if they devastated an island or a continent in order to make sure. No one could ever know how far its seed had been spread, or how far its roots extended deep within the earth. Its progress might be interrupted, or set back a step or two, but it could never be stopped. The tide of true progress can't be turned back, Miss March—not permanently. You might as well try to turn back the tide of time itself."

She wanted to have the last word, but she couldn't formulate it properly. After trying for thirty seconds or so she admitted defeat. All she could eventually contrive to say was: "I feel rather strange."

It was a comment more apt than most of the ready alternatives.

* * * * * * *

Although I had to devote almost all of my attention to Hilda March in the days that followed I fed the fruit to two dozen goats and thirty fowl. Then I set them all loose, and chased them into the interior. That was a simple precautionary measure; I knew that someone might come looking for the woman within the next few days, even if she were exactly what she claimed to be. Hilda herself I removed to one of Grandfather's inner sanctums, deep within the bosom of the hill.

The helicopter arrived two days later, with ten men aboard. I explained that I'd seen no one, but I gave them permission to search the island as assiduously as they could. They set off with determination, but it was only a matter of hours before they began trailing back to the house. Their wounds were very slight, but their internal technology could only do so much in damping down their reaction to the thorn-poisons and they were in some discomfort. I applied some external palliatives, oozing sympathy the while, assuring them that they would be in no mortal danger were they to carry on—but the men of the modern world have grown unused to petty discomforts. They're all cowards at heart.

I didn't ask the leader of the search-party many questions about the person they were looking for lest I should arouse their suspicions, but I did ask how old she was. Anyone would have done the same. They confirmed that she was contracted to die in a few months time under the provisions of he lifetime treaty, but pointed out that they were obliged to search for her nevertheless. I was fairly certain that he was sincere; they really were trying to rescue her, not tracking down a renegade suspected of ducking out of her deal with the new world order. I wished them the best of luck with their search when they left, having found nothing.

THE TREE OF LIFE, BY BRIAN STABLEFORD

Hilda remained alive for more than a week. Perhaps that was due entirely to her internal technology, but I couldn't help feeling that perhaps—just perhaps—she might have been better off without her protective nanotech. The molecular machines were programmed to fight against any disturbance of their environment, and that included the effects of the seeds that had possessed her as soon as she had consumed the fruit of the Haeckel tree. There was no way of knowing what might have become of her flesh, or of her many-layered brain, had kindly civilization refrained from filling her with stubborn resistance.

Her ontogeny showed no outward sign of recapitulating her phylogeny while she changed, but most of the changes were internal, invisible to my inquisitive eyes. I hoped that she might find a voice again, in order to give me some indication of what might be going on—indeed, I hoped that her intelligence might be augmented rather than suppressed, and that she might awake from her second coma far more exuberantly than she had awakened from her first—but we were both out of luck. It was far too much to expect, given that this was my first experiment with a human subject; the hazards of fate are never as generous as that.

One day, I firmly believe, one of the children of the tree will speak to the world with the voice of a prophet, and will have much to say—but the time is not yet.

I made my usual encrypted record of the changes that did take place, as any dutiful scientist would have done, but I knew that the record would not be valuable and that Hilda would not be returning to the tree. I did everything I could to keep her alive as long as possible. Although she couldn't hear me I urged and pleaded with her to make what efforts she could to come to terms with what was happening to her, but she couldn't respond.

I suffered several severe fits of remorse over what I had done. I called myself a murderer a dozen times over, and refused to excuse myself on the grounds that she would otherwise have wasted her life, her health and her potential. Nor did I think myself any less guilty on the account that she would have sanctioned the destruction of the Haeckel tree, and would probably have done everything in her power to achieve that end had she come to believe in its existence. She was not, after all, capable of understanding that the tree's life was infinitely more precious than the life of any merely human being; it was stupidity that would have moved her—and perhaps had moved her, if she really was a UN spy—rather than malice.

With the passage of time, though, my bad conscience eased and I was able to look at things more calmly. I buried her carefully, where she would never be found, and then I set out to make what study I could of the other creatures I had given to the avid fruit. Several were still healthy, and I knew that one or two, at least, would eventually return to the tree, but when I came to tabulate the results of the experiment they seemed remarkably poor by comparison with my optimistic hopes.

A tree's time is not ours, and evolutionary progress is slow, no matter how it may be achieved or cunningly assisted, but with every year that passes I become more conscious of the threat of my own mortality. I cannot resist the conviction that I shall not live to catch the merest glimpse of the Promised Land that this island will one day become.

I now believe that I have been far too cautious in reintroducing vertebrate species to the island. I must make every effort to import many more. I must have monkeys and rodents, perhaps even snakes. The risk of destabilizing the island's ecology must have receded by this time, and if one of the imported species does run riot and become a plague I shall simply have to tackle the problem and solve it. Like the birds and the bats, the new populations will doubtless become circumspect, but the tree needs them, desperately....

No, that isn't true; the tree is self-sufficient. What I told the woman is true—no power on earth can destroy it now. In the long run, even I am irrelevant to its fortunes, and anything I feel a desperate need to do is for my benefit and edification.

The tree is, after all, the tree of life itself; it stands outside the empire of man, utterly unconcerned with the knowledge of good and evil or the follies of temptation.

* * * * * * *

Two weeks after the helicopter left, the fishermen from Bahu came to Moro, according to their habit. We had a banquet on the beach; they provided the fish and the palm wine while I provided the meat and the fruit. The fruit was, of course, quite innocuous.

"It's a pity that woman who was lost from the tourist boat didn't wash up on your island," one of the girls said to me, as we lay under the stars with full bellies, caressing one another according to a fashion that the people of the night-dark continents abandoned long ago. "She might have thought it paradise and decided to stay."

"I'm glad that she didn't," I told her. "I value my solitude too much. I was put upon the earth to do my grandfather's work, and it's best that I do it alone."

"No man should be alone," she said, teasingly. "A man without friendship and love is hardly a man at all, and might as well be made of wood."

"We are what we eat," I told her, warmly and with genuine affection, "and I dine on hope and glory, while common men cannot."

THE SKIN TRADE

They say that you can't judge a man by the color of his skin, but a good tailor can. A state-of-the-art skin is an adept chameleon, of course, but it can only do so much to cosset and shape and mask its wearer. Nowadays, when everybody has a skin of some kind, you never hear people saying "Dead clothes make dead men" any more, but the fact is that a person who's hollow inside can take the luster off the finest skin. A tailor can always see that slight discoloration at a glance, and a good tailor can make a pretty fair diagnosis of the particular kind of soul-sickness involved.

I'm a very good tailor.

There's a saying in the trade that all customers are good and that bad customers are best. It means that if there weren't a steady supply of clients who stubbornly insist on changing their skins at ludicrously frequent intervals a lot of competent tailors might go bankrupt. That's why tailors are so scrupulously polite to neurotic fashion-victims and so patient with those freaks whose bodily secretions are so prolific or so noxious that even the most avid skin has difficulty turning them to good effect.

I suppose it's true that it'll be a sad day for the business when the presently-hectic advancement of skin technology slows down to a mere crawl and the world finally attains the kind of collective sanity that will allow everyone to keep their first post-pubertal skin until the day they choose to die. Speaking purely for myself, though, I won't be unhappy to see it. There's something infinitely depressing about constant customers who simply cannot find a skin that suits them, and insist on blaming their tailors for their failure instead of themselves. It's always a bad day for me when someone like Ritchie Halliday walks through the door of my fitting-room.

Ritchie thinks of himself as a very smart person, and in his way I suppose he must be. At any rate, he earns a good deal of money—enough to change his skin as often as he likes, for any reason that occurs to him, and always for the most up-to-date model. He likes to boast that no one in the world has greater expertise than he does in handling very distant machines by ultra-remote telepresence. I believe him, although I'm not as certain as he is that it's a gift and not a flaw in his personality.

"Your average run-of-the-mill Waldo can't adapt his stream of consciousness to deal efficiently with the time-delay involved in being on the moon," he usually tells me, as soon as I begin rubbing him down with the virus-solution that instructs the skin to go into fission mode. "I'm the only man I know who can lag down for the kind of meld you need to worm around in the Trojans, get in the groove, and stay there for as long as it takes. When we start in on the Jovian satellites, Mr. Invisible Mender, I'll be there, at the cutting edge of human progress."

He has a rich assortment of silly nicknames by which to address me; I think he does it to everybody.

"I suppose you think working my kind of machinery is pretty boring," he often adds, chuckling over the double-meaning, "but believe you me, there's a real art to it—just like there is to your game."

I've always swallowed the implied insult, the way any good tailor would. That's part of his problem; he thinks of each of his skins as just another machine for living in, essentially similar to the metal creepy-crawlies that provide him with other-worldly eyes and other-worldly hands. He can't quite grasp the fact that there's all the difference in the world between skins and cybersuits.

Ritchie parades his ignorance and his misunderstanding every time I peel him, as little bothered by the fact that he's said it all before as by the fact that it's all nonsense. A lot of people talk all the time while their tailors are laying them bare. These days, tailors and parents collecting their newly-decanted offspring from the hatchery are the only people who ever get to see the naked flesh of their fellow human beings. Everybody gets embarrassed about being peeled, and many of them react to that embarrassment with obsessive garrulity. I suppose people of that kind are preferable to the few who retreat into awful silence, requiring that I should talk incessantly to them, but Ritchie isn't the easiest man to listen to, and he usually doesn't take a blind bit of notice of my replies.

I'd heard Ritchie's spiel so many times before that I was quite astonished the day he suddenly veered away from his usual script and started telling me a story. Not unnaturally, he turned the story into a catalogue of complaints about his latest skin, but I didn't mind that at all. What could be more revealing of a man's true self than the complaints he makes against his skin?

* * * * * * *

"It's a great skin, Old Needleman, from a purely functional point of view. Never a moment's chill, mops up the nasties like a dream. I've never been in better shape, and that sweet tooth of mine has put an unsightly bulge into more than one skin in my time, but this one mops up surplus calories like a hungry rat. I did some bad psychedelics a few weeks back and the skin had me sorted in no time—no hangover at all. The colors are great—dutifully sober by day and a riot of imagination by night. You really have a flair for kaleidoscopics, you know—best in the West, I reckon. As for the gentle caress, well, it's just fine...as far as it goes. No, that's the wrong way to put it. It might be more realistic to put it the other way around...maybe it goes just a little too far. Hell, I'm not explaining this very well, am I? Look, I never thought much about this before, so I'm still trying to figure it out. These things're alive, right?"

"Of course they're alive, Mr. Halliday. That's why they're called skins." My tone was as mild as milk, but I have to confess that I was trying to make him feel like a moron. Why not? It was the ninth skin I'd made for him and the ninth he'd thrown back at me. Usually he said it just didn't feel right—or laid some spurious charge against its self-cleaning capacity, or its analgesic facility, or whatever—without feeling the need to offer a fuller explanation. His fumbling inarticulacy seemed to me to be adding insult to injury.

"Yeah, I know. They have a biochemistry and a physiology, or they couldn't do all the kinds of jobs they do. But is a skin only alive the way a house or a chair is alive, or is there something more than that? Is it an organism? Has it got a life *of its own*?"

"That's a deep philosophical question, Mr. Halliday," I said, soberly. "A skin isn't capable of living long in isolation from a host, of course, but one could say the same about many natural organisms, from viruses to liver-flukes. A skin is entirely benign—all its biological functions are designed to benefit the wearer, so it's by no means a parasite—but there are some natural species that live in benign association with others."

"Symbiosis, right?" he was quick to put in, to show off the fruits of his research. "You're saying that a man and his skin are symbiotes?"

"Not exactly, Mr. Halliday," I purred, with only the faintest trace of sarcasm. "For the relationship to be symbiotic, the skin would have to benefit too."

"That's what I'm trying to get at," he said, triumphantly. "Is the latest generation of skins alive in the sense that they expect to get something in exchange for what they do for us? Is it possible that skin-technology has now advanced to the point at which the critters are evolving on their own account and getting ambitious?"

"Skins aren't sentient, Mr. Halliday. "Lacking minds, they can hardly entertain ambitions. They're actually more like organs than commensal organisms. After all, we call them skins precisely because they bond to the skin that nature gave you, in order to perform all the useful tasks that natural selection didn't equip natural skin to carry out. They can't reproduce themselves, so they're not subject to any kind of natural selection and they can't evolve the way even synthetic organisms can and do. They're *tailored*; the only purposes they have are those built into them by their designers. Stand up now, please, and remain very still."

The Tree of Life, by Brian Stableford

"Well, I'm not so sure," he said. "You might think I'm a little bit crazy, Mr. Stitch-in-Time, but I think that skin you're stripping off has ideas of its own. I have this definite suspicion that it's not content to confine its medical functions to domestic cleaning and everyday antibiotics. I think it's been interfering with my hormones for reasons of its own."

It was a remarkable allegation, but it was by no means unprecedented. People have always been inclined to deny some of their own emotions, to alienate them as external forces. Since the dawn of consciousness people have been only too ready to deny responsibility with the aid of formulations like "I couldn't help it," "I don't know what came over me" and—perhaps most revealingly of all—"I fell in love." It's only to be expected that skins would become convenient scapegoats for that kind of moral cowardice.

The skin was gracefully sliding away from Ritchie's upper body, letting his real face and his true colors show through, even in the dim light of the fitting-room. He was stirring a little—fission can be very itchy—but he wasn't imperiling the integrity of the skin. That was one of his few virtues; he might reject a lot of skins but he always managed to give them back in good condition.

"What makes you think so, Mr. Halliday?" I asked, offhandedly. I was concentrating on the delicate task of gathering the sloughed skin, but not so intently that I couldn't keep track of his unfolding story. I figured that it had to be a case of *cherchez la femme*, and I gave myself a metaphorical pat on the back when he continued.

"I met this girl, see. Not in virtspace or at a metalorgy—on the tram to the Control Tower. I say *met*, but in the beginning I just saw her. I was on my way to Mars, and I was trying to get into the right frame of mind—I have to do that, you know, it's not just a matter of logging on and jogging off—but I just couldn't stop looking at her, and I couldn't figure out why. Her face wasn't lit up or anything—she was on her way to work, same as me, so she was masked as Audrey Anon. I mean, there's no rational explanation for it—no reason at all why *I* should want to look at *her*. She could've been anybody...only she wasn't. I didn't get excited, mind.

I'm not one of those guys who get excited at random. But there was something drawing me to her like a magnet."

The skin was almost off now; he raised his feet one at a time without being asked.

"She was on the tram again that evening," he went on, "and there again the next day, in the same seat. Obviously a creature of habit, slipping right into a slot, even though it was her first week on the route. I got exactly the same feeling...couldn't shake it, no matter how hard I tried. Next day, I gave in. As soon as I got on I went and sat down next to her, and introduced myself. I said we obviously lived and worked close by, with exactly the same shift-commitments. She was surprised—which was only to be expected—but there was something else too, right from the beginning."

He remained standing there, shivering slightly. The air was warm and still, but everybody shivers when they're skinless. I gave him a soft sponge to wipe himself down.

"She told me she worked for the 3-V company that owns the studios right across from the Tower," he said, as he ran the sponge over his torso. "She'd been working from home, splicing live and synthetic footage for ads, but she was doing some kind of complex digitization—I don't really understand why—and she felt she needed a supercomp-station with better display facilities than she had in the capstack.

"I could tell right away that she wasn't my type at all. Shy and shallow, locked in real time and local space, straight as straight can be. No money, no class. She wasn't even *physically* my type. I mean, a skin can only do so much in shaping a face and a figure. I like tallish women with curves and style; this one was short and skinny—like if she stood sideways she'd almost disappear—and she acted exactly the way you'd expect a 3-V splicer to act, too precise by half, without an ounce of spontaneity—as delicate and tedious as the job. I'm not one of those guys who says that as long as the skins are smooth enough you can fuck your granny and enjoy it; I'm really very picky, a bit of a perfectionist...as you've probably noticed from the way I keep changing my skin, waiting for the technology to catch up with my standards."

I'd turned away briefly but now I was returning with a fresh skin limply draped across my arms. It wasn't gossamer-light and he was a big man, but it still weighed less than a medium-sized grapefruit. I began to hang it, very carefully. The texture of his flesh was quite disgusting, but a true professional takes such things in his stride. I made sure I had the skin *just so* before I triggered the melding process that would complete the job.

"And you think that your skin might have had something to do with this...unusual attraction?" I said, making every effort to sound like a man trying to be civil in the face of appalling provocation. I had to help the skin a little, teasing it with my fingers. I didn't have to tell him to stand still; he had stopped shivering.

"I know it sounds weird," he said. "But when a guy clicks with a girl, these days, it isn't just a matter of him and her, is it? I mean, the *contact* is skin to skin, and lots of people...well, I don't know what people get up to in the privacy of their own virtserts, but according to rumor...I mean, nobody really needs a *second* skin nowadays, do they? Some say that actual fucking is really just a hangover from the olden days, when they made babies the hard way—a habit we'd all have shaken off if only we hadn't figured out how to extend the habit of living....

"Well, anyhow, we got together. Not just once, either— and I have to say that I'm normally a once-is-enough kind of guy. I don't get hung up the ways some guys do. Even when I do take a fancy, it usually wears off after a couple of scrimmages. A long-term relationship with an asteroid-miner is one thing, because you can really get inside a gimmick like that, but getting together with a person is just friction, you know...well, maybe you don't see it that way, being a tailor, but for a guy like me....

"I don't say that I didn't have fun with the girl, because I did, and so did she...but after a little while, I got the distinct impression that my skin was having more fun than I was. Does that make any sense?"

It isn't polite to say no to a question like that. Cold denial is a form of brutality. What I actually said was: "A skin has no sensations of its own, Mr. Halliday. It only has nerve-endings which link up to yours, becoming extensions of your own sensory apparatus. Although it can be stripped away, a skin really is part of you. In fact, it's more intimately a part of you than many of the organs rough-hewn for you by nature. In the old days, when people wore dead clothes, the outermost layer of their skin was also dead, the underlying flesh being in a constant state of self-renewal; tailored skins aren't subject to that necessity. For the first time in human history, people are wholly and truly alive, thanks to tailor-made skin. Your skin removes malign chemicals from your blood and pumps benign ones in, so it does help to regulate the balance of your hormones, but there's no sense in which it can be said to be separate from you, let alone controlling you."

"I know you're right," he said, implying by his tone that he knew no such thing. "After all, you're the tailor—I'm just the dummy. But I just couldn't get it out of my head, you know—the idea that it wasn't me and her so much as my skin and her skin. I don't say the damn thing was thinking, or that it had any kind of desire...nothing that complicated. It was just that the whole business seemed so peculiar. It really was as if my skin were being drawn to hers no matter what either of us might have had to say about it if we'd been able to look at it dispassionately. When we got together, at least after the first few times, I began to feel that the whole thing was a little weird, maybe even a little unnatural. I truly believe that it was an internal difference of opinion between me and my skin. I knew there was no future in it, that we had nothing in common, nothing to say to one another, nothing to hold us except the rolling and writhing, but the skin....

"The simple fact is, Mr. Invisible Mender, that I knew I needed fitting out all over again. I had to get out of that relationship, and I just didn't think I could do it while I was wearing that skin. I really felt, deep down, that unless I could get a complete change, I was all dressed up with nowhere to go. Anyhow, I read this article in the *Biotech Bulletin,* which says the newest models can work your muscles up to perfect pitch, adding ten kilos and more to the average clean and jerk."

THE TREE OF LIFE, BY BRIAN STABLEFORD

The average jerk, anyway, I thought—but I didn't say anything of the kind. Like any good tailor, I knew a cue for sales-talk when I met one, and we all have to make a living. Those of us incapable of magical rapport with the ever-faithful but severely time-lapsed inhabitants of the asteroid belt simply have to hold communion with lesser beings.

"You can move now, Mr. Halliday," I told him. "This is a very good skin—the best there is. It'll do everything the *Biotech Bulletin* says, and more. How does it feel?"

"It feels great," he confirmed, as he went to look at himself in the mirror—the mirror which he'd been studiously ignoring for the past thirty minutes. "This could be the one. This could be the one that's really *me*."

I could see even then that the colors weren't right, but that wasn't the fault of the skin, which was one of my very best. It was the fault of the man inside.

* * * * * * *

I half-expected Sally to come in within a matter of days, but she didn't. When she didn't appear in six weeks I even began to wonder whether Ritchie had continued to see her— which would, in a way, have made sense. I even began to wonder whether I ought to feel guilty about it, although I knew it was silly. After all, I knew perfectly well that it was all in Ritchie's mind, and that the skin he'd made into a scapegoat had absolutely nothing to do with his peculiar infatuation. In the end, though, the day came when the door opened and in shuffled Sally, in her usual shamefaced fashion.

"I'm terribly sorry about all this," she said, as I started the slow business of persuading the tenacious molecules to let go. "I really am."

"That's all right, Sally," I said, evenly. "Everyone has the right to shop around until she finds a skin that suits her."

She was still lying face down at that point, so I couldn't see her blurry blue eyes. Nor could she see mine.

"It's one thing to have the right," she observed, "and quite another to find the money. Especially when I know, deep down, that the problem isn't with the skins at all.

THE TREE OF LIFE, BY BRIAN STABLEFORD

You're the best tailor in the neighborhood—everybody says so. It's me that's all wrong. I don't know why you bother, just because we had a thing once. It was a long time ago. You really don't owe me anything."

She was right; I didn't. But I do take a pride in my work, and I really did want to find a skin that might solve her problems, if they were in fact soluble.

Even before she started to tell me about it, I'd deduced that Ritchie Halliday had run true to form. Once he'd shed the skin on which he'd fixed the blame, his head had had no difficulty straightening itself out. Sally had hung on for two months, hoping that he might come round, but in the end she'd given up. I didn't know whether to feel glad or sad about that. After all, I'm a tailor, not a matchmaker. There are no matchmakers any more; the world no longer has any need for them.

"I had to use the on-site facilities on a particularly complicated job," she told me, as I gently stood her up so that the flaying process could get under way, "so I started going into the studios. I met this man on the tram. He really wasn't my type—big, brash, plenty of money—but he was rather beautiful. I was astonished that he even noticed me. I was in my working drab, face set like porcelain. Heaven alone knows what drew him to me. He was awfully arrogant, always bragging about the slowness of light-speed being no limitation to his efficiency—he operates remotes way out in space from that tower place across the road from the studios—but there was something cuddly about him that made me want to wrap myself around him. Normally, as you know, I don't bother much with actual people—after all, when you have virtual partners available at the touch of a button, why bother with all the knees and elbows?—but this was different. For the first time I felt as if I might really be getting close to somebody. We had this *rapport*...we really connected. I know he felt the same way, at least for a while, but there was something in him that kept wanting to pull back. I guess it must give a person a peculiar outlook on life, spending six hours every day way out in the system, where the sun's just another star. A person like him doesn't just operate his machines, the way factory-drivers do; he *becomes* the mind of each and every one, like the queen of some strange kind of hive, and it just becomes normal to have a reaction time of fifteen or twenty minutes. I don't think, in his heart of hearts, that he ever wanted to come down to earth. Does that sound crazy?"

"No," I assured her, as I carefully collected the skin that was falling away from her slender body. "It doesn't sound crazy at all."

"While he was with me," she said, looking down, "I felt completely at home in that skin. For the first time in my life I thought: *This is what it's supposed to be like. This is what a skin is supposed to feel like.* Maybe that was the problem. Maybe if I'd been able to hold myself back, just a little, I wouldn't have forged such a tight link between that feeling of being comfortable and being with him. Because, you see, when he went cold on me, I suddenly didn't feel at ease in the skin any more. The comfort went when he did.

"He wasn't unkind, of course—at least, he didn't mean to be. It was just that he broke it off the same way he did everything else, not very gently. He actually got a new apartment, so that he wouldn't have to travel on the same tram any more. Imagine that! Moving expenses are a minor hassle to a man like him; they pay him a lot of money to sort out the problems those space-slugs run into if they're left to their own devices for too long. He reckons he'll be the first man on the Jovian moons, you know—maybe the first to go swimming in the Great Red Spot itself. It was understandable, of course. What did he ever see in me in the first place? He has lots of rich friends—he knows actresses whose tapes I've spliced and whose images I've souped up by enhanced digitization. I've never even been to a metalorgy. We really didn't have anything in common. It's such a shame that I got to associate feeling at home in my skin with being with him. I know it makes no sense, but I just can't shake off the feeling. I just can't go on living in the same skin that he used to fondle, that meant so much to him...while it lasted. It's as if I can still feel the echo of him while I wear it. Silly, silly, silly."

"You mustn't worry about it," I said, as I gathered up the remnants of the tattered shroud. "If only you didn't take these things so hard you'd find it much easier to get along with your skins."

It wasn't her fault that there was no hope of recycling the skin as a whole entity; even if she'd stood as still as a statue it wouldn't have been any use. Its cells would have to be reduced to blastular innocence, returned to the crucible to reproduce and respecialize before being born yet again.

"I know," she said. "I'm an atavism. I don't really belong in the modern world at all. I was made to go naked, or to dress myself in all manner of lifeless paraphernalia."

"That's nonsense," I told her. "You're a citizen of the twenty-second century, just like everyone else, and you have all the time in the world to find a skin that will make an appropriate interface between your inner self and the world at large. With luck we'll *all* have all the time in the world—even tailors who've grown old waiting for rejuve technology to hit the jackpot. Skintech is making such rapid progress that even people like me, who feel deeply and uniquely attached to skins we put on half a lifetime ago, will have to shed them or be left high and dry by the great tide of human evolution."

"I'm thinking of getting a new job," she said. "It'll mean retraining, but I'm not a machine, am I? I can't keep on doing the same old thing forever. My work isn't like tailoring, which is constantly changing...the problem with digitizing images is that when you've reduced everything to ones and zeros there really isn't much further you can go, and splicing real-to-synth is just cut-and-stitch, cut-and-stitch."

It's not as bad as that, Miss Patchwork, I thought—but all I said was: "That's not a bad idea. Change your life along with your skin and start from scratch. Give yourself the chance to build a coherent whole and it'll all work out. Trust yourself a little. Give your new skin a chance to get comfortable and maybe you'll be comfortable inside it."

I started the hanging. That was always the easy part with Sally. She was strangely unselfconscious about standing naked with her head back and her arms outstretched; she never flinched or shrugged the way some people do.

"It's really not very nice to keep casting them off, is it?" she said, murmuring through tightened lips. "I mean, the ones I bring back have all been brought back before, haven't they? I suppose, with me being so small and thin, they don't get any more chances. They die, don't they? And it's not their fault, is it? It's my fault, for being so bloody difficult."

"They don't die, Sally," I said, soothingly. "They're not individuals. The cells are immortal—they simply get recycled into new skins. Everything in the world gets recycled, molecule by molecule and atom by atom. The air we breathe has been breathed since time immemorial by all the human beings who ever set foot upon the earth. The air doesn't care who breathes it in and who breathes it out, and the cells that make up our skins just get on with the job, no matter how they're recombined. There's no need to feel bad about bringing your skin back to the tailor's—no need at all."

"You're very kind," she said. "I don't deserve it, but I'm very grateful. You're the best man I know—far better than Ritchie Halliday, no matter how he made me feel."

"I'm just a tailor," I told her. "Fitting people into skins is my job. This one will be just right. Take my word for it."

****

Sally's new skin suited her. All her skins did, no matter how uncomfortable she felt inside them. I suppose that's a tribute to my cutting and seaming skills—all the more so because it was a recycling job—but it's also testimony to the fact that there was something precious in *her*, whose full value she didn't yet know. Maybe I'm sentimental, but my judgment in such matters has always been sound. I could tell that Sally was authentically beautiful by the way the colors glowed; in time, I felt sure, she'd come to know it too.

I'm profoundly glad that the olden days are long gone; it must have been a terrible thing to have to rely on clothes to create the images by means of which we display ourselves to the world at large. Skins are so much better in every conceivable way, and they're getting better all the time. It isn't their lack of technological sophistication which makes so many people uncomfortable within them; it's our lack of emotional sophistication that's to blame—but I'm not one of those people who think that we're unready for the authentic immortality that rejuve technology will very soon deliver to those who can afford it. I figure that true sanity will be easy enough to cultivate, once we have all the time we need to do the job.

I'm confident that future generations will be more easily able to reap the full reward of the tailor's art, and I reckon that it mightn't be such a bad thing if a few of my mediocre competitors were to go bankrupt. Of course, it's easy for me to say that; I'm already rich, and I have absolute faith in my own ability.

I expect to hear a hundred more stories like Ritchie's and Sally's before I move on to some other kind of art-work, but there'll come a time when tales of that pathetic kind will be as obsolete as birth and death. One day, everybody will be able to look into a mirror and say "That's *really me*," and know that it's true—and always will be.

This time around I gave Sally a skin that had been sloughed by one of the actresses whose tapes she cut and pasted and whose images she patiently repaired with the aid of a fertile stream of dots and dashes. There was no element of strategy in the choice, because I knew full well that it really didn't matter at all where a skin had been before I passed it on to a new owner.

I knew that the answer to Sally's problem, like the answer to Ritchie's, was simply a matter of trial and error, and of having faith in the things that are worthy of our faith. If we all keep going long enough, we'll hit the winning combinations in the end. That's the nature of human evolution—and, indeed, of all evolution.

Ritchie Halliday's ninth skin had already been re-cut and sold on, of course, but there was no possibility at all of anything strange happening again—if anything strange had happened at all. Personally, I don't think anything had.

I'm just about willing to concede that Ritchie might have been subconsciously drawn to the wearer of his previous skin. There are all kinds of subtle ways in which a second-hand skin might conceivably be recognized, no matter how well it blends with its new owner. What I can't believe is that Sally's decision to go into the studios for a while, on the same tram that Ritchie caught to work every day, could be anything but coincidence. Skins don't have a memory in that sense, and they don't have that kind of control over their wearers.

In any case, it would be absurd to imagine—even for a moment—that one of Ritchie's cast-offs would want to get back together with him, if it were capable of wanting anything at all.

OUT OF TOUCH

When he'd moved the cases out on to the roadway and locked the door behind him Jake went round to the back—or, as he'd always thought of it, the front—of the house so that he could watch the breakers rolling up the deserted beach. The sea was on the retreat, having delivered the usual cargo of rubbish to the ragged tide line. When he and Martha had first moved into the Village there had been bits of kelp and dead crabs mixed in with the beached flotsam, but nowadays the waste was all man-made. Red plastic bottle-tops stood out like warning lights.

While he stood there watching the dull grey waves Peterson, the caretaker, came to say goodbye. "Your kids comin' to pick you up?" he asked, although he knew perfectly well that they were.

"Sam and Doreen," Jake said, although Peterson could hardly be interested in knowing their names. "Sam's my son. They've been married twenty years, but there are no grandchildren. Kids don't seem to have kids of their own any more."

"Comes of expectin' to live forever," Peterson said, laconically. "Guess you won't be seein' no old people any more. Quite a change. Never figured on endin' up as one of an endangered species."

"There are old people in the cities," Jake told him. "Lots of them."

"I warn't includin' the Third Worlders."

"Neither was I."

"Well there won't be lots of 'em for long," Peterson said, with a sigh. "What'd you give to have been born twenty years later, hey?"

"I'd give a lot not to have been born thirty years sooner," Jake countered, trying his damnedest to look on the bright side. "We missed the worst of the wars, you and I. We missed the worst of a lot of things."

"An' the best of everythin'," Peterson added, sourly. The closing of the Village had only cost the residents their so-called retirement homes but it had cost the caretaker a living. Peterson had managed to avoid accumulating enough social credits to qualify for the full welfare handout—which presumably meant that he'd spent time in jail, although Jake had never asked and Martha's gossip grapevine had never picked up a reliable rumor—and he didn't seem to have any kids to him help out. Who could blame the old misery-guts for being bitter, when he had cause to be envious, not merely of the younger generations who had been granted permission to drink at the fountain of youth, but also of his own peers?

"I'm going to miss this place," Jake said, softly, as he heard the sound of a car drawing up out front—or out back, the way he preferred to figure it.

"It was allus just a waiting-room for the graveyard," Peterson assured him, his voice grating like an old hinge. "Have everything you need and more where you're goin', includin' ocean views."

I won't have Martha, Jake thought, suffering the now-familiar pang whenever that particular thought resounded in his head. All he said out loud was: "It's not the same when you can only see, and not touch."

* * * * * * *

"It's not the same," Jake said, while Sam's nimble fingers ran through twenty or thirty of the most popular outlooks to which the window had access.

"Yes it is, Dad," Sam said, patiently. "The image is optically perfect—parallax-shifts and everything. It's exactly like looking through a real window, except that you have the choice of a million different windows to look through. Sure, some of them are taped and edited and some are digitally synthesized, but there are more than two hundred that are relayed live. You see exactly what you'd see if the house were really there: South Sea atolls, Alaska, the Himalayas...even fifteen fathoms deep off the Great Barrier Reef. With the remote control in your hand you can surf the whole world. This is *everywhere*."

By way of illustration Sam summoned the Great Barrier Reef—which, by virtue of being entirely artificial, was abundantly stocked with pretty fish and virtually litter-free. Apparently, there really were dwellings on the ocean floor, which could be picked up relatively cheaply now that the wave of fashion had passed them by.

"It's downtown Brownsville," Jake insisted, stubbornly. "There's nothing the other side of that wall but another wall. If there really were a window cut there, there'd be nothing to see but bricks."

"We don't have bricks any more, Dad," Sam reminded him. "The outer tegument of the house is overlaid with plates of reinforced dextrochitin."

"I'll try to forget that," Jake replied. "It makes it sound like we're living inside a giant cockroach. The point is, Sam, that it's not a real window. It's a fake. You can look through, but you can't open it to breathe the air. There's nothing to *touch*."

"You can touch if you use the VR set," Doreen put in, helpfully. "It's only a headset and a pair of gloves, I know, but you really do get the sensation of moving through the environments, and the tactile simulators in the gloves are really very good. You don't have the same range as the window, of course, but they're developing so fast...every week there's a dozen new scenarios available."

"And you don't have to worry about the cable bill," Sam added. "You can call up what you want when you want—no limit. Honestly, Dad, we want you to be happy here. We want you to be free."

"That's the modern way of looking at things, is it?" Jake said, awkwardly conscious of the depth of his ingratitude. "With a window and a fancy flying-helmet you can be free, even in a prison. Anyplace is everyplace, just as long as you have the right gadgets."

"Hell, Dad, you had a VR set in the Village, and a cable hook-up for space-sharing. It's not like you were living in some mud hut, compared to which this is Disneyland. You're only twenty-seven years older than I am, and you worked all your life with robots and spy-eyes. Okay, you were a hardware man, a real engineer, but you're no dirt-farmer sucked into the twenty-first century wilderness through some time-warp. You understand all this stuff just fine. We're trying to make a home for you here and we're doing the best we can, okay?"

"Sure it's okay," Jake said, sitting down on the bed and tiredly laying out his trump card—the one they'd never be able to beat or face down. "After all, I'm not going to be here for long, am I?"

Sam switched the window to a starry night, so dark and so very starry that it had to be on the moon. Doreen picked an invisible speck of dirt off one of the roses that were growing out of the wall around the bathroom-unit. They didn't bother with the customary reassurances; they thought he was behaving too badly to deserve even that. Maybe he was, but the fact remained that although Sam was only twenty-seven years younger than his father, Sam didn't look a day over twenty-five and would never look any older, whereas every one of Jake's sixty-seven years was indelibly marked on his face and his hands and his irredeemably-spoiled heart.

If he were lucky, Jake thought, he might get to occupy this plush cell for twenty or thirty years. Nobody could tell how long Sam might outlive him; perhaps a hundred years, perhaps a thousand. There was insufficient data, as yet, on which to base an estimate of the life-expectancy of the eternally young, and the data was likely to remain insufficient for a very long time.

"We'll leave you to unpack and get settled in," Sam said, probably as gently as he could. "You have your own dispenser, of course, but if you'd like to join us for dinner you'd be more than welcome. We generally eat at seven-thirty. If there's anything you need that you don't have, you only have to say."

"Thanks," Jake said, as sincerely as he could. "Thanks for everything. You too, Doreen."

"It's okay," Doreen said, as she followed Sam out of the door. "We do understand."

THE TREE OF LIFE, BY BRIAN STABLEFORD

They thought they did understand. They understood that he'd been set in his ways long before he went to the Village, but was set no longer now that he'd lost both Martha and the Village. They understood that he was an old man, who didn't have their adaptability, their patience, their confidence. They understood that he was a member of a species that was soon to be extinct, who had to be treated with the utmost care and consideration and kindness. Unfortunately, that still left an awful lot still to be understood.

"I should be in a zoo," Jake whispered, so softly that no one could have heard him even if the room had been crowded. "People with windows should be tuning in to watch me. Maybe I should call Peterson and suggest that he should hire himself out as a specimen for twenty-four-hour-a-day surveillance. Maybe they'd pay him enough to get a window of his own, so that people all over the world could watch him peering myopically out into infinity."

He picked up the remote control and switched off the staring stars. He tried, unsuccessfully, to get a blank screen, or a brick wall, but he had to settle for a beach scene. He could tell that it wasn't an American beach because the dark wrack marking the tide line was all seaweed and driftwood, without a red bottle-top in sight, but he figured that it would have to do—for now.

There wasn't much to unpack—which was perhaps as well, given that there wasn't a vast amount of space in which to put it. Every square meter of wall that wasn't host to bio-machinery of some kind was fitted out with cupboards and drawers, but they filled up in no time at all with clothes and antique junk. There were books and tapes and photographs and other similarly-useless things: things that had been Martha's, and which she wouldn't have wanted him to throw away; things that had been his, and which Martha would have kept if she'd been here instead of him; things that were his own personal museum of the life he'd led, and which—given that he was fated to be one of the last of his kind—he felt he ought to keep.

In the end, after some sifting and rearranging, he managed to find a place for everything. He wasn't entirely sure whether that was a good sign or not.

THE TREE OF LIFE, BY BRIAN STABLEFORD

* * * * * * *

"It's really very easy to make friends," Doreen assured him.

"It's very easy to make *virtual* friends," Jake corrected her.

"The people you meet in virtual space are just as real as you are," she said, allowing a hint of exasperation to creep into her voice, "and they can be real friends too. Yes, you only see their simulacra, not them, but when you think about it, what do you ever see of people you meet in the flesh except the masks they put on for the sake of politeness? Really, you know, all social space is virtual space. There's no real difference between putting your headset on and logging on to a network and putting your coat on to go walking in the neighborhood, except that the scenery's nicer and nobody ever got mugged in virtual space."

Doreen and Sam both worked in virtual space. Doreen was some kind of trader dealing in futures; she made more money than Sam, who reprogrammed neurotic AIs, although Sam's seemed more like real work to Jake. Because they both worked in virtual space, Sam and Doreen thought it entirely natural to socialize there. If they could have moved there lock, stock and barrel they probably would have. Jake, by contrast, always felt like a stranger in a strange land, like some Third World migrant in the Jersey Sprawl.

"The only people who never get mugged in virtual space are the ones who never tune in the shopping channels," Jake told his daughter-in-law, tartly. It seemed a more pertinent comment than pointing out that hardly anyone ever got mugged in the neighborhood because the surveillance bugs were far too good at seeing in the dark. The Third World might have come to camp on the doorstep of the First, as the newstapes were forever assuring the nervous citizens of America, but the migrants tended to steer clear of streets where they were under constant observation by thousands of electronic eyes. In any case, Brownsville had far less than its fair share of migrants. It was only just over the border, much too close to home.

Doreen flopped down on the bed, lay supine and threw her arms back in an exaggerated gesture of defeat.

"Okay," she said. "You win. If you're that determined to be miserable there's absolutely nothing Sam or I can do about it. If you're absolutely dead set on not having a moment's pleasure between now and the moment you finally pop your clogs nobody in the world can prevent you. But why, Jake? Why are you doing it? Is it yourself you're intent on hurting, or are you trying to make Sam and me feel guilty about something? About what? About giving you a room in our house? About not getting older? Tell me, Jake—what would you have done if you'd been in Sam's shoes? Would you have said 'No! I won't take the treatment unless my dear old Dad can benefit from it too'? Would you have said 'No! I can't insult the wrinkly old curmudgeon by inviting him to come live in my house'? Just tell me what you want, will you?"

Jake stood over her, extending a helping hand. When she finally condescended to take it he hauled her back to her feet—or tried to. He no longer had the strength he had once been able to take for granted.

"I'm sorry," he said. "I'm really not criticizing. I'm grateful to Sam and to you. I ought to be more cheerful, if only for your sakes, because I certainly don't want to make you miserable. I wish I could be cheerful, but...."

There was a long pause before she said: "But what, Jake?" She honestly didn't know. How could she?

"I really miss Martha," he said, simply, knowing that it would go down better than the truth. Not that it wasn't true, of course. He did miss Martha. It just wasn't the whole truth, or anything like.

Doreen's face softened, as he'd known it would. "I know," she said, reaching out to hug him. He let her, because he knew how much better it would make her feel. At least she didn't launch into a speech about life having to go on, and what Martha would have wanted.

What Martha would have wanted, if she'd had a choice, was still to be alive. Maybe she'd have settled for a window in her grave, but only as second best. She was always ready to compromise, always ready to split the difference. She'd have had an easier life if she'd married a more generous haggler than Jake had ever been.

"I miss lots of things," Jake added, as Doreen released him.

"Of course you do," she said. She could probably have made a list. He missed his youth, and his health, and the world in which he'd been a force to be reckoned with—inasmuch as any fairly mediocre human being could be a force to be reckoned with, in a world that had come storming back from the edge of the ecocatastrophic abyss, eventually to win the greatest prize imaginable.

"I honestly don't want to make friends," he told her, when the tension seemed to have unwound and they were no longer at odds. "People kept urging me to make friends in the Village, but I wouldn't. Martha always wanted me to be more sociable—I think she'd have been happier if her friends had been *ours*—but I never really saw the need, or the point. I don't want to spend my days jabbering away to other old men about the past we've all lost but never really shared, and I certainly don't want to while away my time playing games. I was never one for games, ever. I suppose I was never one for people, much. Martha used to say that I spent so much time with robots that I could only relate to disembodied arms and freaky hands, and then only if they weren't working properly."

"That's okay," Doreen said. "It's fine. Sam and I don't want you to do anything you don't want to do, or anything you're not comfortable with. But what *do* you want to do, Jake? What will it take to make the life you've got left worthwhile?"

A miracle, he thought. *Another breakthrough just like the one you got. A way not simply to put the brake on the aging process but to throw the bastard into reverse gear, to undo the damage that's already been done, to turn back the clock....*

"I don't know," he said, truthfully. "I'm trying. It may not look like it sometimes, but I am trying."

"If you want to join us for dinner," she said, "we'll be eating about seven-thirty."

She and Sam always ate at about seven-thirty. There was never any possibility of either of them being late home from work, and they never had anywhere to go except the further reaches of the virtual universe."

"It's okay," Jake said. "I'm not that hungry. I'll get something from my own unit a little later."

"That's fine," she said, stoutly refusing to be offended. "If you change your mind, you know where we are."

When Doreen closed the door behind her Jake felt a perverse urge to lock it, but he wasn't even sure that door had a locking function and if it had he didn't know how to operate it. There was so much to learn, and so little time to learn it. His room was no more than four meters square, and yet there was so much to be done within its boundaries and barriers that even an eternal youth like Sam couldn't be expected to exhaust its possibilities in the space of a single lifetime.

For a man like me, Jake thought, *it's just a cell on Death Row. No use making myself too much at home.* He opened a cupboard and took out one of his old paperback books—a book printed before he'd been born—and sat down on the bed to read. He gave up before he reached the third page, wondering what on earth he was trying to prove. *I'll be chipping flints next*, he thought.

Outside the window, a brontosaurus whose enormous body was half-submerged in swamp-water was patiently and methodically chewing its way through the lush foliage of a huge gymnosperm. Jake tried to catch its eye, but he couldn't. He could look out easily enough, but there was no way the brontosaurus could have looked in, even if it had been real.

* * * * * * *

Jake didn't warn Sam and Doreen that he'd bought the tamarin, so they were somewhat disconcerted when it arrived at the door. He hadn't consciously planned to lay down a challenge to their insistence that he could treat their home as his own, but he was interested to see their reactions nevertheless.

"It's okay," he assured them. "It's engineered for maximum tidiness and programmed for social responsibility. It won't make any dirty messes and it won't press any buttons it isn't supposed to."

"I don't doubt that," Sam said, although he evidently did feel uneasy on both scores. "I'm just surprised, that's all. Why do you think you need it? I wouldn't have thought cute and fluffy was quite your style."

"It's just a sophisticated biochip that does the talking," Doreen chimed in. "It's exactly like talking to a conversational program on the net. It's not really an animal—just an organic robot."

"It won't give you any trouble," Jake insisted, doggedly. "It'll live in my room. It won't bother you at all."

This turned out not to be entirely true. The pet's programming had to be open-ended to allow it to adapt to its owner's conversational habits, and it did tend to wander if Jake wasn't paying attention. If it wasn't authentically curious it gave a very good impression, and its restless fingers did occasionally push buttons that would have been better unpushed. It caused no disasters, but it did produce a measure of exasperating inconvenience. Perhaps it was all Sam's fault for making too much of an effort in the first couple of weeks; he only had to speak to the creature a few times to be included in its rapidly-evolving response-system as an honorary co-owner, and thus to be pestered whenever he was available for pestering and Jake was otherwise occupied. Even though Doreen never said much more to the creature than "Go away!" she too was awarded a special place in its scheme of things, and its constant craven apologies to her quickly became as much of an annoyance as jeers and insults would have been.

Jake could not have liked the creature half as much had it not been so subtly and insistently wayward.

In the early days of their relationship, the tamarin's conversation left much to be desired. It had a memory-chip that carried a potential vocabulary far larger than Jake's, but it was programmed to limit its competence to match his, so he had to spend time telling it elaborate stories, using as many words as he could squeeze in. For a time, this educative process was enjoyable. It injected new purpose into such activities as looking out of the window and watching the TV news, because Jake was able—indeed, required—to deliver a running commentary on everything that could be seen, so that the tamarin could be familiarized with his descriptive powers and his attitudes. After a while, however, the whole thing began to seem like a chore, and the increasingly prolific contributions made by the pet came to seem like mockingly convoluted echoes of his own thought-processes.

"The trouble with you, little monkey," Jake said to the tamarin, as they looked out of the window on to a busy street in the market quarter of some tropical city, watching the crowds go by, "is that you're too good to be true. You're the whole goddam world in a nutshell: bland, obliging, and fundamentally mechanical."

"The trouble with you, Jake," the tamarin replied, airily, "is that you don't know what you want from me. You change your mind from one day to the next, or one minute to the next. I could have had a nice kid for an owner, you know—a lovely little girl, full of hope and excitement and curiosity. You think this is an easy ride for me? Believe me, it isn't."

"There you go again," Jake said. "I call you bland, you immediately start compensating. Too goddam obliging."

On the other side of the window a young street-Arab made an obscene gesture. He was looking straight at Jake and the monkey, but Jake knew that it was just a performance—something he probably did in front of every spy-eye he passed, on the off chance that someone might be watching. Jake wished that there were some way that the kid could have known for sure that he was there, so that the gesture could have been personal instead of merely ritual.

"Why did he do that?" the tamarin asked, almost as if it had read Jake's secret wish. "It's not as if he can see us."

"That program of yours is too clever by half," Jake complained. "It's better at reading people than people are. Heaven help us if your kind ever get the all clear to run for office. On the other hand, you'll probably run the world a lot better than we do, at least until you master the Machiavellian arts of greed and corruption. He did that because he's saying *up yours*! to the entire First World—because he knows that the things we have today, he'll have tomorrow. He knows that his time is coming, and that he'll have all the time he needs to get what he wants. The treatment's too easy and too cheap, you see. It can't be hoarded or controlled. It's spreading like an epidemic, and the only people who can't benefit from it are the people who are already old, already damaged. He knows that he won't always be on the outside being looked at from within, no matter how many rich folks hereabouts are screaming blue murder about population problems and social utility."

"There are a lot of old people out there," the tamarin observed, scanning the street scene with his little dark eyes. "A *lot* of old people. And a lot of people so very nearly old that they can't wait long."

"That's right," Jake said. "But they're going about their business in a quiet and orderly way, because they don't dare to do otherwise. All their fear and resentment is held in check, because this is one cause it wouldn't make sense to risk death for. They all believe that their time is coming, if only they'll be patient, and they're right. All except the ones who've already missed out."

"I'll die too," the tamarin said. "Artificial flesh is designed to be mortal."

"I know," Jake said. "I read the specs."

"Is that why you bought me? Because I'm in the same boat as you, and Sam and Doreen aren't? Is that why you needed me?"

"I wish I knew," Jake said, tiredly. "I wish I knew."

* * * * * * *

The tamarin was designed for indoor life; it didn't need space or exercise. Even so, Jake began to take it out for "walks." It clung to his shoulder, ducking low to get under the wide brim of his hat; when he talked to it out of the corner of his mouth its replies were discreetly murmurous. He took it to places where there were trees, so that he could watch it playing in the branches. It was quite an athlete. Sometimes, he wished it would take the opportunity to make a dash for freedom, but it never did. It had its inbuilt limitations.

On occasion, when the sun was at full blast in a cloudless sky and the temperature was over a hundred in the shade, the tamarin complained that it would rather stay home, but Jake was never quite sure whether it was protesting on its own behalf or being protective of him.

"The species on which you're modeled used to live way down south," he told it, on one occasion. "I never could understand why natural selection handed out fur coats to tropical monkeys, but it can't have been an accident. By rights, you ought to like the hot weather."

"The species on which you're modeled evolved on the plains of equatorial Africa," the tamarin pointed out, "but that didn't stop you inventing air-conditioning."

"The monkey's right," Sam told him, as he stepped out the door. "Neither of you is fitted by nature for wandering around under the noonday sun. It's not as if you were mad dogs or Englishmen."

"I wear a hat," Jake retorted, pausing in order to make an argument of it. "Anyway, I'm not primed for skin cancer. My weak spot is the heart. You know that. Congenital weakness emphasized by wear and tear. That's the way I'll be going."

"I wish you'd talk some sense into him," Sam said to the tamarin. "He never listens to me."

"He always listens," the tamarin riposted, loyally. "He just doesn't take any notice. He's old enough to make up his own mind."

"He sounds more like you than you do," Sam said, wearily—to Jake, not the monkey.

"Better buy one for Doreen," Jake suggested. "Pretty soon it'd have everything she's got and good looks too." But that was uncalled-for, and they both knew it. He cleared out without further delay

He didn't enjoy the outing. Sam and the monkey were right, as usual; it was far too hot outdoors for anything that moved. Even the trees seemed to be wilting under the sun's relentless assault. The tamarin put on its usual acrobatic display, with all possible zest, but it wasn't really having fun. It was only pretending. Everything it did—everything it was or might become—was mere pretence.

On the way back to the house they passed thirty-three beggars—four more than the previous record count—but they weren't menaced in any way whatsoever. There was nothing in the dark and silent eyes that watched them go by but reproach...and perhaps, in the younger ones, a little pity.

"So much for trying to make the migrants stay home by promising to give full-aid priority to long-established populations," Jake said. "They don't believe us any more. Time was when the word of our politicians was our bond."

"Would that be Lincoln you're thinking of, or George Washington?" the tamarin enquired.

"Saint Thomas More," Jake answered.

"He wasn't an American."

"In spirit he was."

"In spirit," the tamarin told him, "so are they. For that matter, so am I."

"I was myself, once," Jake was quick to add, always desirous of claiming the last word. "But that was a long time ago."

The tamarin politely conceded the game. It always did, but Jake never felt that he'd won. Time after time after time, come blazing heat or pouring rain, he claimed the last line—but he never felt that he'd proved anything.

* * * * * * *

They'd been walking for a long time, but it wasn't until they got to the head of the sliproad leading up to the highway that the tamarin finally asked him, wearily, where they were going this time.

"I don't know," Jake replied, truthfully. "I thought we might hitch a ride someplace. Anyplace would do."

"Do you think that's wise?" the tamarin asked.

"No," Jake said. "If it was wise, I wouldn't want to do it."

"I can understand that," the tamarin assured him, "but isn't it just a little too haphazard. You might count it a bonus that Sam won't like it, but he really will be worried if you go missing and turn up three days later in New York or Vancouver."

"Nobody drives from Brownsville to Vancouver," was all Jake said in reply. "We'll be lucky to get as far as Corpus Christi." He had already noted that at least nine out of every ten vehicles that passed them by were on automatic, and that the few manual drivers tended to stare at his outstretched thumb as if he were out of his mind.

"There's nothing out there, Jake," the monkey said, very softly, as it plucked at the lobe of his ear with its tiny hand. "You know that. We've looked at the whole goddam world through your window, and a thousand places more. We know there's no rainbow's end, don't we?"

"That kind of window is just a wall with delusions of grandeur," Jake said, knowing that he was repeating himself. "You can look, but you can't touch. The road is real. It goes someplace real."

"What is it you want to touch, Jake?"

"I don't know. Maybe I'll know when I see it, maybe I won't. Either way, I don't want to sit around the rest of my life just *watching*. Just for once, I want to go somewhere. Just for once, I want to *be* somewhere. Anywhere. Nowhere. You can go home if you want to. You can spill the beans to Sam if you want to."

That was unfair, not least because it was untrue. The tamarin couldn't go home unless he gave it a definite order properly confirmed—but Jake wasn't about to compromise the perversity of his mood by being fair.

The car that finally skidded to a halt thirty meters beyond them was just about the oldest model Jake had seen all day. So was the driver, who must have been seventy-five if he was a day. The driver didn't ask Jake where he was headed; as soon as the door was closed he put his foot right down and roared off.

The car's dashboard was an absolute mess, with circuitboards exposed here, there and everywhere. The top of the windscreen, where all the virtual displays should have been, was quite blank.

"I guess you like tinkering," Jake said. "My name's Jake, by the way."

"Never ride in a car that can be hijacked by remote control," the other advised him. "I'm Conor O'Callaghan. That's Irish. Family goes right back to the great potato famine. Much better class of immigrant in those days. Not like now. Country's going to hell."

The vehicle jagged from lane to lane in the same staccato style as his speech, out to the fastest track and then halfway in again. Most of the traffic on the highway consisted of disciplined convoys of robotrucks, which Conor seemed to take a profound delight in disrupting. A forlorn red light was blinking in the centre of the steering-column like a stranded bottle-top.

"I believe that's a police warning, Mr. O'Callaghan," the tamarin remarked. It was the first time the creature had ever displayed knowledge that Jake didn't have, and it was that fact, rather than the red light itself, which belatedly alerted Jake to the fact that all was not well.

"That monkey of yours a fink?" the driver asked. "If it is, I'd be obliged if it'd get the hell out before the sirens start screeching."

"This is a stolen car," Jake said, wonderingly.

"Well hell, a man wouldn't want to do all that to his own car, would he?" the driver said, presumably meaning the exposed circuit-boards and the various kinds of sabotage that had doubtless been worked upon them. "Don't worry—she might be old but she's got all the safety features. I don't think I could kill us if I were to throw her off a bridge. Course, that thing on your shoulder ain't belted in, so it might bounce around a bit when we cut to the chase."

In the distance, Jake heard the wailing of sirens. They seemed to be getting closer with remarkable rapidity.

"They're fast," Conor conceded, as if he'd caught the thought crossing Jake's mind, "but they ain't allowed to be reckless. Gettin' on our tail is one thing—catchin' us is somethin' else."

Again the car began to zigzag from lane to lane. Conor recklessly hurled the vehicle at the wheels of mammoth robotrucks, which dutifully swerved and altered pace with lumbering grace. The juggernauts always managed to avoid the car, if only by a seeming thumb's-width. Jake remembered, though, that nearly one in ten of the vehicles that had passed him on the sliproad had had human drivers. He wondered how many of those drivers had failed to switch to automatic after filtering into the highway traffic, and how many had been messing about with their own circuit-boards.

"Do you do this often?" he inquired, astonished by the mildness of his tone. He was afraid, but the fear didn't seem to hurt. Thus far, it was just a kind of excitement.

"Not as often as I'd like," Conor confessed.

"Do you always pick up hitchhikers when you do?"

"Don't usually see any. Wouldn't pick up a Third Worlder, of course, or anyone under the age of irresponsibility, but I figured you might be grateful. Am I wrong?"

Jake wasn't sure what the answer to that question was, but he was saved from the necessity of offering one by the nervous tamarin, which leapt down on to the dash-ledge to stare through the windscreen with evident alarm.

"Central Traffic Control is slowing the traffic down," the monkey said, in a decidedly officious tone. "It would be dangerous in the extreme to maintain our present speed."

"Naw," said the driver. "It gets even more exciting when they turn the road into an obstacle course."

Jake saw that the rest of the traffic was indeed being brought to a gradual standstill. Soon, theirs would be the only vehicle on the move, except for the pursuing police vehicles. The robotrucks were drawing inwards by careful degrees, leaving the outermost lanes of the highway empty, but Conor didn't immediately move out there; he continued weaving in and out of the middle lanes, cutting across other vehicles with reckless abandon. They continued to avoid him with marvelous agility and patience.

Jake realized, somewhat to his disappointment, that the experience wasn't so very different from a VR "ride," and that his familiarity with such rides, although limited, was determining the oddly-qualified and carefully-muffled terror of his responses.

I'm so out of touch with reality that I can't even grasp it any more, he thought. *This is what it's come to. I'm going to die, and it's just another virtual experience.*

"Do you have any idea how many people you're inconveniencing, Mr. O'Callaghan?" the tamarin asked, in a censorious manner that was certainly no reflection of Jake's personality.

"Sure do," Conor said, enthusiastically. "Putting a roadblock across a twelve-lane superhighway is one hell of an operation. Snarls up twenty, maybe twenty-five thousand vehicles. Last lot of fines bankrupted me—from now on, I'm dying on credit."

"They'll put you under house arrest," Jake said, wonderingly. "You'll never be able to go out again, ever."

"Depends how good their locks are," Conor replied. "I've been a cracker since I was so high. Takes solid walls and heavy bolts to keep me inside—software won't do it. Nice day trip, hey?"

Jake laughed, feeling a strange wave of relief pass through him as the car was forced back into the empty outer lanes. There was now a solid wall of robotrucks to their right, and nothing ahead of them for at least a kilometer. As the wave passed, though, Jake began to eye the barrier protecting the grassy meridian, wondering just how crazy the old man was.

He turned in his seat. The pursuing police cars were coming up fast. Conor began to jiggle the wheel from side to side so that the car veered from one empty lane to another. The pursuers' safety mechanisms held them back; they couldn't overtake unless he left them an adequate gap, and he was a very good judge of adequate gaps.

"I strongly advise you to slow down, sir," the tamarin said, leaping back on to Jake's shoulder and then slipping down behind the seats. It was taking protective action; it had seen the roadblock that was looming up ahead of them.

Conor didn't slow down. He just drove full tilt at the roadblock.

The distance separating the car from the block disappeared with terrifying fluidity, and Jake felt his heart—his weak, unstable heart—pounding in his chest like an earthbreaking drill of a type he hadn't seen in fifty years. The terror inside him back-flipped out of its virtual mode and became suddenly, overwhelmingly forceful. It was mortal terror now; he knew that they were going to crash, that the car and the whole damn world were going to be torn apart.

The only thing he didn't know was why.

In spite of his authentic terror, that was the thought which seized hold of him as they hurtled towards the barrier: *Why is the crazy man doing this? Because he knows that he won't die, or because he hopes that he might?*

Conor had obviously done this before. For him, it was just a joyride, just a day out—but it was Jake's first time, and he had never been in a crash of any kind. As the barrier hurtled towards them like the black horizon of death itself, Jake's poor heart leaped and lurched and tried with all its pathetic might to explode.

He never felt the impact. He saw it, but he never felt a thing.

* * * * * * *

Jake woke up in his own bed, feeling dreadful.

Sam was stationed to the right, Doreen to the left. Sam was pale, exhausted and anxious; Doreen was flushed, agitated and solicitous. It didn't take long for their tender enquiries to give way to harsh recriminations.

"You could have been killed," Sam said. "You very nearly were."

"The car had safety features," Jake muttered. "Crazy Conor by-passed all the software checks, but the hardware was still in place."

"That's not the point," Sam persisted. "You had a major heart attack, Dad. If there hadn't been an ambulance waiting behind the barrier, you'd be stone dead. As it is, you might have lost five or ten years. It wasn't trivial, Dad—nothing is, at your age."

No, Jake thought. *At my age, nothing is.*

"Where did you think you were going, Jake?" Doreen wanted to know. She was fussing over him, fluffing the pillows, checking the many wires and catheters that connected various parts of his prone body to the house physician, reading the various displays that were monitoring his all-too-frail flesh. Somehow, she gave the impression of being in her element—which was odd, given her actual vocation.

They've got me where they want me now, he thought, uncharitably. "Nowhere," he said out loud.

"Well," said Sam, "you nearly made it. You won't be going out again for quite some time. Fortunately, that lunatic you were with won't be going out for the rest of his life. Why on earth did you hitch a ride with a maniac like that?"

"He offered," Jake said. "Where's the tamarin?"

They had both been bending over him, but now they straightened up like twin pillars. He felt as if he were somehow suspended between them and drawn unnaturally taut.

"The monkey didn't have a belt or an airbag," Sam said, reluctantly. "It must have tried to use the back of your seat as a cushion. It would have been okay if only the back seat hadn't been sheared from its moorings. That's why your back hurts—you bruised several vertebrae. The monkey was caught and crushed. There was nothing the medical team could do."

"I'm sorry," Doreen was quick to say, as if someone might have suspected her of being glad if she hadn't said it.

"Oh shit," said Jake.

The silence was hard to bear, but not as hard to bear as the things they were too diplomatic to say out loud. Things like: *it was only a kind of robot, not really alive at all*; or, *you can get another one if you want*; or, *it was your own stupid fault you stupid, senile old fool*. He noticed, for the first time, that his back really was in a bad way. He'd be walking stiffly for some time, if and when he was able to get up again.

He tried to twist himself around so that he could look at the monitors that were collating an objective record of his distress, but his spine wouldn't tolerate the torque and the displays were too high up on the wall.

"It's my data," he said, sourly. "I ought to be able to read it."

"You can," Doreen told him, in matronly fashion. "All you have to do is put the VR helmet on. It'll put a full display right before your eyes. You can watch your insides churning away through a fleet of internal cameras if you want to."

Suddenly, it didn't seem like such a good idea.

"No charges have been filed against you," Sam said, obviously thinking that there was safer conversational ground in that direction, "but we had to extradite you from Mexico as an illegal alien. There's a certain irony in that, I suppose."

"I didn't even know we were heading south," Jake told him, bitterly. "I guess I'll be forgetting which way's up next. But I can still die with a clean sheet. You can put that on my tombstone if you like. *Here lies Jake, died with a clean sheet*. Better set up a spy-eye so you can look out of your window at it any time you like. Show your kid, if you ever get around to having one. One's still the ration, I suppose, for all right-thinking immortals?"

He didn't add: *We could've had two, if we'd wanted to*. It was true; he and Martha could have, if they hadn't had a conscience about Third World overcrowding. Nobody had known way back then that the next generation wouldn't have to bother with dying, or that the surplus personnel of the Third World would simply come and set up house in the interstices of the First.

"Don't be like that, Dad," Sam said. His voice was light, but he meant it.

"I am like that," Jake retorted, stubbornly. "Always was, always will be."

* * * * * * *

Doreen finally had to get back to work; however uncertain they might be, the world's futures still had to be bought and sold. Sam stayed for a while longer.

"You had a bad shock, I guess," Sam said.

"Let that be a lesson to me," Jake countered. "It's dangerous out there, what with all these crazy old people. A man can lose his best friend as easy as snapping his fingers."

"Was the monkey really your best friend?" Sam asked, skeptically—displaying a perspicacity of which even the tamarin's clever biochip might have been incapable.

"No," Jake admitted. "I spent too much time with smart machines to start grieving for one. It's not like losing Martha was, not in a million years. Don't say I won't miss him, mind. Hard to find people I have that much in common with."

"Doesn't it get a little claustrophobic, talking all the time with an echo?"

"About as claustrophobic as a cell on Death Row with a million windows and a doorway to a thousand virtual worlds. Okay, so he wasn't really as smart as he sounded—who is?"

"You never used to call it *he* when it was alive," Sam observed. "You never even gave it a name."

"Maybe they ought to make them with sexual organs," Jake said. "Just for decoration, of course. It'd be easier to give them names if they were one thing or the other. It'd be easier to think of them as real animals. I mean, that's the idea, isn't it? We're supposed to be able to think of them as real animals, just like us. That way, we really might be able to make friends with them, the way we sometimes can with one another."

"Someone called from the Village," Sam told him. "Saw the news, wanted to know if you were okay. Name of Peterson. Was he a friend?"

"Not really."

"Good of him to call, though."

"Not really."

Sam sat down on the bed and looked his father right in the eye. "If you want to die, Dad, you can," he said, very soberly. "It's easy enough. If you want to live and get nothing out of it, that's even easier. It must be hell, having fallen through a trapdoor that was sealed and made safe a few years after it caught you. I ask the same question, you know: *Why you?* I hear the same answer: *Why anybody?* Whenever it came along, someone was bound to miss out: a whole generation. I won't try to fan the flames by saying that they might still discover a way to undo damage already done, although they might. All I'll say is that I'd feel a lot happier and a lot prouder if *my* father was one of the guys who did his level best to make the most of the time he had, even though he'd lost almost everything that made what he had seem worth having. But then, I always was a selfish little toad, wasn't I? Comes of being an only child, I guess. In the future, there'll only be only children. What a world, hey?"

Jake said nothing, because there was nothing he could say that wouldn't make him seem like an old fool. He wriggled and writhed a bit, knowing that the physician would read it as a sign of increasing discomfort and up the endorphin input. He figured that it was time to float for a while, and to feel sensibly detached.

"I'll come in and see how you are in a little while," Sam said. "Doreen'll pop in and out as and when she can. You want peace and quiet and all those wires out, you'll have to recover. Okay?"

"Sure," said Jake. "I'll be fine. Back on my feet in no time."

"I've moved the window nearer the bed," Sam pointed out, as he paused in the doorway, "so you can see out."

"Thanks," Jake said, lukewarmly.

At first he turned away from the window, and even shut his eyes for a while, but he couldn't go to sleep. In the end, he turned back again, to face the reconfigured wall. Beyond the imaginary window-pane snow was gently falling on a meadow.

After watching the scene for a few tedious minutes, Jake found the remote control and switched off the snow. Then he switched off the meadow. Idly, he started surfing through the channels.

Worlds came and went, each one flaring up in a blaze of light and then dying. Some of them were here and now, others elsewhere and anywhere, in the present or the distant past or possible futures or pasts that might have been but never were. Jake couldn't tell the real ones from the unreal at this sort of pace; they were all whirled in together, all part and parcel of the same infinitely-confused and infinitely-confusing whole.

What an old fool I am, Jake thought, *trying to go anywhere and nowhere on the highway, when all the anywheres and nowheres anyone could ever want to see are right outside my window.* But he knew, as he thought it, that the window was really a wall, just like the one Central Traffic Control had thrown across the highway: a wall to keep him from getting out no matter how fast or how far he decided to go.

He could see everything—a world of infinite possibility, full of people, young and old—but he couldn't actually go there. He wriggled around a bit, to remind the invisible physician's programs that he was still there, still in distress.

It could be worse, he reminded himself, sternly. *It could be a great deal worse, and a man my age should be wise enough to count his blessings. At least I have a son, and a home, and a few more heartbeats to count—and I have a window right next to my bed.*

He waited, numbly, for the brave words to take effect. He was sure that they would, if he only gave them enough time and cajoled enough endorphins from the systems hidden in the wall. They had to. What else was there to take comfort from but words, shaped and given life by bravery?

By slow degrees, the caress of the clean sheets on his bruised and careworn skin became breathtakingly and luxuriously soft. Somehow, it reminded him of Martha, of fine sand warmed and glittered by the sun, and of the tenderness of youth.

For the moment, at least, it was something he didn't want to lose.

SKIN DEEP

"You really don't have to go all the way, Piggy," said Melissa Sai, gently. "No matter what the 3-V pundits say, total infatuation is simply not necessary."

"You don't understand, Missy," Orchisson complained, with more than a trace of bitterness in his voice, as he studied himself in the mirror. "I've had my fair share of media hype, and I'm not stupid enough to let it get to me the way some people do. There's really no need for you to be utterly cynical about emotional matters. You may have given up your finer feelings for Lent in 2349 and never got them back again, but that doesn't mean that no one in the whole world can ever fall in love."

Melissa looked down at her neatly-crossed legs in order to hide her injured frown, and then made a show of surveying the delicate curve of her forearm. Roy had never talked to her this way before, and it wasn't just her pride that was hurt. She really was trying to help him, and she was disappointed by her inability to get through. There had been a time when he had listened to her, respecting her judgment—but that had been before he got his "fair share" of media hype.

She felt that she owed it to herself, if not to him, to put in one last plea for sanity. "It's a joke, Roy," she said. "Don't you see that? I won't even dignify it by calling it a myth. Sure, we all play along—it's a plug for the whole facetech business. But if I'd ever thought that there was the slightest chance of your falling for that kind of crap, I'd never have started calling you Piggy."

"Actually, Missy," he said, "turning away from the mirror at last, "I wish you wouldn't. Not in front of Helena, anyway. It's undignified. How do I look?"

He looked fine. Melissa didn't need a mirror to reassure her that her own face was just as flawless. She was, after all, in the business, and could get her looks wholesale. But hers was a very ordinary perfection; she was not a Work of Art with a capital W and a capital A. The biotechnician who had restructured her had been a first-class craftsman, but he had not been a Saul Steinhardt or a Roy Orchisson.

Whenever she was asked, Melissa always said that the reason she had never let her partner work on her own face was that she couldn't trust anyone else to take her place as his tissue-texturer, but that wasn't true. The reason she had never let him turn her into a Work of Art was that she had been in the business for a long time—she was forty years older than Orchisson—and she had long ago grown sick of all the 3-V babble about the Quest for Perfect Beauty and the Wisdom of the Loving Eye. She had seen too many would-be Pygmalions come to grief. Roy was the third featurist she had adopted and promoted, and she had nicknamed them all "Piggy" in the hope that she might immunize them against that kind of disease; but it hadn't worked with the other two, and now Roy had fallen for it too. Why, oh why, were first-time-young men so incredibly crass?

The fact that he had fallen for it at all was bad enough, but Roy wasn't a man to do things by halves. Instead of becoming besotted with some first-time-young ingénue he'd gone straight to the bottom of the barrel, and fallen in love with Helena Wyngard. Helena was a third-time-young rejuvenate, old enough to be his great-grandmother, who had already had at least eight stabs at becoming the Most Beautiful Woman in the World in the tender care of other Piggies, and was arrogant enough to believe that she'd succeeded every time.

"She's such a bitch," Melissa said, well aware of how feeble it sounded. "She's mad, bad and dangerous to know. She'll chew you up and spit you out the way she does with all the idiots stupid enough to think they love her. Look at her form, for Heaven's sake. What do you think you've got that the other three thousand didn't have?"

She knew that she was leading with her chin, but she just couldn't help herself. The upper-cut was duly delivered with merciless force and just sufficient accuracy to send her reeling. "If I didn't know you better, Missy," he said, as the door-chime rang, "I could almost believe that you were jealous."

* * * * * * *

Melissa Sai was second-time-young, but she had never been in any other line than facetech. Such single-minded application to one kind of work was almost unheard of in modern times, but she had never been a respecter of fashions and trends. If other people wanted to spend their artificially-extended lives collecting higher degrees and juggling three jobs at a time that was their business; she was happy with constancy.

Once, when she was *very* first-time-young, she had considered going into medicine. That had been in an era when saving lives and repairing injuries seemed to be the proper function of tissue-restructuring techniques, and cosmetic restructuring was still widely regarded as a luxurious exercise of vanity. But she had realized, even before social attitudes underwent a general *bouleversement*, that such crude utilitarian thinking was out of date. The human race had passed through the historical phase in which technology served only as a defense against the cruel ravages of nature; all kinds of repair-work and protection had been thoroughly routinized and could be taken for granted. The real work that was to be done no longer had to do with matters of health, but with matters of happiness. Death had lost its sting, old age had had its fangs drawn, and the task now in hand was to improve the business of living. So Melissa became an expert on facework, using her carefully-cultivated gene-switching skills to recover the blastular innocence of the facial tissues, so that they could be remolded by artists.

She was not an artist herself; she was a technician. Without the support that technicians provided, though, artists could not work, and the greatest artists required the most expert gene-switchers to back them up.

Everyone in the world was an art critic nowadays, and there were millions of people who thought that they could spot artistic talent, but Melissa knew better. Only an expert facetechnician could really identify a great featurist. She had worked with hundreds of artists in her time, but in recent times she had devoted herself entirely to her own discoveries. She had found them, trained them, promoted them, and lent her not-inconsiderable influence to the building of their careers. She had not been sorry, in the end, to lose the first two to the Pygmalion Syndrome, but Roy Orchisson was the best of the three, and she had dared to think that he might be different—that he might have the strength of mind to resist the outdated myth that represented love as a kind of madness.

The jealousy she felt was not sexual. She and Roy had romped a few times like any other people of compatible tastes, but their relationship had never been polluted by infatuation. Nevertheless, she was jealous. Roy Orchisson was her *protégé* and her partner, and she did not want to see him hurt, humiliated and played for a sucker by a woman who had made a career of acting out a silly myth fit only for the vidveg.

For the 3-V pundits, it wasn't enough that facetech was a way of making millions of ordinary people feel better about themselves; the 3-V thrived on hype, and in 3-V-ese, the heart and soul of facetech was The Quest for Perfect Beauty. Nor was it sufficient for Beauty to be pursued by calm and careful professionals coolly exercising their skills; in the world of 3-V, Perfect Beauty had to be the product of Unbounded Love, and Magnificent Obsession, and the Ultimate Inspiration.

The vidveg had been fed the story of Helena Wyngard's personal Quest for Perfect Beauty for more than a hundred years, and the fact that she was now third-time-young seemed only to have increased the interest of her loyal public. According to the hype, of course, she had already succeeded in the Quest at least three times, but that had never made any difference to future expectations; according to the

3-V celebrity-brokers, facemakers were continually Pushing Back the Horizons of Beauty, constantly raising the standards of human perfection.

It was all rather pathetic. But the artists kept falling for it. The more media attention they got, the more they got sucked into the vortex. Eventually, they got talked into the belief that only the extremes of passion could inspire them to produce their finest work. And they started looking avidly about for someone to fall in love with—someone who might play Galatea to their Pygmalion.

It had always been inevitable, in spite of Melissa's hopes, that Roy Orchisson would eventually get his fingers burned just like all the rest. But she couldn't help feeling that insult had been added to injury by the fact that he'd fallen head-over-heels for Helena Wyngard.

* * * * * * *

The door of the ante-room slid soundlessly aside to reveal the woman in question. She was followed into the room by her personal assistant, Wilson Shafran, a delicately effete third-time-young man whose perennial privilege it was to hover in the background, while his employer strutted her stuff.

Even Melissa had to concede that Helena's present face was probably the best thing Saul Steinhardt had ever done. It hadn't yet begun to show any signs of wear and tear—it was only fifteen years old, and with proper maintenance it could have stayed on the road for another thirty years, even on a double rejuvenate like Helena Wyngard. But that wasn't Helena's way; Helena liked to have a new look just as soon as the old one began to seem over-familiar. The news that a new genius might be emerging among the ranks of the top-flight featurists was a magnet that infallibly drew her attention. She liked to catch her Pygmalions at exactly the right point in their careers. She liked to get the very best out of them—and then she would do her best to see that they never went one better. Had the law of the land offered her more tactical latitude she would probably have had them murdered, but things being as they were, she contented herself with conscientious attempts at spiritual destruction.

"Roy, darling," she said, in a super sweet tone that only expertly retuned vocal chords could have produced, "it's so wonderful to see you again. And this must be Dr. Sai—such a pretty name, my dear. Roy has told me so much about you."

Orchisson bowed in an over-theatrical fashion, while Melissa contented herself with a very formal nod. When they all moved through to the inner sanctum in order to inspect the mock-ups on the big screen, Helena gravitated towards Orchisson, immediately reducing the distance between them to one that boasted of intimacy. This invasion of his personal space did not bother Roy in the least, and it was obvious that he had already granted her an exclusive territorial claim. Melissa, politely but carefully excluded, permitted herself a tiny sigh.

Melissa could see that any chance she might have had to make Roy see sense had already perished. Helena had already taken over. Roy must know perfectly well what had happened to all his predecessors, but the fact that Helena Wyngard was the ultimate *femme fatale* seemed to make her more attractive to those she lured and then attempted to destroy. The first victim of infatuation was always common sense; every new lover she took hoped and believed, in frank defiance of the calculus of probability, that *he* would not be as easily discarded as the rest.

Shafran came forward to inspect the mock-ups too, but he took up a position on the far side of the gravitating couple.

Orchisson began to display his designs on the screen, delicately playing with line and tint, explaining the logic of his approach. He spoke rapidly, but quite clearly, cleverly picking up the thread of some earlier discussion while Helena Wyngard hastened him along with little nods and seductive upward glances shot from beneath slightly-lowered eyelids. Melissa, momentarily lost in her study of their body-language, had to make an effort to tune in.

"...It's not contrast for contrast's sake, of course," Roy was saying, with the casual ease of a showman who has mastered his patter, "nor is it a mere matter of fashion. I don't pay any attention to vidchatter about what's in and what's out—I aim to make the trends, not follow them. But the ivory-complexioned ash-blonde look is so classically severe and symmetrical that it's come to seem mechanical. The reason I'm suggesting the black hair and eyes, and the fuller lips, is to give me the latitude to play with sultriness, sensuality and mystery, all at the same time...."

Melissa looked on impassively. It was a charade, of course. The faces sketched out on the screen were essentially insipid, in spite of all the skill the computer had in the matter of rendering them lifelike. The program could ring the changes on six hundred independent variables, altering each one by the subtlest fractions, and the software engineers claimed that it could represent every human face that ever had been worn and ever could be created; but at the end of the day, a face was a living thing, and the true artistry involved in creating faces more beautiful than any that had previously been seen or made only showed up in the living flesh. Orchisson could tell Helena Wyngard what kind of face he intended to make for her, but he could not show it to her as it would really appear; she would have to trust him to add the touch of magic that would turn a dead design into a fabulous fantasy.

When Helena finally said, "It's marvelous," her voice was like the purr of a cat—supremely generous and contented, but with a hint of the predatory about it.

"I'm so glad," said Orchisson, loading his own words with carefully-modulated sincerity. "I know that I'm taking on a lot, to work with a face that has been sculpted by Steinhardt and De Cosimo—not to mention Vulović and Bačik—but I really do think I'm ready, and more than ready. The gift which an artist has can only be caught once at the fullest point of its flowering. This is *my* time; I feel it in my bones."

This concatenation of clichés was too much even for Helena, who turned gracefully away from Orchisson to look Melissa full in the face.

"I do appreciate the importance of your part in all this, my dear," she said. "I've undergone reconstruction enough times to know that an artist is nothing without appropriate technical support. You have a genius too, Dr. Sai, and I know what a debt I will owe to you, as well as to Roy, if this works out as we hope it will."

"It will work out," Melissa promised, coldly. "But my part really is routine. Roy is the sculptor—I just make sure the clay is malleable, without doing any damage to the model."

Helena Wyngard smiled, and in that smile Melissa saw how casually she had been dismissed. The woman's real purpose in looking at her had not been to pay her a compliment or reassure her that her supporting role in the planned operation was a worthy one, but simply to make sure that there was no possibility of Roy's affections being deflected from their intended target. She had judged at a glance that there was not.

"I'll show Helena round the theatre," said Orchisson to Melissa. "Then I'll take her back to her hotel. Could you possibly look after Mr. Schafran?"

Melissa raised an eyebrow, but nodded dutifully. She bowed to them both as they moved towards the door, leaving her behind with the personal assistant. She looked at the face displayed on the screen, which would soon be the face about which every 3-V frontperson would be asking the vital questions.

Has The Most Beautiful Woman in the World done it again?

Has the New Boy from the Mid-West topped the great Saul Steinhardt?

Has Helena found The Love of Her Life at last?

"How could anyone ever have believed that love was blind?" said Shafran, silkily, "or that beauty was only skin deep? You must let me take you to dinner, Dr. Sai, so that we can settle the financial details. I happen to know the most wonderful little bistro, just around the corner."

* * * * * * *

Melissa saw very little of Roy during the following week. He was too busy letting his hormones run wild, honing his Magnificent Obsession to just the right pitch of intensity. He was also busy being seen out and about with his inamorata, making sure that all the world's vidveg knew exactly what was going on. All the preparations for the long series of operations were left to Melissa.

She tried to console herself with the thought that he would get over it, in time. In a hundred years, when he was newly third-time-young and she had taken her turn to test the prevailing wisdom which said that third rejuvenations never took, they would surely be able to laugh about it. There were thousands of Helena Wyngard's ex-lovers in the world, and well over half of them showed no emotional scars at all after the first thirty years or so. Roy would still be a first-rate facemaker when Helena had finished with him.

She should have been reassured by such observations, all of which were true, but she was not. She had wanted something else for Roy: she had wanted him to rise above the morass of media mythology, to be his own man. She had hoped that she would never have to take refuge in reminding herself that although love might be the last of the unconquered diseases of man it was very rarely fatal.

Melissa had always wanted to find a partner who would mirror her own coolness, her own control, and she had thought for a while that Roy might be the one. The historical moment had seemed ripe for men to stop conducting themselves like poodles on heat, and start growing into the clothes of reason—but she had been too optimistic. The sad fact was Roy had taken it into his head that he had fallen in love, and he fell hard. By the time they began the Great Work, he was in a veritable fever of excitement.

In the past, he had always been a quick worker. Melissa had always admired the deft gracefulness of his hands. This time, though, he was posing as a perfectionist. It was not enough that the right result be achieved; it had to be achieved effortfully. She had never seen him poke and probe so much to such little effect, nor so doubtful about the results of his sculpting. But she bore with him, never uttering a word of criticism; she was, after all, a true professional.

Slowly, Helena Wyngard's latest face took shape. Twenty-four hours into the series it looked like a complete wreck; forty-eight hours passed before it even began to look salvageable. By the time the third day was coming to an end, though, Melissa had begun to see in her mind's eye what Roy must be seeing in his. She began to appreciate the cunning and the daring of his approach, and she began to see the genius shining through.

Melissa had little sympathy with those cynics who said that there was only so much that could be done with the human face and that all the possible permutations had already been exhausted; for all her dislike of 3-V-ese phraseology she really did believe in Pushing Back the Horizons of Beauty, and she knew that Roy Orchisson was doing exactly that while he worked on Helena Wyngard. However unworthy his motives and methods might be, Helena really was his Galatea; this was his finest work to date, and it was difficult for Melissa to imagine that he could ever surpass it.

On the fourth day, he began to introduce innovations at the technical level, which was something she had never known him do before. She was deeply hurt that he hadn't checked it out with her, given that the technical side of the operation was her business.

"I don't like it, Roy," she told him, as soon as they took a break. "You're not supposed to introduce novel DNA without a full discussion of its probable effects. You're certainly not supposed to use novel DNA without even telling me what it is or what it's supposed to do. I carry the can if anything goes wrong at the technical level—it's my responsibility. Whatever you're using, it's not even registered."

"Nothing will go wrong," he assured her. "It's no big deal, biochemically. It's just one more special effect—but it's my secret, okay? A great artist is entitled to his idiosyncrasies."

"It's not okay, Roy. We're working together. You've never used any novel DNA before without checking it through with me. I don't like it at all."

"I'm a big boy now, Missy," he told her. "You don't have to mother me any more. I don't have your practical skill in de-differentiation, but I know my genetics. An artist is entitled to mix his own colors if he can't get the tints he needs off the shelf. Trust me, Missy—this is the big one, and I really need to do it my way."

She knew, at that point, that she had lost him for good. From now on, he would go his own way. He had stopped thinking of her as the person who had detected and nurtured his talent, and had begun to regard her simply as a tech—an assistant, whose role was to do as she was told. He had become convinced not merely of his own genius, but of the fact that his genius was his alone, and that no one else had any right to interfere in its deployment.

She was hurt by this, but she went back to the operating table and got on with the job. She continued to support him throughout the operation, to the very limit of her skill. That, she thought, was the professional thing to do.

Whatever the novel DNA was that Roy had used to transform the tissues of Helena Wyngard's face, it certainly did no harm. She came out of the operation more beautiful than she had ever looked before—perhaps more beautiful than *anyone* had ever looked before. Roy was certain of it; Melissa was certain of it, and even Wilson Schafran was certain of it.

"If ever I were going to go straight," said Schafran, at the first public show, "I'd go straight for *that*." It made headlines on the 3-V, in spite of the fact that he'd said it at least three times before in the course of the last seventy years. Vidveg had notoriously short memories.

* * * * * * *

The pantomime romance continued on its inevitable course, mapped out in painstaking detail by the insatiable 3-V cameras. Helena and Roy were deeply in love; Helena and Roy were traveling round the world; Helena and Roy were greeted everywhere with wild acclamation.

Meanwhile, Melissa knew, Helena would be sharpening her claws. The demands that she made on her partner's time, attention and bank balance would gradually grow to take over his every waking moment, and would still be unsatisfied. Other would-be lovers would be queuing up to drink in the delicious smiles of her new face and offer up their unqualified adoration. At first she would be content with flirting and tantalizing, but not for long. Soon she would begin complaining about Roy's possessiveness, and would make the point that his creation was, after all, *her* face, to do with as she wished. Eventually, she would explain to everyone how unreasonable he had become, and how he had fallen victim to the same disease that had claimed so many of her earlier facemakers: the disease of thinking that he owned her.

"I had hoped, you know," she would say with a sigh, fluttering her new eyelashes at the cameras, "that Roy would be different. I hoped that he might be capable of a mature relationship. Unfortunately...."

But it never quite got that far.

It transpired that Roy *was* different, in a way that neither Helena nor Melissa had anticipated.

It was Wilson Schafran who was delegated to bear the bad news. He called to say that he had traveled all the way from Queensland to California for the privilege of having a very quiet word with her, in person and in the strictest confidence. He wouldn't meet her in a hotel or in one of his wonderful little bistros; he wanted to be well away from the nearest microphone or camera—which wasn't easy to arrange in a world whose walls were so liberally equipped with eyes and ears.

She finally agreed to meet him on a lonely stretch of private beach. They left their separate robocabs to wait with meters running while he took her for a walk along the moist sand below the high-tide line.

"We have a problem," he said. "And by *we*, I don't just mean Helena and Roy. Your neck is on the line too, if what your favorite facemaker says is true."

"What does he say?" she asked, frostily. But Schafran wasn't that direct,

"Helena did him a big favor, you know," he said. "Coming to him to have her face done. It's the best publicity a guy in his line of work can ever have—it'll set him up for life, and that can be a long time nowadays. And she took a risk doing it, you know. She's third-time-young, and you know how rare it is for anyone to get a fourth turn. Barring miracles, she's only got two more faces left—three at the outside.

I don't mind telling you that it wasn't just Orchisson's talent that brought her to the two of you. She knew about you, too. She knew that there wasn't a safer pair of hi-tech hands in the world, and she wanted to be absolutely sure that nothing could possibly slip on the technical side. She trusted you."

"Are you trying to suggest that something did slip on the technical side?" asked Melissa.

"Could be," he said, glumly. "We're not entirely sure. It might be that Orchisson's telling lies—he wouldn't be the first guy to try something crazy when brush-off time rolled around. You'd think that after all this time they'd know the score, wouldn't you? They must, in their heart of hearts—but every damn one of them gets it into his head that he'll be the one to tame her...the one who'll give her the face that she can't bear to trade in. That's what gets them, you know: it's not so much that she starts using her faces to reel in other guys, but the thought that once they're history she'll start looking around for a new facemaker. It really hurts them deep down, to think that their great work of art won't even last until her next rejuve. Like I say, they all tend to go a bit crazy. More than one guy has threatened to vitriolize her—talk about cutting off your nose to spite your face. But your boy has come up with a new twist on that one."

"What new twist?" she asked, sharply. She was unhappy at the turn which the conversation had taken, and her stomach was already knotted up with alarm at the thought of what Schafran was implying.

"Orchisson says that he and his work of art are a package," Schafran told her. "He claims that when he rebuilt her face he built in a booby-trap of some kind. He says that if and when he gets tired of her, and decides to let her go, that will be okay—but he's not prepared to be cast aside like a worn out sock until he's good and ready. He says that if he's forced out before he's ready, he won't leave the face behind—he says that he can trigger its decay overnight, and that it will leave such a mess behind that it will be impossible for any other facemaker to rebuild her. Personally, I think it's all bullshit, because a trap like that would have to be laid by you rather than by him, and I know that you're not crazy—but he says that he sneaked some unregistered DNA into the op without your okay, and I have to check it out. Tell me, Miss Sai, is it true?"

Melissa stopped and turned to watch the waves playing with the shore. The wind that spurred them on was surprisingly cool, but she felt uncomfortably warm.

"I don't know," she said, after a few moments.

"What do you mean, you don't know?" said Schafran, icily.

"I mean that I didn't do anything of the sort, and I can't really believe that he would. But he did use some novel DNA—unregistered stuff. We both know it's illegal, but we both know that it happens all the time. He didn't check it with me, or clear it with me—I gave him hell at the time, but I took it for granted that it was something trivial, something harmless. I could be wrong. But he's wrong too, even if he did lay some kind of booby-trap. Nothing could stop a new facemaker doing a rescue job—nothing short of outright murder."

Schafran smiled wryly. "I told her that," he said. "But Orchisson has a cunning streak. Helena won't take chances with her face—not even million to one chances—and he has her running scared. You have to talk to Orchisson, Miss Sai. You have to get him to back off. I don't have to tell you what it would do to him—and to you—if he did do what he says he did, and he really does mess up her face, even temporarily. It would be the end of everything for both of you."

"Yes," she agreed, dully. "It would, wouldn't it?"

That was the natural end of the conversation. Schafran had said what he had come to say. But as they walked back to the highway, he surprised her by saying: "You love him, don't you?"

"Not the way you mean," she retorted.

"I know I play the fool," he said, soberly, "but that's only a job. Believe me, Miss Sai, I mean what you mean. You love him the way I love her: cleanly; aesthetically; platonically."

"I thought you only liked men," she said—but it was surprise, not bitchiness, that made her say it.

"I only have sex with men," he said. "But this is the twenty-fourth century, Miss Sai. We're all born from artificial wombs and we're all sterilized at birth. The idea that love and our redundant animal instincts are flipsides of the same coin should have been laid to rest three hundred years ago. You understand that, and so do I—but the vidveg don't, and Helena doesn't, and Orchisson doesn't. It's a shame, but you and I are the only sane players in the game and it's down to us to save it. Talk to him, Miss Sai. Explain to him that we're different now—that we can be *human* beings, if only we're prepared to make the effort."

It was a good exit line. She had to give him that. She couldn't really respect a man who could make a career out of playing court jester to Helena Wyngard and call it love, but his way of putting things had a certain piquant charm.

* * * * * * *

Needless to say, Melissa had to fly all the way to Oz to talk to her wayward *protégé*; he wouldn't respond to any kind of a summons. Once she was there, he still tried as hard as he could to avoid seeing her in any place where they couldn't be overheard. She finally managed to corner him on a traffic-island in the centre of Brisbane, and he conceded defeat when it became obvious that he could only get to the button which would stop the traffic by shoving her violently aside. He consented to let her engage him in conversation while the robocabs whizzed around them in a hectic but perfectly-programmed collision-free whirl.

"You have to stop it," she told him. "You have to tell Helena that this booby-trap nonsense is all lies."

"Why should I?" he said, refusing to meet her eye. "And what business is it of yours anyhow?"

"Firstly," she said, trying not to sound too much like a co-parent scolding the household brat, "because it *is* all lies. Secondly, because trying to resurrect a dead relationship is a fool's game even if you forgo blackmail and stick to relatively dignified methods like crying your eyes out and begging. And it's my business because anything you say in public about this makes me an accessory or a dupe, either of which is enough to crucify my career along with your own."

"You don't know for sure it's a lie," he told her.

"Yes I do," she said. "You don't think I let you use novel DNA in the theatre without checking it out afterwards, do you?"

He looked up at that, surprised but still furtive. "You told Schafran you couldn't be sure," he pointed out.

"I lied," she said. "Maybe I shouldn't have, but I did. I wanted a chance to talk some sense into you."

He looked at her speculatively. She could see that he was trying to judge from her expression whether or not she was lying now; she knew that he wouldn't be able to. Whatever people claimed, it really was impossible to tell the second-time-young from the first-time-young by looking at them, but when it came to reading their features for guilt and guile, rejuvenates had all the advantages of their actual years.

"Okay," he said, finally, "so I spun her a line. But it wasn't what you think. I'm not the lovesick moron that everyone seems to think I am. It's just that...well, I wanted to stop her. Maybe not even that...maybe I only wanted to slow her down, make her think about what she is and how she lives. I really did love her, for a while...and that face I gave her really is a masterpiece—even you have to admit that. In fact, it's *because* her face is a masterpiece that I didn't want it treated like one more product on the conveyor-belt. I mean, Missy, that woman is sick. I just couldn't let her do it—I couldn't let her destroy a work of art like that. It's *my* face, Missy...it's *our* face. Surely you can understand why I didn't want to just kiss it goodbye and let her drag it through the dirt."

"You didn't have any objection to her destroying Saul Steinhardt's masterpiece," Melissa said, quietly.

"That was different," he complained.

"Not to Saul," she said. "Saul was very proud of that face. Very proud indeed."

"Mine's better."

"His was the best he could do," she pointed out. "And though it may seem like heresy to say so, these things really are a matter of taste. Beauty is in the eye of the beholder."

"Crap," he retorted. "Chemistry and electricity are in the eye of the beholder—chemistry and electricity that respond to cues which were written into the genes millions of years ago. Even you can't rebuild brains so that they think beautiful faces are ugly and *vice versa*. Beauty is real, Missy, and that's why there's such a thing as art. Keats was right about truth being beauty and beauty being truth. And that's why Helena Wyngard needs to be tamed. She's not an art-lover, she's an art-destroyer, and her career stops here, with *my face*. Okay?"

"You know perfectly well it's not okay," she told him, sorely annoyed at having to listen to so much bullshit. "You just wanted to give her the boot, instead of letting her do it to you. You just wanted to scare her a bit, to punish her for not having the grace to treat you just a little better than she treated all the rest. Well, you've done it, and now it's time to stop. Tell her that it was all nonsense, and come home with me. There are faces to be made, Piggy—lots and lots of lovely faces."

"No," he said. "I won't do it. I want her to stay scared—and she is scared, you know. She's coming up to the end of the line, and she knows it. Even if her fourth rejuve adds a few more years to her span, she'll never be truly young again. Even if she doesn't die, she'll have to grow old. She doesn't like that idea one little bit, Missy. She's really scared. Even Schafran doesn't know how scared she is, but I do. That's how close we became, Missy—that's how close we were, until she got bored."

"If you don't tell her," Melissa said, "I will."

"She won't believe you," Orchisson countered, trying as hard as he could to seem smugly certain. "Unless it comes from me, she won't believe it. She might have grown tired of me, but she isn't free—not yet, maybe not ever."

Missy pursed her lips, and watched the traffic whizzing around the island come smoothly to a halt when the lights changed, allowing a party of pedestrians to cross over. Roy could have escaped then, but there was no longer any point. As they passed Roy and Melissa the pedestrians stared at them in the frankly disbelieving fashion that Australians always had when they encountered anything out of the ordinary. Missy waited until they were gone and the traffic was moving again before she spoke again.

THE TREE OF LIFE, BY BRIAN STABLEFORD

"I don't want to hear this kind of thing from you, Roy," she said, radiating disappointment. "It's not worthy of you. You're a better man than that. You accepted a role in Helena Wyngard's real life soap opera, and you played it to the best of your ability, but now it's time to get on to something else. She's been stuck in the same fantasy for three lifetimes, but you don't have to be. You can find better scripts by far than the one you're trying to foist on her. Give it up, Piggy, please."

She came forward to take his arm, intending to link it with hers—but the more intimate territories of his personal space were still pledged to Helena Wyngard, off-limits to her. He stepped back reflexively in order to avoid her. He recoiled so urgently that he stumbled.

He caught his heel on the raised curb of the island, and he fell backwards into the road.

Robocabs had far better reflexes than anything ever driven by human beings, but even they couldn't repeal the laws of motion. The one that was zooming along the lane into which Roy Orchisson fell had too much momentum to stop in time, and its near-side wheel went right over his face—the face that he wore in front of his own head. The weight of the vehicle pulverized his skull and the brain within.

Melissa screamed, and went on screaming for quite some time, while all the lights in the area changed to red, and the whole world came belatedly to a halt.

* * * * * * *

The funeral was a very grand affair. Violent deaths were rare in the modern world, and tended to be represented as awful tragedies by the professional hysterics of the 3-V even when they involved people of no particular significance or celebrity. When a man with Roy Orchisson's high media profile was killed by falling off a traffic island it was a suitable occasion for an orgy of public mourning such as was seen only twice or three times in a decade.

Thirty thousand people turned up at the cemetery, and the eulogies—which took up three hours of the primest time—set a new ratings record in the extended documentary category. The world wept for a great genius laid to rest at the absurdly early age of thirty-nine, bemoaning the loss of all the fabulously beautiful faces he might have made in the course of the next two-and-a-half centuries.

Not unnaturally, the focal point of all the media attention was Helena Wyngard—who, it was widely alleged, had at last found the One Great Love of Her Life, only to have him cruelly snatched away at the very height of their passion. There was now no shred of doubt that her face was the greatest work of art Roy Orchisson would ever produce, and the fact that it was marked so obviously with a very special grief added tremendously to the natural attraction that it exerted over the cameras which crowded around it. All Helena's faces had been newsworthy for a while, but circumstances had made for this one a whole new order of magnitude of newsworthiness. Its tears became, for a while, the most poignantly familiar image in the world.

The moment would have passed, of course, in the normal course of affairs. Nine days was still a respectable lifetime for a media-hype wonder, and very few *causes célèbres* could survive one rejuvenation, let alone two. But at the end of nine days, the tears that stained Roy Orchisson's masterpiece had begun to have an uncanny effect.

Helena Wyngard's face was changing. Its astonishing beauty was beginning to fade.

Melissa Sai discovered this at exactly the same time that everyone else did, and in spite of what she and Wilson Schafran had discussed, she assumed at first—as everyone else did—that it was only an effect of crying so many tears, of an understandable over-indulgence in extravagant lamentations. She knew, after all, that there was no booby-trap—that Roy Orchisson's threat had been quite empty. She had, of course, taken the trouble to inform Helena Wyngard of that fact, in no uncertain terms—and Helena had believed her, or had seemed to.

But as the days wore on, and the cameras which might have resumed their ceaseless search for other images lingered just a little longer, it became gradually obvious that the fading of Helena's beauty was no mere illusion or temporary effect of emotional strain. Her face—the most famous face in the entire world—was falling by degrees into ruin. Nor was the change any mere acceleration of normal aging; it was worse than that.

Incredibly, Helena was slower to realize what was happening than the vidveg, who saw her from a great distance, but always in intimate close-up. Wilson Schafran told Melissa, when he called to plead with her for urgent assistance, that it was not Helena's mirror that had first convinced her that something was dreadfully wrong, but seeing herself on 3-V.

While Melissa crossed the world for the third time in as many weeks, Helena Wyngard was already trying to go into hiding; but there was no beach or traffic island in the world remote enough to evade the cameras, if the cameras did not want to be evaded. Helena continued to be headline news, and the world watched her beautiful face become gradually derelict.

Oddly enough, no rumor of Roy Orchisson's malicious threats ever escaped—or, if it did, it was quietly disregarded by media frontpersons who were busy building a different story around the compounded tragedy.

Helena, in their representations, was pining away. Having lost the One Great Love of Her Life she had lost the Will to Be Beautiful.

It was a marvelous story, because it was at once so utterly unprecedented and so utterly familiar. It had been said of countless people that they had lost their hypothetical will to live, but that was back in the Dark Ages, before the sophistication of modern medicine. In today's world, it seemed so much more appropriate that one should lose instead the Will to Be Beautiful, and if there was tragedy to be found in the contemplation of anyone suffering such a fate, Helena Wyngard was the ideal candidate. She had the heartfelt sympathy and unbridled pity of the entire world.

* * * * * * *

Melissa Sai and Wilson Schafran eventually found a place where they could talk privately, although they had to leave Helena behind in order to arrange it safely. It was in the protected wilderness of an unreclaimed sector of the Nullarbor Plain. There they discussed the possibilities before them.

"Technically," said Melissa, "there simply isn't a problem. The deterioration is purely psychosomatic. But that's why it's difficult to issue a confident prognosis. I can rebuild her face in a matter of days, working with or without an artist—but if the shock, or the fear, or whatever caused this is still there...it might just start again. I'll do my best, but there are things beyond any geneswitcher's control, and I can't promise anything. I'm sorry. I'm sorry for everything."

"That's okay," said Schafran. "It's not your fault. It's not even Orchisson's fault. She knew, all the time, that his juvenile bullshit was all hot air. She always knew it...but she just couldn't quite make her face believe it. Deep down, the fear is much more powerful than anything she knows. Her mind believed what you told her, but her body is saturated by anxieties that won't be quieted by mere thought. She's very old, you know...much older than she used to look."

"Aren't we all," said Melissa.

"So we are," he agreed, in a low tone. "But we haven't yet learned to cope with it, have we? Most of us have emotions that are still rooted in the distant past. We can change our faces, but the rest of it still defeats us. We want you to operate as soon as you're ready, Dr. Sai. She doesn't want to use an artist. She just wants a face: a face like yours or mine. This time, she doesn't think she needs a work of art. She's decided to leave the task of pushing back the horizons of beauty to others, at least for a while."

Melissa nodded. She expected Schafran to say something more, but he didn't. He just stared at the horizon, and all the wilderness displayed before it.

"He *was* a genius, you know," said Melissa. "And I did love him, in spite of everything. Cleanly, aesthetically and platonically—the kind of love that ought to be *true* love, now that we're what we are, instead of what we were. You were right about that."

"I always am," said Schafran. "It's the one and only privilege of agreeing to play the fool without actually being one."

"It's not so bad for you," said Melissa. "After all, my Pygmalion's dead and buried. At least your Galatea's still alive."

"But she's not beautiful any more," he said, in a voice as flat and bleak as the plain. "She's not a work of art. She's only a woman. What good is that to me?"

"Beauty," she said, forgiving herself the lapse into cliché for once, "is only skin deep."

"Aesthetically," he said, "skin deep is all there is. That's why we could be living in Utopia—if only we could adapt."

"If only," she agreed.

Then they turned away from the unappealing wilderness, and headed back towards civilization.

CARRIERS

Bowring heard the noise of the two helicopters while he was in the bloodshed vamping the sows, but even when they'd crossed over three times he didn't hurry out to take a look. He carried on linking up the needles to the sows' necks, working with practiced precision. A few of the younger ones stirred in their hammocks, mewing faintly, and he gentled them reflexively with his work-roughened hand. Not that he thought of them as feeling creatures—no farmer of any kind could afford to be sentimental about his stock, and bloodfarmers least of all. To him the sows were just fleshy factories, automated production lines for all the useful products harvested with their cytogenically-augmented leucocytes and erythrocytes.

It wasn't until he had completed the round that he went outside and stood there, shading his eyes from the early morning sun, peering up at the helicopters as they roared overhead for the fourth time. They were dark green, and carried army insignia. They were only sixty or seventy feet off the ground, and gave the impression that they might tear the satellite dish off the chimney if they got too close to the house.

"Get the hell out of my airspace!" he said. He spoke aloud, but he didn't bother to shout, because they'd never hear him. "Just get the hell out, and don't come back."

Army vehicles always reminded him of the *Ares*. Even ordinary vehicles did, sometimes. He always preferred to stay indoors when the bloodtruck did its rounds, leaving the driver and his mate to load the daily cargo by themselves.

The soldier sitting beside the pilot in the bubble of the leading machine was pointing down at him and chattering away into a hand-held microphone, but both the helicopters went straight on, without making any attempt to land. This time, they didn't come back—they zoomed away down the valley, towards the distant sea.

"What was that all about?" said Bowring, still speaking aloud although there was no one to hear him. He was quite unselfconscious about talking to himself; it was one of the privileges of being a recluse.

He went back into the bloodshed to check the lines, detaching them one by one. As he went he collected the bladderpacks, laying them out with meticulous care in the huge steel vacuum-flasks where they were stored for their journey to the city, nested in ice. He sealed each drum carefully, making sure the labels were fully filled out, and then began rolling them into the yard to await collection. He stacked them in the shade of the lean-to beside the gate, and covered them with a tarpaulin. The truck was due at ten, and was rarely late, but he was always careful. The legacy of his training was still imprinted on all his habits and customs; when it came to routines he was a real machine.

The moment he entered the house he knew that something was wrong. Nothing had been disturbed and there were no tell-tale footprints in the hall, but he knew that while he had been in the shed someone had opened the unlocked door, come in, and closed it again. The balance of the odors that inhabited the house had been disturbed, and even though the sour-sweet scent of the sows' blood still lingered in his nostrils he sensed the change.

He knew his personal space as minutely as that, and always had done since the long months of that interminable homeward journey in the *Ares*, when his personal space had been restricted to the interior of an imperfectly-functioning spacesuit.

He went into the kitchen, and took the shotgun from the cupboard beneath the sink. He went to the drawer to get two shells, and loaded it. Then he simply stood still and listened very carefully, trying to catch the sound of a surreptitious movement.

What he heard instead was a muffled whimpering sound, like the sound the young sows sometimes made when they were too full of their over-prolific blood—or when some cowboy in a chopper disturbed their peace. It was coming from the bedroom.

Bowring shuffled off his yard-boots, and then tiptoed to the stairwell in his stockinged feet. He went up slowly, avoiding the stairs which creaked, with his right forefinger balanced on the trigger-guard of the gun.

The bedroom door was closed, and he hesitated before it. He had seen enough television to know what to do in such situations, but he knew that the door was solid and that the catch was sturdy—and that he didn't have the strength to break it down with a single charge.

He heard the crying sound again, a little louder this time. He reached out and turned the handle of the door. Rather than throwing it violently back and leaping through, as melodramatic tradition demanded, he pushed it slowly inwards while he stayed outside, gun at the ready.

The girl who was sitting on the bed started violently as the door opened, and looked at him in stark terror. She leaned sideways reflexively to shield the whimpering baby that she had laid down on his bed.

"Don't!" she implored him. "Please don't!"

He let the muzzle of the gun fall, so that it was pointing at the floor.

"What the hell are you doing here?" he said, harshly. The tension had not yet eased out of his anxious muscles. "You've no right to come into my house."

"I had to!" she said. "Please don't turn me in. Please! I haven't done anything. It's all a mistake. *I haven't done anything!*"

"The helicopters," he said, belatedly making the connection. "They were searching for you?"

She nodded. "It's a mistake," she said, again. "I'm not what they think. They want to take the baby, but it's all a mistake. She's all right. She's not what they say."

She couldn't be more than seventeen, maybe less. She was wearing a dingy green anorak, faded jeans, and battered trainers. Her pale face was dirty and her mousy brown hair was disheveled. The blanket in which the baby was wrapped was soiled both inside and out. They looked totally harmless and utterly pathetic—but they were in his house.

He opened his mouth to ask her what "they" thought she was, and what they said the baby was, but before he could form the words the doorbell rang. Evidently the helicopters had only been the spearhead of the operation; there were men on the ground too.

Shit! he thought. *She's brought the whole world on to my land, knocking at my door.*

"Don't," she pleaded, her voice faint, as if terror had robbed her of the power to voice more than the single word.

He went back down the staircase and went to the door, still carrying the gun.

Three soldiers waited outside. One of them was a sergeant. All three tensed when they saw the gun in his hand, and moved as if to unship their own rifles from their shoulders, but he altered his grip, and leaned the shotgun against the wall just inside the door, butt down.

"Sorry," he said, insincerely. "I don't get many callers away out here."

"We're looking for a woman and a child," said the sergeant, unceremoniously. "We need to search the farm."

"No you don't," said Bowring. "It's my land. You've no right. Just leave, will you—and go quietly. I've got two hundred bloodstock sows in the bloodshed, and their yields are affected if something starts them pumping adrenalin."

The sergeant frowned. "I'm sorry, sir," he said. "But we do have the right, and we do need to do it. We'll go as quietly as we can, but we do have to check."

Just get them out, Bowring told himself. *Don't drag it out—just get it over with.*

"All right," said Bowring. "Check the barn, if you must, and the storage-bunkers. The henhouse too. But don't go blundering about in the bloodshed—there's nowhere in there to hide, and you can see everything you need to see from the doorway. There's no need to check the house. She isn't in here."

The sergeant's frown turned into a scowl. "Maybe she got in without your seeing her," he said.

"She couldn't have," said Bowring, stubbornly. "The back door's bolted, and the windows are screwed down. I can swear that no one's come through this door. But when I was upstairs a little while ago I did see somebody moving along the hedgerow beside the path that leads down the valley—just a glimpse, as they moved into the wood. It may have been one of your men, I suppose, but I don't think so. About four hundred yards that way, twenty or twenty-five minutes ago." He pointed.

The sergeant turned to one of his companions. "Take MacArdle and Flint, and get along to the wood," he said. Then he turned back to Bowring. "We'll still have to search the farm," he said, trying to match him for stubbornness—as if anyone could be as pig-headed as a bloodfarmer.

"Do it quickly and quietly," said Bowring, maintaining his position in the doorway, so that no one could go past. "Be careful with the drums by the gate—and don't go into the bloodshed."

"And the house," said the sergeant. "I'll have to search the house."

"That's not necessary," said Bowring, staring the sergeant in the eye.

The sergeant stared back determinedly, but then his forehead furrowed in a slight frown and his gaze flickered. "Don't I know you?" he said, uncertainly.

"No," said Bowring, firmly. "You don't."

"Jesus," said the remaining soldier, as enlightenment dawned. "It's that guy who came back from Mars. It's Bob Bowring. What the fuck're you doing in a place like this?"

"I live here," said Bowring, flatly. "It's my home." Still he didn't move—but now the sergeant backed off half a stride, and didn't seem ready to meet his stare. The fact that he recognized Bowring's name had changed his attitude. He knew now that Bowring was an ex-military man himself, officer class—not to mention an ex-hero and an ex-VIP. He didn't want to get into an argument with someone who could make trouble for him.

"Okay," he said, finally. "We'll check the barn and the other places. I'll do the shed myself—carefully. Thanks."

"Don't take too long about it," said Bowring, closing the door and thumbing the deadlock. But he was under no illusion that he had won anything more that a little time. He knew that they'd be back. He hadn't dared ask them what they were looking for.

"I should have turned her in," he murmured, "And got it over with, once and for all." But he couldn't convince himself. He still had curiosity, no matter how much he valued his privacy. He was interested to know why the army was out chasing a girl and a baby. But curiosity had its price, and he shivered with a sudden complex flash of remembered odors, remembered pains, remembered loss and the memory of bright, bright stars in the long, long Martian night.

Slowly, he went back upstairs, remembering the way the soldier had described him: not as the man who *went* to Mars, but as the man who *came back*—as if the horrors of the homeward journey were all that counted, as if *being there* had meant little or nothing, and had accomplished nothing at all.

* * * * * * *

While the girl and the baby were cleaning up in the bathroom Bowring turned on the news channel. He didn't expect that there would be anything about the search on the news—he assumed, almost unthinkingly, that the operation would be secret—but he was wrong. He caught the headline almost immediately and thumbed the remote until the latest edit came up on screen. The shots of army helicopters were library stock, and they had to show a map to indicate where the search was taking place, but the commentary was fairly specific.

"...carriers of a notifiable disease," the voice-over was saying. "Neither the mother nor the child shows any outward sign of illness, but members of the public should not approach them under any circumstances. Anyone who has seen the woman should contact the police on one of these numbers...."

The unsmiling picture of the girl that they flashed up was a standard Central Directory still, which made her look older than she was. Her name was Janine Stenner. She was seventeen.

Bowring looked down at his hands as he contemplated the phrase "carriers of notifiable disease." He had handled the baby and come into contact with more than one of its bodily fluids, and had touched the girl's hands too. But the hands were quite steady and he was slightly surprised by his own lack of anxiety. His reclusiveness was not born of a fear of contamination.

"It's a mistake," the girl had said. "I'm not what they say." And the soldiers had not been wearing any protective clothing.

"Carriers of what?" he said, aloud. "The black death?"

"It's a mistake," said a small voice, behind him. "It's not true."

She came into the room, looking nervously around at the bank of PCs against the wall. She could see through the open door into the lab, and she glanced at the equipment, as though she were anxious about what it implied as to the nature of his profession.

"Emma's asleep," she added, as she sat down on the swiveling chair at the workstation—he was already occupying the one and only armchair. "I left her on your bed."

He touched the remote to switch off the TV.

"Why do they think you've got a dangerous disease if you haven't?" he asked, brusquely. "Or is that just for public consumption—a lie to cover up some other reason?"

She shook her head. "They wanted to abort the baby," she said, softly. "They said I was carrying something—that the baby would be carrying it too. They had me shut up in some private clinic, way down south, but I ran away. It wasn't difficult to disappear, to begin with. I've been in Heysham for the last five months—but when Emma started to come...I couldn't do it alone. I knew they'd trace me, but I had to get help...and it's not so easy to hide now. But I'm not ill, and neither is Emma. They don't know what they're talking about. They had others at the clinic, but none of us were ill—and they didn't mind touching us, being with us, even...it doesn't make any sense. It's all lies. I'm not going to let them take Emma. I'm not...but I don't have anywhere to go, now."

"Do your parents know what's happening?" he asked, trying to sound gentle and caring.

She shook her head. "Mum died," she said. "I only ever had Mum."

"What about Emma's father?"

She looked up at him, very strangely, as if she knew that she was about to say something that would offend him. She opened her mouth, but then she shut it again, and shook her head. She looked around again, evidently desperate to change the subject, and said: "What is this place?"

"It's a farm," he said.

"What's a bloodshed?" Evidently she had been listening while he talked to the sergeant.

"This is a blood farm," he told her. "The bloodshed's where I keep the transgenic sows. They're genetically engineered to produce blood with various kinds of antibodies, hormones and co-factors in it. It's not as nasty as it sounds—the sows are genetically-lobotomized, so the higher brain-functions are reduced. They're engineered for overproduction, and they need regular vamping—taking off the surplus isn't much different from milking cows. There are milk farms up the valley where they take augmented milk from transgenic ewes, but sows are better for human-transfusible blood. Don't be fooled by the lab—it's not real scientific work. I don't do research. I'm just a farmer."

She looked at him speculatively, but there was no trace of horror or repulsion in her gaze. She was a child of the genetic revolution; she took such things as blood farms for granted. "Are you really the man who came back from Mars?" she asked.

"Yes," he said, curtly.

"And now you're running a blood farm?"

"It's an honest job," he told her. "I was in pretty bad shape when the *Ares* reached Earth orbit. They patched me up as well as they could, but I was unfit for any kind of military service—or most kinds of heavy work. My bones deteriorated, you see, while I was so long in free fall, and the suit wasn't intended for continuous wear over all those months."

"It must have been absolute hell," she said, with all the ingenuous frankness of youth. "Stuck inside your suit for so long, with two dead men for company." It was what she'd learned in school. When it had all happened she had been a babe in arms, not much older than her daughter.

"Exactly what is it they think you're carrying, Janine?" he asked. "And why are they so desperate that they called the army out?"

"I don't know," she said. "What was it like, being on Mars?"

It was obvious that she was trying to steer the conversation away from areas too uncomfortable for her to bear. Curiosity was a kind of refuge for her: a way of keeping her mind off her fears. She didn't really care what it had been like, being on Mars—which was just as well.

"Cramped," he said. "Like living in an overcrowded tent."

"I mean, what was *Mars* like?"

"Arid. Very red, and very dead."

"But you found life there."

"No we didn't. We found that there had *been* life there, billions of years before. When the solar system was younger." He stopped, but he could see that she wanted him to go on. Her eyes were so pale and frightened. He took a deep breath. "Once," he said, awkwardly, "Mars had an atmosphere, and liquid water. Long before life on Earth emerged from the sea there was life of a kind on Mars, but it all died out. *All* of it—nothing survived, even at the bacterial level. Not that there were many other levels, even in the good old days. They're still arguing about its biochemical basis; the evidence I brought back was woefully inadequate and inconclusive." After another pause, he said: "They're going to come back, you know—the soldiers. That kind of operation doesn't get called off. They'll comb the area, back and forth, until they find you. As you said, *you* might be able to get away and hide, but the baby certainly can't."

She stared him in the face, and said: "You can hide us. This is a big place. There must be somewhere you can hide us."

"I don't think so. I really ought to turn you in."

"I'll do anything you want," she said, dropping her stare. When he didn't reply, she added: "You don't have to worry about catching anything. At the clinic, they knew, but it didn't...stop them."

"What's that supposed to mean?" he said, a little sharply.

She shrugged. "One of the male nurses," she said. "He...."

"Raped you?"

She shook her head. "Not exactly," she said. "But he shouldn't have. I was a patient...I was a virgin."

"Is that how you got pregnant? With Emma?"

She shook her head again, more violently. She was starting at the floor. "I was already pregnant," she said, in a low tone. She knew exactly what she was saying, and she was telling him for a purpose. She was implying that it had something to do with the reason they'd taken her into the clinic in the first place, and the reason they'd wanted to abort her baby, and the reason they had mobilized the army to chase her up hill and down dale as soon as they'd traced her. Did she think she had borne a new messiah or something?

"Do you have any idea at all why they're so keen to catch you?" he asked, keeping his voice perfectly level.

She shook her head yet again—but then she added: "I look like my Mum."

He was only a farmer, but some knowledge of genetics was essential to his business, and he had two hundred cloned sows out in the bloodshed, not one of which had a father.

"You mean that you were a virgin birth too?" he queried. "A parthenogenetic clone?"

She shrugged. The word *parthenogenetic* meant nothing to her. "I look like my Mum," she said. "That's why they took me to the clinic. As for Emma...maybe she'll look like me and maybe she won't. They think she will. But I'm healthy, and so is she. You can hide us, Mr. Bowring. I'll do anything you want, but you mustn't let them take Emma!"

Is there anything I want? he asked himself, silently. *Is there anything I want, except space in which to move, and air to breathe, and solitude?*

It was an easy question to answer. There was nothing he wanted, except of course for the impossible things. He might have wanted to be someone else. He might have wanted to be someone other than the man who had come back from Mars. He might have wanted not to be the one and only carrier of that experience, that memory, that burden of sickness, horror and guilt—not that there was anything to be guilty about; chance and chance alone had dictated the pattern of misfortune and malfunctions that had determined that the others should die while he survived...and yet, guilt was part of the burden.

In time, of course, others would go back to Mars, to carry forward the work, to carry forward the mission, to carry forward the hopes and ambitions of outward-looking men. It might be easier, then, to forget the bright stars and the alien sky, and the endless night-black desert which was only red by day. In the meantime, he wanted...nothing that lay within the realms of possibility.

"It's impossible," he said. His mouth was curiously dry. "You must see that it's impossible. We all have to live within the limits of possibility." He thought as he said it of his two dead companions, riding the *Ares* home in their coffin-suits. All the ingenuity in the world wouldn't have been adequate to the task of saving them. There had been nothing he or anyone else could do.

Why on earth do they want the girl? he wondered. *Why are they saying that she and the child are carrying some dread disease? Who's lying to whom, and why?*

The doorbell rang again, loudly and insistently.

* * * * * * *

This time, it was an officer—but the sergeant was with him, and so were the two men who'd been with the sergeant before. The officer was in his fifties, only a year or two younger than Bowring. He looked at Bowring with unfeigned respect, the way a man ought to look at a living legend "I'm Captain Clarke, Lieutenant Bowring," he said. Bowring could tell that he hadn't cited the rank to stress that he was a superior officer, but simply out of politeness. Captain Clarke was a gentleman.

The gun was still propped up against the wall just inside the door. Bowring picked it up by the barrel, left-handed, and swung it up and around so that his right hand gripped the stock.

Clarke was genuinely astonished. "There's no need for that, sir," he said. It was odd to hear a captain calling someone he'd just addressed as lieutenant "sir."

"What do you want?" said Bowring, coldly.

"I need to talk to you. I'm very sorry, but it's necessary to search your farm again—including the house." The captain was trying hard not to shed his own amiability in response to Bowring's hostility.

"No," said Bowring.

Clarke hesitated, and then switched into humoring mode. "The woman's here, isn't she?" he said "We're already fairly sure about that, Lieutenant—and nothing less than a comprehensive search will convince us otherwise."

"You can't come in," said Bowring.

"Yes, we can," said the captain, quietly. Bowring judged that if he hadn't been who he was, they would have come in already. If he'd been nobody in particular, they'd simply have brushed him aside. They wouldn't even have fetched a captain to do the job: a sergeant's stripes would have been authority enough.

"This isn't a trivial matter," Clarke continued, when Bowring didn't budge. "We have to take the girl and the baby into custody. I assure you that we don't intend to harm them."

"Why is she running away from you?" Bowring countered, even though he knew that it was half way to a dangerous admission.

"Because she doesn't understand. She knows that the doctors thought it might be best to abort her baby, and she thinks they'll harm it now it's here—but they won't. It's just that...we do need to have her in our care."

"Because she and the child are carrying some disease or other?"

"In a manner of speaking, yes."

Bowring moved his hand to the trigger-guard of the shotgun. This time the sergeant had his own gun in his hands, and he moved it in response—but the captain was in his way.

The captain somehow reminded Bowring of *the* captain: the real captain, who had died on Mars; The captain whose rotting body, in spite of all their attempts to sterilize it, probably still harbored a measure of bacterial life: the only life that now existed on Mars.

"If she's infectious," said Bowring, "you and your men are taking a hell of a risk. Where are your masks and rubber gloves?"

"She's not infectious," said Captain Clarke. "At least, not yet."

"Are you going to explain that?" asked Bowring, when the captain showed no sign of elaborating.

Clarke sighed, letting his impatience show but keeping it under strict control. "We're wasting time, Mr. Bowring. We do intend to come in, and you really can't stop us. You know that."

"You little shit," said Bowring—inaccurately, because the captain was as tall as he and at least thirty pounds heavier. "Take one step inside my house and I'll blow you away, no matter who you are and no matter what you one day hope to be." He didn't mean it, and he was ashamed of the thought that he was making a fool of himself, but he couldn't move. He couldn't give way. He couldn't let them in.

The sergeant raised his weapon, but it was only a ploy to distract Bowring's attention; as Bowring moved half a step forward, to menace the sergeant with his own gun, Clarke grabbed the barrel and forced it aside. Bowring's finger, caught inside the trigger-guard, tightened reflexively, and the gun went off, but no one was in danger. Even so, the other soldiers were quick to react. The butt of a rifle came crashing down on his head from the side, and Bowring crumpled up, wishing that pain didn't always make him think of the *Ares*, and the long, long journey home.

* * * * * * *

THE TREE OF LIFE, BY BRIAN STABLEFORD

When he came round he was lying on his bed, and Captain Clarke was standing at the window looking out over the fields at the distant sea. Bowring's head felt fizzy, but not as painful as it might have. He guessed that he'd been dosed with analgesics. Even so, inside his head he had the stink of his damaged suit in his nostrils, and two dead men for company.

As soon as he moved, the captain turned round.

"Don't try to sit up," Clarke advised him. "I'm truly sorry about that. The silly sod hit you too hard—but there's no fracture. There's a lump, but it'll go down in time."

Bowring raised a tentative hand. There was no bandage wrapped around his head. As Clarke said, there was indeed a huge and tender lump, but no blood matting his hair.

"You shouldn't have waved the gun like that," said the captain, seemingly uncertain as to whether he should try to sound annoyed or pitying. "It made things awkward, for no good purpose. You must have known you couldn't keep us out. Why didn't you just let us in?"

"Because I didn't want to," Bowring answered, his voice grating slightly.

"And because you didn't want to do it, you thought you didn't have to—because you're the man who came back from Mars?" Clarke sounded disappointed, like a man discovering feet of clay beneath an idol's wasted limbs.

"Something like that," Bowring agreed. He sounded and felt vindictive. Because, after all, he *was* the man who had come back from Mars. He was no longer famous, but he was remembered. He was a living legend. He was in a position to make his voice heard—to raise awkward questions whenever and wherever he wanted to, and demand answers.

"You can see her whenever you want to," said Clarke, seemingly reading his mind. "You can make sure that she's being well looked after, and that the baby's fine. Anything you want to set your mind at rest—even an explanation. But as of now, Lieutenant, you've been called up from the reserve. You're on active service again, and the active service you're required to provide is keeping your mouth shut. That's the deal. If you were anybody else, we'd fob you off with lies and threats, but you're supposed to be on our side. You're supposed to understand."

"Well, I don't," said Bowring, sourly, sitting up in spite of Clarke's advice. It hurt, but it was bearable. "Just what the hell is it that you think she's carrying?"

"She's carrying what you failed to bring back from Mars," said Clarke, coolly, as he leaned on the window-frame. "Alien life."

"What?" said Bowring, foolishly. It was beyond belief, but it didn't sound like a lie.

"We've been invaded," said Clarke, matter-of-factly.

Bowring took a few seconds to adjust his frame of mind before he said: "When?"

"The best guess is 1915—give or take three years."

"By a gang of parthenogenetically-reproducing females who just happen to look perfectly human?" said Bowring, sarcastically. "No doubt they've been in hiding ever since—and in the course of the past hundred-and-some years they've naturally forgotten who they really are, or failed to pass on their wisdom to subsequent generations. That's worse than some Hollywood antique.

"She told you about the virgin birth, then?" said Clarke, quite untroubled by the B-movie scenario.

"I didn't believe her," Bowring said, nursing his throbbing head. After a few seconds it began to get better again. The soldier hadn't hit him *that* hard; he was, after all, an old man.

"Well, it's true," said Clarke. "You, of all people, shouldn't have been overly surprised by that."

"Because I came back from Mars?" said Bowring, failing this time to make the connection, although he'd made it readily enough before.

"Because you make your living in a bloodshed," Clarke came back at him. "A shed stocked with animals that have no fathers, because it's more convenient if they're forced to breed absolutely true...for exactly the same reason that it's convenient for the invaders' hosts to breed true, for ten or fifty or a hundred generations. Forget Mars, Lieutenant Bowring. Think bloodfarming. And then think how a biotech-minded species might go about organizing an alien invasion. No fleets, no firepower, no resistance, just...."

He paused, expectantly. Even though his head was aching, Bowring could see where he was at. "Just cytogenes," he said, completing the sentence. "Just artificial cytogenes. Engineered parasites—not so very different from the ones we implant in the cells of sows and ewes and all the other kinds of transgenics, to make them produce what we need."

He could follow the chain of logic easily enough. Cytogenes were packages of genetic material which functioned exactly like the genes in the nucleus of a cell, using the cell's constructive systems to reproduce themselves and to manufacture proteins. They were hereditary in the sense that they could be passed on from parent to child, but they could only be passed from mother to daughter, because ova retained their cytoplasm during the reproductive process and sperms didn't. They could be passed on as passengers in ordinary sexual reproduction, but once they had harmonized with a particular set of nuclear genes it was safer and more convenient simply to duplicate the entire set. Otherwise, there could be problems with the host's immune system. The transgenic sows in the bloodshed were all clones produced by induced parthenogenesis. Natural selection had never done much with cytogenes, but maybe that was just a freak of chance—genetic engineers had seen their potential quickly enough.

"How do you know she's carrying *alien* cytogenes?" Bowring asked. "Maybe they're the product of mutation—haven't we always found that all our best ideas were anticipated by nature, even if we didn't know it beforehand?

"They're too complex," Clarke answered. "And they aren't made of DNA. They're closely related, chemically speaking, but not identical. All life on Earth, from viruses and paramecia to trees, mice and men, has a common chemical ancestor. Janine's cytogenes and our genetic systems may have a common ancestor too, but if they do, it existed several billions of years ago, probably not on Earth. We've never seen anything *exactly* like them before, although opinions vary as to whether we've seen some other kin of theirs."

There was only one place anyone could ever have seen "some other kin" of an alien cytogene, and Bowring had no difficulty at all in following the idea through to the appropriate spectrum of alternative possibilities.

"You're saying that this thing that Janine and the baby are carrying is related to the stuff I brought back from Mars?" he said. "You think Earth was invaded in *nineteen fifteen* by spores produced by Martian life-forms that died out more than a billion years ago?"

"That's one hypothesis," Clarke agreed, equably. "Maybe Mars was invaded, from somewhere else. Nobody knows. Nobody knows whether these things were designed by engineers or whether they just evolved somewhere out there in the infinite universe. Nobody knows whether we were targeted, or whether the things just drifted here. Maybe the whole damn universe is lousy with opportunistic cytogenes. Maybe our common chemical ancestor was something of the same sort. Nobody knows. But we're trying to find out—and while we do, Janine Stenner and all her blood relatives have to be in our care. We have to study them...and we have to control them, at least until we figure out what all the cytogenes are for, and what the future phases of their preplanned evolution may produce. There could be nasty surprises yet in store, and we don't want to be taken unawares—as you'll readily understand, Lieutenant Bowring."

Little shit, thought Bowring, without much conviction. He knew full well that the other was right. Clarke, and those who gave him orders, had known that he would understand, had known that he could safely be brought aboard. He was, after all, a man who had already done his bit for humankind, and for the Great Adventure. He was one of the pioneers of the attempted conquest of the high frontier: one of DNA's first ambassadors to the universe at large.

At the end of the day, he thought, *that's all we are. Just carriers of our genes, instruments of their struggle for existence.*

He stood up, feeling a little weak at the knees but quite able to move. He came to stand beside Clarke at the window, as if to concede without actually having to admit that Clarke had been right all along. It was late afternoon now, and the sun was staining the curved roof of the bloodshed with angry yellow light. The truck that had collected the day's produce was long gone, and so were the helicopters and the soldiers. Everything was quiet. When Clarke was gone, everything would be back to normal—or almost normal. He was back on active service again. He had a secret to keep, and something to think about.

"You should have explained it to her," he said, after a pause to steady himself. "You should have told *her* what it was all about."

"She's just a child," said Clarke, reasonably. "She doesn't have your intelligence, and she doesn't have your sense of responsibility. We really do think it would be best if this didn't become the substance of rumors and wild reportage. Can you imagine what the press would do with a story of this kind? We may have seemed to you to be out on a witch-hunt, but can you imagine the kind of fears that could be stoked up by popular misconceptions of what's going on? There are those in our midst who are carriers of alien life— would you really want to explain that to the kind of people who think that what *you* do is some kind of voodoo? You must be very well aware of all the reasons why bloodfarming's the perfect job for someone who wants to cut himself off from all kinds of social intercourse. People really don't understand."

"You should have *explained*," said Bowring, stubbornly. "She has a right to know, to be given the chance to understand. She's a child of the revolution."

Clarke moved towards the door. He didn't touch Bowring, or even offer to shake hands. "You can see her whenever you like," the captain repeated. "In the meantime, you'd better take it easy until the lump goes down." He made as if to leave, but paused. "Did she ask you what it was like?" he said, softly. "Did she ask you how it felt to stand on alien sands, and look up at alien stars? Did she ask you what you were doing here, running a bloodfarm in the middle of nowhere?"

"Yes," said Bowring, faintly.

"And did she understand what *you* told her? Did she grasp what that all meant?"

Bowring thought about the bright, bright stars of the glorious Martian night; and the unbelievably rosy evenings;

and the infinite deadness of the barren sunlit land; and the awful loneliness of the long, long ride home in the desolate, sick coffin-ship...and about the frail, inadequate relics of something once-living but long, long dead that he had carried with him, along with the bodies of his friends.

The images crowded in his mind, dissolving into a chaotic confusion of sensation that made him dizzy, derailing his train of thought and overwhelming his awareness of the present moment. Five or six seconds passed before he could suppress it and take command again.

Was it really possible, he wondered, that something more of Martian life had actually survived—or something of a common ancestor uniting the living Earth with the corpse that was Mars?

"I couldn't explain it," he said, awkwardly, in answer to Clarke's challenge. "I didn't even want to. But I will try. Given time, I think I can make her understand. She has the right to try. She's a child of the revolution, after all."

"Maybe we all have a right to try," said Captain Clarke, "and maybe we all can"—and left him, then, to his solitude and to the dull pain of his as-yet-unending grief.

ROGUE TERMINATOR

Dorset pharmers are old-fashioned folk—as you can readily see by the fact that we still spell the word "pharmer" rather than "pharma," the way the trendies in Berkshire do. Food-growers, of course, still spell the word with an f, but there haven't been many food-growers around Yetminster during the last twenty years. Even the apple-growers in Somerset have given up the cider business in the interests of packing their Coxes and Braeburns with plantigens. Up in Taunton they rub their hands in glee every time one of the tabloids tells us that the first plague war is bound to break out any day now.

It's because we're so attentive to tradition in these parts that we still do our serious drinking on a Sunday. Pharming is just as much a seven-day-a-week job as farming used to be, and no one hereabouts actually rested on the Sabbath even in the days when there were still a few wives and pensioners addicted to religious observance, but you have to make room for drinking somewhere in the calendar and the best pub in Yetminster happens to be just across the road from the biggest church. Pharmers, like farmers, aren't the kind of folk to do their drinking willy-nilly; it's the kind of vocation that requires its followers to get together on a regular basis to swap news and tips—especially tips. The science is still moving forward at breakneck pace, you see, and nobody but a fool ever waits until the AgMin field tests are complete before improving his stocks. It's not enough to be up with the Honest Joneses if you want to make real money—you have to be a step or two ahead. We like to think of it as Dorset's heroic contribution to the cutting edge of progress.

THE TREE OF LIFE, BY BRIAN STABLEFORD

The bravest—and, as it turned out, strangest—of all our contributions to the cutting edge of progress began on a cold night in February 2034, when there were so few townies about that we didn't even have to wait for chucking-out time before getting down to the meat of the conversation. Naturally enough, it was Jack Gridley who had the tip. The Gridleys have always been fashion-leaders, ever since Jack's granddad, Old Freddy, came up with the wheeze of using a plank and a bit of string to make mysterious circles in our cornfields so our folks could charge tourists and scientists a pound a head to see them. Come to think of it, though, it was also Old Freddy who couldn't be content with circles, and got so carried away with more complicated designs that he became obsessed with the idea that he was being inspired and guided by beings from a higher dimension—which did rather undermine the whole point of the exercise.

"You doing rape this season, Lukey?" Jack asked me, in a quasi-confidential manner, as he stared contemplatively at the froth on his third pint of the night. That furtive way of speaking was the signal for everyone else to prick up their ears, and everyone did, although they continued to maintain the polite pretence that Jack and I were having a private discussion.

"Course I am," I told him. "The arse's dropped right out of wheat and corn's way past hackneyed. Oilseed's where it's at. Everyone knows that. Fifty-seven new varieties last year alone. I'm thinking of sowing the whole top field with morphine precursors, the ones either side of the stream with hyped-up beta-two agonists and cytochrome-P450 assistants, and maybe splitting the rest between dystrophin repair agents, telomere extrapolators and transposon suppressants."

"Good mix," Jack said, approvingly. "Except maybe the dystrophin repairers and the transposon blockers. That's Fancy Dan stuff. My old granddad always used to say *stick to the basics and you won't go far wrong.*"

"Pity he could never follow his own advice," I observed, refusing to allow myself to be nettled.

"Well, that's as it may be," Jack conceded, "but I'm a Gridley through and through, and I'm content to leave it to the big boys to muck about with so-called orphans. I'm going for the new generation of coryza inhibitors myself."

I'd had my fingers burned back in '31 dabbling in cold cures, and I wasn't prepared to bet that the new generation would be any more effective in the long term than the last three, but I could tell that Jack had something else on his mind apart from pick-and-mix pharm stocks, so I didn't argue.

"Mind you," he went on, when the pause had been pregnant long enough, "it's a real pain in the arse having to buy new seed every year. Gives us the scope to experiment, of course, and it certainly wouldn't do to keep on planting the same old stuff in a rapidly-evolving market, but how long is it now that you've been producing those morphine precursors? And how much better are this year's beta-two agonists than last year's?"

"No way around it," I said, cautiously. The seed companies loved their terminators, and the AgMin was behind them all the way. Nobody wanted to go back to the old days, when there were townies coming out and trampling our business left, right and centre just in case we gave a butterfly a stomach ache. The only way the civil serpents at the AgMin had been able to weasel the GeneMod legislation through the New Lords was to promise faithfully that the only crops grown on English pharms would be incapable of producing fertile seed, so that anything that went wrong would be a once and once only affair.

"Well," said Jack, "that's what people think—but I've always been a Gilbert and Sullivan fan, and I've always been exceeding fond of *The Mikado*, which makes the very wise point that as long as the public at large believes that the executioner has done his work, whether he actually has or not, the ends of justice are served."

I wasn't about to argue with Gilbert and Sullivan, even though I knew they'd been dead far too long to have any meaningful opinions on the Genetic Revolution, so I cut straight to the chase. "Are you saying that you can lay your hands on some engineered rape stocks that haven't been neutered?" I asked.

"Naw," he said, disgustedly. "Anyone can do that—but what do you get out of your crop except soap and cooking oil? What I'm saying is that I know where I can lay my hands on a terminator decoupler. A way to turn the reproductive potential of *any* GM seed back on."

"And where did *that* come from?" I asked, skeptically.

"From a pharm, of course," he told me. "A YAC pharm, as it happens. Hasn't yeast always been the agriculturalist's best friend, ever since the day that the first beer was brewed?"

YAC production isn't what I'd call proper pharming. Yeast Artificial Chromosomes are just molecular machines used in genome sequencing, not real pharmaceuticals. I have to admit, though, that molecular artificers are clever buggers. If anyone was going to come up with a terminator decoupler, I figured, it was highly likely to be some bored YAC pharmer stirring up his vats to see if anything interesting floated up with the scum.

"I'd still have to buy this year's seed," I pointed out, "And every time I wanted to try something new in future, I'd have to buy it in."

"You'd have to keep buying new stock anyway, to avoid suspicion," Jack pointed out. "We wouldn't want the Minispies to come poking their long noses in, would we? But think how much you could save if you could plant, say, half your fields with seed from the previous year's crops? You'd have your choice, after all. If the dystrophin repair business happens to go belly-up you can just chuck the seed away, but telomere extrapolants might last as long as you do—and if they work the way they're supposed to, that could be a *very* long time."

He had a point—and he'd finished his pint.

"Let me get you another," I said. "Maybe we can do a bit of business."

I wasn't the only one, of course. By the time Jack left the pub at four in the morning he'd sunk at least sixteen, and hadn't had to pay for a single one. His walk was as steady and forceful as ever, though, and I knew that his landrover wouldn't hit anything he hadn't aimed it at during the five-mile drive back to his place. It's wonderful what a man can accomplish with a little ingenuity, a good stock of home-grown rapes stuffed full cytochrome-P450 assistants, and a contact in the YAC business.

* * * * * * *

The best thing about the terminator decoupler was that it was so close to being alive that it could reproduce itself almost as easily outside the infused seeds as inside. As long as I kept the culture well-fed with enriched glucose substrate, Jack assured me, I'd never run out. He wasn't spreading the stuff around with the intention of making a big profit, you see. He was doing it because we were mates, all in the same business and all in the same boat. That was why we were happy to let the little miracle-worker be known by one and all as Jack's YAC, although it wasn't, strictly speaking, a YAC and he hadn't actually invented it. Matiness has always been the strength of English farming folk—except, of course, for those located east of Salisbury, west of Chard and north of Wincanton. We stick together, and we guard one another's backs. We like to think of it as the spirit of the Cerne Abbas giant.

I decided to be careful, and not to expose the entirety of my newly-bought seed-stocks to the terminator decoupler. I knew full well that the first law of genetic engineering is that you can never do *one thing*. Every alteration of the metabolic flux inside a cell has consequences, and the feedback mechanisms regulating that flux are so complicated that some of the consequences are always unforeseeable. So I carefully split each parcel of seeds into two, exposing one to Jack's YACs and leaving the other uninfected. I also divided the stocks between different fields wherever it was practicable, or different halves of the same field where it wasn't. Never let it be said that mere pharmers are too stupid to understand the underlying logic of the experimental method.

We had a very good spring, even by comparison with the early Greenhouse years before the UN Forestry Commission got its plant-a-billion-a-year program off the ground. My fields turned green, then vivid yellow, in a very satisfactory manner. There wasn't any obvious difference between the crops that had been treated with Jack's terminator and the ones that hadn't—but I hadn't expected any, so that was all right. The morphine precursor producers seemed to be having a particularly good year, but the plants whose oils were engineered to be full of transposon suppressants were slow starters. I thought for a while that we might have a problem in the boggier ground with some kind of facultative pest that had made the jump, but once the flowers were out the plants came on well enough, much to my relief. The Biodiversity Lobby had become so strong that the Ministry wouldn't let us use any but the most specific biopesticides in case we took out a few innocent bystanders along with the rapemunchers, but every five years or so natural selection would throw up a new subspecies that was ready, willing and able to take our pride and joy apart, and the AgMin troubleshooters never found a fix in time, no matter how quickly the bug was reported.

All in all, though, things were going very smoothly by midsummer's day, when family tradition dictated that I take a few hours off to drive Shelley and the kids up to the top of the downs for a good old-fashioned picnic. We always sat on the edge of one of the Ministry's woodland sanctuaries, where we could listen to the birds that still knew how to sing while looking out over the vast ocean of yellow that extended all the way to Sherborne in the north and all the way to Dorchester in the south.

The rapesea was dotted everywhere with islands, some of them green, some of them red-tiled and not a few of them grey, but it had no obvious boundaries except the railway and the Frome. About half the green islands were wildlife minisanctuaries; the rest included a few relict oak woods, a couple of dozen test crops—mostly strawberries, but some potatoes and even a few beets—and a few fugitive fields of barley.

"It's all very impressive," Shelley admitted, when I called her attention to the stately calm of the lovely yellow expanse, "but I can never quite get over the fact that it's called *rape*. Remember all those old jokes about the rape of the English countryside?"

THE TREE OF LIFE, BY BRIAN STABLEFORD

"It's *oilseed* rape," I reminded her, not for the first time. "If it makes you feel better, pretend that it's mustard. And if you think this is impressive, imagine what it must be like in India." South-East Asia was so oil-poor that the second generation of oilseeds adapted for tropical and sub-tropical habitats had been taken up by native farmers almost as enthusiastically as the rubber trees and bananas that secreted vaccines against hepatitis-C, malaria and every other pestilence endemic to the region had been taken up in Indonesia and Malaysia.

I tried to explain to the kids that the climatologists loved the Indian rapeseas even more extravagantly than the politicians because of the contribution they were making to rainfall distribution, but they weren't in a mood to be lectured. Shelley told me that they weren't old enough to grasp the significance of the fact that the age-old tyranny of the monsoon was finally giving way to an era of environmental fraternity, but she was just trying to let the brats off the hook. Liz probably wasn't old enough to take it all aboard, but Joe could have taken an intelligent interest if only he'd been that way inclined.

"It's all so *boring*," Joe complained, just to make certain that I knew that he'd far rather have stayed at home to play VR-games. "It's all the *same*."

"No it's not," I assured him. "There are more than thirteen thousand variants of oilseed rape in Dorset. Shall I explain why we can't simply grow all the different drugs in the same plant?"

"Anything but that, Dad," he complained. "Anyway, I know already—I'm not stupid, you know."

"It's not just because it's a good idea to keep your products separate, although it certainly is," I soldiered on, regardless. "The real problem is that if you carry out multiple transformations on a single set of chromosomes the risk of buggering up the developmental process increases exponentially."

Shelley frowned, because she didn't like me saying "buggering" in front of the kids, but she didn't say anything. She left that to Joe, whose response was: "Boring, buggering *boring*!"

It was true that he wasn't stupid, even though he was easily bored. He was smart enough, in his own way, but I'd begun to worry that he'd never make a pharmer. That, I supposed, was down to Shelley's genes. I'd countered their influence as best I could, but there's only so much DNA a man can provide. It wasn't her fault, of course—she hadn't designed the mechanics of inheritance. I'd often wondered what kind of parent would foist a name like Shelley on a Yetminster girl, but her Mum and Dad had died the year before I met her, killed on the M3 north of Winchester by a lorry driver busy arguing on his mobile phone. That was one problem the pharmacogenomicists would never get to grips with—infinitely more intractable than souping up the liver to provide instant sobriety on demand. We'd agreed readily enough to call our own girl Elizabeth.

"The birds are pretty, aren't they, Mummy?" was Liz's contribution to the cause of family harmony.

"Yes they are," Shelley assured her. "Every year we come there are more and more. One day, they'll learn to sing again the way they used to. They have the voices. They just have to learn to use them musically."

She was being sentimental, but it was okay by me. I missed the birdsong too, and lots of other things besides—but I was a pharmer through and through, and pharmers have to think of the future. The pharmacogenomicists may be the ones who are designing the future, but pharmers are the ones who actually have to make it. If ever the plague war does come, we'll be the poor buggers digging for victory.

* * * * * * *

I kept a careful eye on the YAC-infected plants as they continued to grow, of course, but the terminator decoupler didn't seem to have had any visible effect on the flowers—in fact, I began to wonder if it had had any effect at all. It occurred to me that I was going to look like a prize fool if I sowed half my fields the following year with seed that turned out not to be fertile at all. The insects buzzing and fluttering benignly around the flowers seemed happy enough, but I wasn't sure whether to take that as a good sign or not. The birds that came chasing the local insects seemed happy enough too, but that didn't seem relevant.

As Shelley had observed during our trip to the downs, the birds still seemed to be increasing their numbers year by year. It was difficult to believe that even chaffinches, tree sparrows and lapwings had been brought to the brink of extinction as recently as '21—the year Joe had been born. All but a handful of familiar species had eventually come through the great depletion pretty well, but they'd had to change their habits considerably. By 2034 the larks, swallows, sparrows and thrushes had been on the way back for a full decade, but the abandonment of their old territorial habits had caused many of them to fall silent, because their singing had always been so closely associated with the marking of those territories. Some people saw that as a disaster, or an accusatory commentary on our management of history, but I wasn't so sure.

Like pharmers, I figured, the pioneers of new avian culture had been merely forced by the ecological revolution to abandon their outdated territorial assumptions and adapt to a more flexible way of life. In so doing, if you cared to look at it like that, they were providing a shining example of the awesome versatility of Nature. Maybe it was a pity that they'd given up on their traditional ditties—but I'd lived on the land all my life, and I'd always thought that their songs were crude and primitive. I'd actually written to the *Guardian* to say so in '25, when the letter column had been besieged by ridiculous proposals to set up educational tannoy systems throughout the south of England to "teach the world to sing again" by using digital technology to "restore the lost heritage of the skylarks and the thrushes."

Personally, I approved of the gutsy way in which the newly discreet birds had got used to flying considerable distances in mixed flocks to feed themselves, returning to their roosting-areas at nights. I like the way they sometimes darkened the sky at dusk while they traded places with the bats. The bats had been having a particularly good time since the last anti-extinction crusade, and there was hardly a loft in Yetminster and Crewkerne in '34 that didn't have a purpose-built batroost as well as a soffit-set of nesting-boxes. My place was an exception, of course, but if any passing towny asked I always said I'd had the chimneys on the house and the roof-space of the barn converted. Who was ever going to know the difference without climbing up to take a look?

I became worried all over again when the time came to bring the crop in and put it through quality control. I was tempted to try to keep the two halves of the various stocks separate so that I'd know if there was any difference in yield between the plants whose terminators had supposedly been deactivated and those which were exactly as the suppliers intended, but in the end I mixed them all up. Any difference that had showed up would have attracted further attention from the scrutineers, and the last thing I wanted was to excite the curiosity of my suppliers' agents or visiting Minispies. Overall, returns were pretty good, especially the morphine precursors and—less expectedly—the late-blooming transposon suppressants.

"What exactly *are* transposon suppressants?" I asked the company's tallyman as he calculated his rake-off.

"As I understand it, transposons are weird DNA sequences that can shift other bits of DNA around the chromosomes during meiosis," he said, off-handedly. "Opinions seem to vary as to whether they're relics of conscripted viruses or satellite spin-off. Anyway, their activity increases the generation-on-generation mutation-rate, especially in mammoth genes. Most of the affected eggs abort, but some don't. The posy gits in PR say it's one of the selective taxes we paid for our rapid evolution from the ancient primates. For the moment, transposon suppressants are officially classified as orphan drugs, targeted at a narrow range of infertility problems, but we're hoping to upgrade them. The lab boys are confident that our present field trials will demonstrate that long term usage can delay menopause, but the real problem is that they're such delicate compounds. We're more anxious about stability than utility. I don't mind telling you that it's quite a relief to see you bringing in the crop at this level of productivity. If only they'll store as well as they grow, they could be big money-spinners. It's possible that they can help reverse falling sperm counts. too—lots of demand for that nowadays."

THE TREE OF LIFE, BY BRIAN STABLEFORD

Not round here, I muttered, under my breath. *We're all Cerne Abbas giants in these parts.* Aloud, I said: "Do they stop transposons shifting the plant DNA around too?" I asked. I wasn't just making conversation or showing off—I really do try to take an interest in these matters. It's a pharmer's clear duty.

"Plants don't have as much intergenic DNA as animals," the tallyman assured me, "so they probably don't go in much for transposons. It wouldn't matter if they did, though. All the suppressants would do would make sure they bred a little truer, if they bred at all—which they don't."

I dropped the topic then, lest the conversation should stray on to dangerous ground.

Come the spring of '35 all the Sunday night regulars were getting a bit worried about Jack's YACs. We all needed reassurance that the seed we'd reserved would actually germinate. None of us had put all his eggs in the one basket, of course—there was the usual range of new variants to try, and we had to buy in some repeat stocks to stop our suppliers getting suspicious. Mercifully, there were so many biotech companies clamoring for our attention that they were all quite used to being in one year and out the next. I don't think any of us intended to plant more than a third of his acreage with the reserved seed, and the more cautious souls were thinking in the region of a fifth or a sixth—but even that represented a considerable gamble, given the other uncertainties to which our profit margins were prey.

"You have to speculate to accumulate, lads," Jack told us. "Anyway, it's our duty as men of Wessex to be the standard-bearers of the revolution. Didn't our ancestors fight tooth and nail to take this land from the Celts? Are we men or mice?"

Now that the patient sequencers have assured us that mice have homologues of ninety-eight per cent of human genes, and protogenes comparable to half of the remainder, the distinction between mice and men doesn't seem quite as clear as it must have done in the good old days when the West Saxons were kicking the shit out of King Arthur and his Romanesque nancy-boys, but it would have been niggardly to point it out. Anyway, we could all remember the money we'd made before the arse dropped out of the corn circle scam, so we were still inclined put our trust in Gridley ingenuity and Jack's YACs.

We were duly rewarded for our faith when the reserved seed sprouted with astonishing vigor, easily outgreening the fields in which we'd planted seeds whose terminators were supposedly still operative.

* * * * * * *

Some people say that pharmers, like farmers, are never satisfied, and I suppose there's a certain truth in that. There's always something to worry about on a pharm. There are so many things that *could* go wrong that every time things go right you can't help feeling that fate is busy storing up trouble. I have to admit that I got more and more worried as the growing-season progressed, simply because its progress was so prodigious.

The new plants did pretty well, but the plants grown from the illicitly-reserved seed did *incredibly* well. They grew fast and they grew tall. Their color was bright even when they were still green, but when they put out flowers the yellow was dazzling. The yellow of engineered rape has always been a little more fervent than the slightly primrosy tint of the natural varieties, and the flowers always feel slicker to the touch, but all the rapes whose terminators had been decoupled caught the sunlight like amber warning-lights and when I pinched them in my fingers they were positively *buttery*. Even engineered rape doesn't have a lot of odor, and I'd never thought of it as particularly sweet-smelling, but Jack's YACs had wrought miracles with the scent of the refertilized stocks. They were so nearly intoxicating that I couldn't help wondering whether I could do a deal with the guys from Country Wines who were doing a roaring trade with engineered elderflower.

None of this was just my opinion, either. There was no particular surprise in the fact that Shelley and Liz approved of the unprecedented lushness, but even Joe felt compelled to comment on it.

"Shit, Dad," he said, feeling free to swear because Shelley wasn't around. "What kind of fertilizer have you been using? It's bad enough going through adolescent hormone hell without getting a blast of raw pheromones every time I open my window."

"Human pheromones are a silly myth," I told him, sternly. "They're the physiological equivalent of feng shui."

"I didn't mean it literally," he assured me. "Mind you, if the wind's blowing towards Cerne Abbas, Old Chalky's likely to get right up and go a'huntin'—and not for rabbits, if you get my drift. Now I understand why they call it rape."

"Don't let your mother hear you talking dirty like that," I said. It didn't seem to be the right time to inform him that the mighty tool of the Cerne Abbas giant was a nineteenth-century fake—probably the work of Old Freddy Gridley's grandfather—although he was certainly old enough to know the truth.

I couldn't help remembering Joe's verdict, though, while I watched the birds and the bees at play. It certainly seemed to me that the friendly insects loved the nectar of the superabundant flowers, and that the ever-discreet birds loved the taste of insects reared on that produce. I had never seen so many swallows and swifts over my fields, even in my father's day, and the thrushes were beginning to flock like the starlings of old. They were chirping a fair bit too, albeit a bit uncertainly—as if they were trying to remember, but hadn't quite got the knack of it. Even the jays and peregrines seemed to be having a bonanza year. It was obvious that if these increases in productivity were reflected in the oil extracted from the plants, the tally-man were going to be just as happy as the birds—and as suspicious as all hell.

"What are you worried about?" Jack retorted, scornfully, when I voiced anxieties on the second Sunday in June. "You know the drill. Deny everything. Must be something in the soil, Mr. Ministryman. Us poor yokels don't understand these newfangled biochemical thingamajigs."

"Suppose the YACs show up on the assay?"

"Suppose they do. Same drill. What's a YAC, Mr. Ministryman? Tibetan cows, ain't they? Are you telling us that those bloody salesmen have been peddling *contaminated stock*?"

"It might not be that easy, Jack," I persisted. "What we have here is an unexpected side-effect. Your bloody YACs haven't stopped at decoupling the terminators. Who knows what else they've stirred up? Suppose they've interfered with the products—what then? It's no good growing giant plants if the morphine precursors won't precurse and the beta two agonists won't agonize."

He didn't bother laughing at the feeble jokes. "Suppose they haven't, Lukey," he said. "Suppose they've done nothing but boost our yields sky-high. We Gridleys have always had a nose for these things, and I reckon we're on to a real winner here. I reckon this could make us rich, boy. Keep your nerve and stick with it, that's my advice."

It was safe enough, as advice went. After all, what choice did we have? We were in for the penny and in for the pound—and as Jack said, if it did blow up in our faces, all we had to do was deny everything. If all else failed, we could always try to blame it on little green men. It had worked before.

"Well," Sid Phillips put in, cheerily, "at least we got the dawn chorus back, don't we? Just like old times. Well, not quite, but even better in a way."

That was true too, I realized, especially the "not quite, but even better in a way." I hadn't really noticed it until my attention was called to it, because the dawn chorus had always sounded raucous to me, and the fact that it was gathering volume day by day had seemed to me like a progressive return to the old days—but it wasn't, quite. It was a more remarkable thing than that. Unprompted by any tannoy systems, the few birds that had begun to sing again had been experimentalists, and now the results of their experiments were beginning to spread. The dawn's heralds were singing new songs, more exotic—and perhaps more accomplished—than the old.

It wasn't until midsummer day that I realized the true extent of the developing problem—if "problem" is the right word. I was too close to it on the pharm, always inside looking out, seeing the details one by one but not weaving them together into any kind of coherent whole. It wasn't until our annual picnic that I got a chance to see the big picture, in all its awful glory.

There was nothing awful and everything glorious about the day itself. Even Joe seemed glad to be dragged out of virtual reality. It was Joe, in fact, who first observed that the scene which confronted us as we sat together on the same old hilltop was considerably different from the one we were used to.

"Your precious sea of yellow looks a lot stormier this year, Dad," he observed, with the kind of sneer that only a teenager can contrive.

From that distance it was easy enough to see that he was right. The illusory ocean formed by the fusion of millions of rape-flowers was much less flat than usual. The plants were growing to such different heights that some invisible and intangible wind seemed to be whipping up big waves, as if in anticipation of a typhoon. Given that the sky was so clear and blue, such choppiness seemed decidedly inappropriate.

"I rather like it," Shelley said. "It's bright, and there's more color in it—isn't there, Luke?"

There certainly was. To Shelley, of course, color was just color, but my pharmer's eyes were already straining hard as I tried to figure out why there was more color in what should have been a seamless place of pure and unadulterated yellow. It wasn't just the unprecedented brightness that had caught her eye; there were pinks and purples too. A man in my profession always has to be on the lookout for the return of the dreaded *weeds*, but I soon realized that the new colors weren't new plants; they were differences in the shading of the rape.

It was Liz, inevitably, who mentioned that the woods were noisier than usual. She had no old memories to awaken, no reflexes of exclusion. There was more birdsong in the carefully-planted wood now than there had ever been during any picnic she'd been on. It was on its way back to what most people would have considered its natural level—but not to its natural state.

"Oh bugger," I muttered.

"What's wrong?" Shelley demanded, crossly.

"Nothing," I said. "Everything's fine and dandy. Exceedingly fine and dandy. It's summertime, and the rape is high. Higher than it's ever been before, and still getting higher. The birds are singing the way they never sang before, the bees are humming fit to bust, and the whole of bloody Dorset's got rosy cheeks. Everything's absolutely peachy. Too lively by half. It's supposed to be tame, but it's not. Jack's bloody YACs have slipped the leash, and they're making the rape run wild."

"What *are* you on about, Dad?" Joe wanted to know.

"Cross-pollination," I said. "Cross-bloody-pollination and hybrid bloody vigor. Switch off the terminators, and the flowers stay fertile—but they don't fertilize themselves and their pollinators don't have enough discrimination to stick to their own kind. It shouldn't have mattered much, because the crossbreeds ought to have been selected out—combining different transformations is supposed to bugger up the developmental process, as every bloody school kid knows. Except that it hasn't. I can see that just by looking. The rogue terminator's running amok."

I realized, belatedly, that I hadn't ever asked Jack the most important question of all. He wouldn't have had an answer, of course, but I really ought to have asked, and I should have insisted that I wasn't going to use his bloody YACs unless and until his genomic wizards spelled out exactly *how* Jack's bloody YACs were going to decouple the terminators in our seeds. Without knowing that, I and all the others had simply had to take it on trust that it wouldn't decouple anything else—and now we were paying the price.

"It's those unstable transposon suppressants," I muttered. "The little buggers have shafted those too. And the process isn't neutral. The decoupled products are *active*. The whole bloody mechanism has gone into reverse."

"Boring," Joe said. "Bloody buggering boring."

"This is supposed to be a picnic, Luke," Shelley said, through gritted teeth. "Can't you forget the ins and outs of pharming for five minutes?"

"Oh, it's a picnic all right," I told her. "It's a right bloody picnic and no mistake!"

THE TREE OF LIFE, BY BRIAN STABLEFORD

* * * * * * *

By mid-August the transformation of south-west England had made the TV news. By the end of August it *was* the news, and not just because it was the so-called silly season. The Ministry men were out in force by then, sampling everything in sight and marveling at the results.

The birds were singing new songs. The bees were making new honey. The wildlife sanctuaries were overflowing, not merely with sturdy and virile individuals but with countless new varieties. The butterflies with psychedelic patterns on their wings were the most obvious, but I knew that the most significant changes would be inside, deep down in the metabolic flux of every cell.

The first rule of genetic engineering is that no matter how hard you try, you can never do just *one* thing. The second rule is that if you try to do too many things, chaos takes over. There isn't a third rule, because everything else is outside *the rules*, but humankind didn't evolve from the ancient primates—let alone from amoebas—by doing one thing at a time or giving up on chaos. Sometimes, when you mix things up, you don't just get a mess, you get *cooking*. What else is civilization about?

To the TV reporters and the curious townies all the new colors were just colors, but we pharmers are physician enough to know that heightened color is a symptom of fever, and I knew soon enough that Jack's YACs had kick-started a real fever of creativity in the fields of north Dorset. If thrushes were composing concertos and bees were packing their honey full of pheromones, and even the butterflies were playing Picasso, what would be going on inside the rape? What sorts of oil would we strike when we brought in the crop? Were we going to get paid for it, and if so, how much?

I suppose I was lucky not to get caught when the white-coated detectives descended on the fields like hail. The way I'd planted everything half and half, in neatly-paired samples, would have been a dead giveaway if Jack's YACs had stayed were they were supposed to stay. Fortunately or unfortunately, they hadn't. They'd spread a lot more widely than anyone had anticipated. The fact that they could survive and thrive outside their hosts had enabled them to migrate out of the previous season's rape-roots into the soil, where they'd infected hundreds of other organisms, including nematodes, annelid worms and beetle larvae. It hadn't made much difference while that first season lasted, any more than it had made much difference to the infected rapes, but that had only been the beginning.

None of YACs' new hosts were in any way inconvenienced by their new commensals, so they had served as a reservoir from which the YACs remigrated to infect *all* the seeds I sowed in the spring of '35. That year's crop was, therefore, divided between second-generation terminator-decoupled individuals and first-generation terminator-decoupled individuals. By the time the Minispies started poking around, the natural conclusion for them to draw was that the whole farm and the whole bloody district had been hit by an unprecedented epidemic, whose symptoms were so various that the decoupling of the terminators didn't leap out at them as a uniquely significant or suspicious circumstance.

The second-generation plants I'd sown included the full range of variants I'd planted in '34, but I'd eliminated cytochrome-P450 assistants and the dystrophin repair agents from the new stocks, doubled my order of transposon suppressants and added a brand new line of novel antidepressants. It turned out that all the products were more-or-less okay except the transposon suppressants, which had done a back flip and turned into transposon enhancers. That made them completely useless for medical purposes, because in the context of higher animal genomes they had become dangerously mutagenic—but, as the tally-man had pointed out to me the previous autumn, plants don't go in much for Fancy Dan stuff like mammoth genes, protogenes and humungous satellite-repeat sequences. Nor do insects. Their DNA is exon-rich, and what the energized transposons were doing, not merely to their host plants but to the insects that fed on their nectar, and anything that fed on the insects, was multiplying the number of functional genes. Polyploidy in plants and invertebrate animals often leads to giantism, and the partial polyploidy promoted by the rogue transposons was encouraging all the local wildlife in that direction, as well as promoting other local super abundances.

If all else had been equal, the work of the rogue transposons would have been strictly short-term, because the augmented chromosomes of the affected plants wouldn't have been able to pair up in the next round of cross-fertilization. In effect, the accidentally-created transposon-enhancers would have functioned as a natural one-step-removed terminator technology—but Jack's YACs had taken care of that by drastically reducing the fussiness of the chromosomes during meiosis.

All of which, as Joe might say, is boring, buggering boring—except in sum. What it added up to in the summer of '35, though, was a spectacular boost to the local pace of evolution, whose like had not been seen since the last supervolcano went off umpteen million years before and scoured all the continents clean, ushering in a new phase of fabulous adaptive radiation.

Fortunately, the main consequence of the fact that the new ecoboom was limited, at least in the beginning, to a triple handful of farms in north Dorset, Somerset and Devon was a dramatic increase in tourism. Townies love singing birds and pretty butterflies, and, above all else, they love novelty. Even if the crops hadn't come in as well as they did, we'd all have grown richer. As it as, we grew *much* richer.

If the Minispies had known what to look for, they might just have been able to figure out that all three of the affected communities had a key member who knew somebody who knew somebody who worked on a YAC pharm, but they didn't. By the time they got involved, the ecosituation had become very complicated indeed, and it would have taken Sherlock Holmes and a Cray supercomputer to work out how it had all started—but just in case, Jack Gridley and I started taking surreptitious trips to Hampshire and Berkshire armed with buckets full of YAC soup, surreptitiously depositing the stuff here, there and everywhere, for all the world as if it had fallen from Heaven. Maybe there is a third rule of genetic engineering, identical to the eleventh commandment: *whatever else you do, cover your arse.*

The Tree of Life, by Brian Stableford

We were as discreet as we were generous, though, in more ways than one. As soon as the townies started flocking westward in droves, inspired by the reports in the *Sun* and the *Mirror*, we had to make bloody sure that our farms were the ones that every tour-guide considered unmissable. They had to be the best of the bunch, so that we could bill them as the English Edens and the twin focal points of the New Genesis. We worked as hard towards that goal as any pharmer ever had, since the day when it all began.

* * * * * * *

The way it all turned out was very gratifying, even if the Ministry did put an end to it when they bred a bug to chase down all Jack's YACs and made sure that normal service was resumed, evolution-wise. It was great while it lasted, and I did my utmost to make the most of it. I think I succeeded.

I was pleased for myself, of course, but what really made me proud that August was the way Joe took to it all like a duck to water. The little bugger had always liked showing off, and suddenly he was in his element. There was no more skulking in his bedroom once the gawkers began to arrive in their hundreds, including teenage girls by the dozen. He was out in the fields, like a true pharmer's son, giving them a proper education in the intricacies of genomics, the mysteries of the transposon and the perennially wayward ways of Nature.

He never meant a single bloody word of it, but it was birdsong to my ears.

Jack Gridley, alas, went the other way. His son was never a talker—the bullshit always seemed to skip a generation in his family—so Jack became the carnival barker himself. If he'd been as canny a scriptwriter as my Joe turned out to be he'd have pleased a more various crowd, but he went all mystical and started talking about the supernatural gifts of providence and the mysterious ways of the divine intelligence.

It wouldn't have been so bad if it had all been insincere, but Jack started going on in exactly the same way after hours on Sundays, lecturing us all on the subject of how he'd obviously been chosen by God Himself to bring the miracle of spiritual renewal to the primal wilderness of Wessex. Some people just don't know when to stop.

Sid Phillips nudged me one night when Jack was holding forth and said that it was the spiritual renewal of the Cerne Abbas Giant all over again, but Jack had always been my best friend and it didn't seem right to laugh at him, even if he was going off half-cocked. If we're going to survive and make progress, we pharmers have to stick together, and mind one another's business as carefully as we can.

After all, if we don't, who will?

THE HOME FRONT

Now that we have lived in the security of peace for more than thirty years a generation has grown up to whom the plague wars are a matter of myth and legend. Survivors of my age are often approached by the wondrous young and asked what it was like to live through those frightful years, but few of them can answer as fully or as accurately as I can.

In my time I have met many doctors, genetic engineers and statesmen who lay claim to have been in "the front line" during the First Plague War, but the originality of that conflict was precisely the fact that its real combatants were invading microbes and defensive antibodies. All its entrenchments were internal to the human body and mind. It is true that there were battlegrounds of a sort in the hospitals, the laboratories and even in the House of Commons, but this was a war whose entire strategy was to strike at the most intimate locations of all. For that reason, the only authentic front was the home front: the nucleus of family life.

Many an octogenarian is prepared to wax lyrical now on the feelings of dread associated with obligatory confinement. They will assure you that no one would risk exposure to a crowd if it could possibly be avoided, and that every step out of doors was a terror-laden trek through a minefield. They exaggerate. Life was not so rapidly transformed in an era when a substantial majority of the population still worked outside the home or attended school, and only a minority had the means or the inclination to make all their purchases electronically. Even if electronic shopping had been universal, that would have brought about a very dramatic increase in the number of people employed in the delivery business, all of whom would have had to go abroad and interact with considerable numbers of their fellows.

For these reasons, total confinement was rare during the First Plague War, and rarely voluntary. Even I, who had little choice in the matter after both my legs were amputated above the knee following the Paddington Railway Disaster of '19, occasionally sallied forth in my electrically-powered wheelchair in spite of the protestations of my wife Martha. Martha was almost as firmly anchored as I was, by virtue of the care she had to devote to me and to our younger daughter Frances, but it would have taken more than rumors of war to force Frances' teenage sister Petra to remain indoors for long.

The certainty of hindsight sometimes leads us to forget that the First Plague War was, throughout its duration, essentially a matter of rumor, but such was the case. The absence of any formal declaration of war, combined with the highly dubious status of many of the terrorist organizations that competed to claim responsibility for its worst atrocities, sustained an atmosphere of uncertainty that complicated our fears. To some extent, the effect was to exaggerate our anxieties, but it allowed braver souls a margin of doubt to which they could dismiss all inconvenient alarms.

I suppose I was fortunate that the Paddington Disaster had not disrupted my career completely, because I had the education and training necessary to set myself up as an independent share-trader operating via my domestic unit. I had established a reputation that allowed me to build a satisfactory register of corporate and individual clients, so I was able to negotiate the movement of several million euros on a daily basis. I had always been a specialist in the biotech sector, which was highly volatile even before the war started—and it was that accident of happenstance more than any other which placed my minuscule fraction of the home front at the centre of the fiercest action the war produced.

Doctors, as is only natural, think that the hottest action of the plague wars was experienced on the wards that filled up, week by week between '29 and '33, with victims of hyperflu, assertive MRSA, neurotoxic Human Mosaic Virus, and plethoral hemorrhagic fever. Laboratory engineers, equally understandably, think that the crucial battles were fought within the bodies of the mouse models housed in their triple-X biocontainment facilities. In fact, the most hectic action of all was seen on the London Stock Exchange, and the only hand-to-hand fighting involved the sneak-thieves and armed robbers who continually raided the nation's greenhouses during the six months from September '29 to March '30: the cruel winter of the great plantigen panic.

I never laid a finger on a single genetically-modified potato or carrot, but I was in the thick of it nevertheless. So, perforce, were my wife and children; their lives, like mine, hung in the balance throughout. That is why my story is one of the most pertinent records of the First Plague War, as well as one of the most poignant.

* * * * * * *

Although my work required fierce concentration and a readiness to react to market moves at a moment's notice I was occasionally forced by necessity to let Frances play in my study while I worked. It was not safe to leave her alone, even in the adjacent ground-floor room where she attended school on-line. She suffered from an environmentally-induced syndrome which made her unusually prone to form allergies to any and all novel organic compounds.

In the twentieth century such a condition would have proved swiftly fatal, but by the time Frances was born in '21 medical science had begun to catch up with the problem. There were efficient palliatives to apply to her occasional rashes, and effective ways of ensuring that she received adequate nutrition in spite of her perennial tendency to gastric distress and diarrhea. The only aspects of her allergic attacks that seriously threatened her life were general anaphylactic shock and the disruption of her breathing by massive histamine reactions in the throat. It was these possibilities that compelled us to keep very careful control over the contents of our home and the importation of exotic organic molecules. By way of completing our precautions, Martha, Petra and I had all been carefully trained to administer various injections, to operate breathing-apparatus, and—should the worst ever come to the worst—to perform an emergency tracheotomy.

Frances was very patient on the rare occasions when she had to be left in my sole care, and seemed to know instinctively when to maintain silence, even though she was a talkative child by nature. When business was slack, however, she would make heroic attempts to understand what I was doing.

As chance would have it, she was present when I first set up my position in plantigens in July '29, and it was only natural that she should ask me to explain what I was doing and why.

"I'm buying lots of potatoes and a few carrots," I told her, oversimplifying recklessly.

"Isn't Mummy doing that?" she asked. Martha was at the supermarket.

"She's buying the ones we'll be cooking and eating. I'm buying ones that haven't even been planted yet. They're the kind that have to be eaten raw if they're to do any good."

"You can't eat raw potatoes," she said, skeptically.

"They're not very nice," I agreed, "but cooking would destroy the vital ingredients of these kinds, because they're so delicate."

I explained to her, as best as I could, that a host of genetic engineers was busy transplanting new genes into all kinds of root vegetables, so that they would incorporate large quantities of special proteins or protein fragments into their edible parts. I told her that the recent arrival in various parts of the world—including Britain—of new disease-causing viruses had forced scientists to work especially hard on new ways of combating those viruses. "The most popular methods, at the moment," I concluded, "are making plantibodies and plantigens."

"What's the difference?" she wanted to know.

"Antibodies are what our own immune systems produce whenever our bodies are invaded by viruses. Unfortunately, they're often produced too slowly to save us from the worst effects of the diseases, so doctors often try to immunize people in advance, by giving them an injection of something harmless to which the body reacts the same way. Anything that stimulates the production of antibodies is called an antigen. Some scientists are producing plants that produce harmless antigens that can be used to make people's immune systems produce antibodies against the new diseases. Others are trying to cut out the middle-man by producing the antibodies directly, so that people who've already caught the diseases can be treated before they become seriously ill."

"Are antigens like allergens?" Frances asked. She knew a good deal about allergens, because we'd had to explain to her why she could never go out, and why she always had to be so careful even in the house.

"Sort of," I said, "but there isn't any way, as yet, of immunizing people against the kind of reaction you have when your throat closes up and you can't breathe."

She didn't like to go there, so she said: "Are you buying plantigens or plantibodies, Daddy?"

"I'm buying shares in companies that are spending the most money on producing new plantigens," I told her, feeling that I owed her a slightly fuller explanation.

"Why?"

"Plantigens are easier to produce than plantibodies because they're much simpler," I said. "The protection they provide is sometimes limited, but they're often effective against a whole range of closely-related viruses, so they're a better defense against new mutants. The main reason I'm buying plantigens rather than plantibodies, though, is to do with psychological factors."

She'd heard me use that phrase before, but she'd never quite got to grips with it. I tried hard to explain that although plantibodies were more useful in hospitals when sick people actually arrived there, ordinary people were far more interested in things that might keep them out of hospitals altogether. As the fear of the new diseases became more widespread and more urgent, people would become increasingly willing—perhaps even desperate—to buy large quantities of plantigen-containing potatoes and carrots to eat "just in case." For that reason, I told Frances, the sales of plantigen-producing carrots and potatoes would increase more rapidly than the actual level of threat, and that meant that it made sense to buy shares in the companies that were investing most heavily in plantigen development.

"I understand," she said, only a little dubiously. She wanted me to be proud of her. She wanted me to think that she was clever.

I *was* proud of her. I did think she was clever. If she didn't quite understand the origins of the great plantigen panic, it was because nobody really understood it, because nobody really understood what makes some psychological factors so much more powerful than others that they become obsessions.

No sooner had I taken the position than it began to put on value. Throughout August and early September I gradually transferred more and more funds from all my accounts into the relevant holdings—and then felt extremely proud of myself when the prices really took off. From the end of September on, the only question anyone in the market was asking was how long the bull run could possibly last—or, more specifically, exactly when would be the best moment to cash the paper profits and get out.

* * * * * * *

From the very beginning, Martha was skeptical about the trend. "It's going to be tulipomania all over again," she said, at the beginning of November.

"No it's not," I told her. "The value of tulips was purely a matter of aesthetic and commercial perception, with no utilitarian component at all. At least some plantigens are genuinely useful, and some of the ones that aren't useful yet will become useful in the future. As each new disease reaches Britain—whether terrorists really are importing them in test tubes or whether the viruses are simply taking advantage of modern population densities to spread from points of natural origin—possession of the right plantigens might well be a matter of life or death for some people."

"Well, maybe," she conceded. "But people aren't actually buying them as a matter of rational choice. It's not just shares, is it? There are plantigen *collectors* out there, for Heaven's sake, and potato theft is becoming as common as car crime."

I'd noticed that the items I'd seen on the TV news had begun to lose their initial jokey tone, but I was still inclined to laugh off the lunatic fringe.

"It's not funny," Martha insisted. "It was okay when there was still a semblance of medical supervision, but now that it's becoming a hobby fit for idiots the trade is entirely driven by hype and fraud. Every stallholder on the market is trying to talk up his perfectly ordinary carrots and every white van that used to be smuggling cigarettes through the tunnel is busy humping sack loads of King Edwards around. You never get out, so you don't know what it's like on the streets. All you ever see is figures on the screen."

"Share prices are just as real as anything else in the world," I said, defensively.

"Sure they are—and when they go crazy, everything else goes crazy too. Soon there won't be a seed potato available that isn't allegedly loaded with antidotes to everything from the common cold and the black death. Have you seen what's happening to the price of the stock on the supermarket shelves since the local wide boys started selling people do-it-yourself transformation kits? It's ridiculous! I wouldn't care, but ever since the gulf stream was aborted the ground's as hard as iron from October to April. No one who buys a magic potato now can possibly cash in on his investment until next summer, so it's open season for con men."

"That's one of the factors driving the spiral upwards," I observed. "The fact that nobody can start planting for another four or five months is making people all the more anxious to have the right stock ready when the moment comes."

"But the hyperflu won't wait," she pointed out. "It'll peak in February just like the old flu used to do, and if the rumors are right about human mosaic viruses, *they* won't mind the cold either, because they can crystallize out. If neurotoxic HMV does break out in London the most useful weapons we'll have to use against it are imported plantibodies from the places where it's already endemic. Why aren't you buying those by the cartload?"

I had to explain to her that putting money into foreign concerns isn't a good idea in a time of war, especially when you don't know who your enemies are.

THE TREE OF LIFE, BY BRIAN STABLEFORD

"But we know who our *friends* are," she objected. "Spain and Portugal, the southern USA, Australia...they're all on our side."

"Perhaps they are," I said, "but it's precisely the fact that we're still semi-attached to the old Commonwealth and the European Federation, while maintaining our supposedly-special relationship with America, that puts us in the firing line for practically every terrorist in the world. Then again, anxiety breeds paranoia, which breeds universal suspicion—how can we be sure that our friends really are our friends? Trust me, love—I know what I'm doing. Whether it's wise money or not, the big money is flooding into the companies that are trying to develop plantigens against the entire spectrum of HMVs, especially the ones that don't exist yet although their gene-maps are allegedly pinned to every terrorist's drawing-board. This bubble still has a lot of inflation to do."

* * * * * * *

There's a world of difference, of course, between wives and clients. Martha was worried that I was pumping too much money into a panic that couldn't last forever, but the people whose money I was handling were worried that I wasn't committing enough. Most of my individual clients were the kind of people who didn't even bother to check the closing prices after they finished work in normal times, but the prevailing circumstances changed nine out of every ten of them into the kind of neurotic who programs his cell phone to sing the Hallelujah Chorus every time a key stock puts on five per cent.

There is something essentially perverse in human nature that makes people who can see themselves growing richer by the hour worry far more about whether they ought to be growing even richer even faster than they do about the possibility of the trend turning turtle. I'd never been pestered by my clients half as much as I was in January and February of '30, when every day brought news of hundreds more hyper-flu victims and dozens more rumors about the killing potential of so-called HMVs and plethoral hemorrhagic fever. The steadily-increasing kill-rate of iatrogenic infections didn't help at all, although there was little evidence as yet of assertive MRSA migrating out of the wards.

I weathered the storm patiently, at least until Petra decided that it was time to start a potato collection of her own.

"Everyone's doing it," she said, when the true extent of her credit card bills was revealed by a routine consent check. "Not just at the tech, either. The playground at the secondary school's a real shark's nest."

"Sharks don't build nests," I said, unable to restrain my natural pedantry. "And that's not the point. You don't know that any of those potatoes has any therapeutic value whatsoever. Even though you've been paying through the nose for them, the overwhelming probability is that they haven't. You're a bright girl—you must know that."

"Well, whether they have or they haven't, I could sell them all on for half as much again as I paid for them," she said,

"So do it!" I told her. "Now!" Even that seemed moderate, given that the profits she was contemplating were entirely the produce of misrepresentation—but there were limits to the extent of any holier-than-thou stance I could convincingly maintain, as she knew very well.

"But you of all people," she complained, "should appreciate that if I wait until next week I'll get *even more*."

"You can't guarantee that," I told her. "If you hang on to them for one day—one *hour*—longer than the bubble takes to burst, all you're left with is debts. Debts that you still have to pay off, even if it takes you years."

"I know what I'm doing," she insisted. "I can judge the mood. *I thought you'd be proud of me.*"

If it had been tulips, perhaps I would have been, but I'd meant what I'd said to Martha. Come the evil day, some plantigens would make a life-or-death difference to some people. On the other hand, it was surely safe to assume that none of them would come from potatoes traded in a schoolyard, or even in the corridors of a technical college.

"If everybody in your class knows you've got them," Martha pointed out, "that makes us a target for burglary. You now how dangerous that could be, with Frances in the house.

You know we have to be extra careful." That was a good tactic. Petra loved her sister, and was remarkably patient about all the precautions she had to take every time she came into the house. The idea of burglars breaking in, dragging who knew what in their wake, wasn't one she could easily tolerate

"Get rid of them, Petra," I told her, seizing the initiative while I could. "If they aren't out of the house by dinner time, we'll be eating them."

"Hypocrite!" she said—but she knew when she was beaten.

When Petra had calmed down a little, Martha joined forces with me as we tried to explain that what *I* was buying and selling were shares in wholly reputable companies with well-staffed research labs, where every single vegetable on site really had had its genes well and truly tweaked, but Petra refused to be impressed. The only thing that stopped her from carrying on the fight was that Frances had an attack, as she often did when family quarrels were getting out of hand. Ventolin and antihistamines stopped it short of a dash to the hospital but it was a salutary reminder to us all that if hyperflu ever crossed our threshold, we'd have at least one fatal casualty.

* * * * * * *

As hyperflu's kill-rate increased, so did the rumors. It's never easy to tell "natural" rumors from the ones that are deliberately let loose to ramp prices upwards, and there's little point in trying. As soon as they appear on the bulletin boards rumors take on a life of their own, and their progress thereafter is essentially demand-led. No rumor can be effective if people aren't ready to believe it, and if people are hungry to believe something no amount of common sense or authoritative denial will be adequate to kill it.

Given that the war itself was a matter of rumor, there was a certain propriety in the fact that rumors of defensive armory were driving the whole economy.

Looking back from the safe vantage point of today's peace, it's easy to dismiss the great plantigen panic as a folly of no real significance: a mere matter of fools rushing to be fleeced. But bubbles, however absurd they may seem in retrospect, really do affect the whole economy, as Charles Mackay observed in respect of tulipomania in his classic work on *Extraordinary Popular Delusions and the Madness of Crowds*, published in 1841. "Many persons grow insensibly attached to that which gives them a great deal of trouble, as a mother often loves her sick and ever-ailing child better than her more healthy offspring," says Mackay. "Upon the same principle we must account for the unmerited encomia lavished upon these fragile blossoms. In 1634, the rage among the Dutch to possess them was so great that the ordinary industry of the country was neglected, and the population, even to its lowest dregs, embarked in the tulip trade."

So it was in February and March of '30.

It was, I suppose, only natural that the mere rumor that a company had developed a plantigen giving infallible protection against hyperflu was adequate to multiply its already inflated share price three- or fourfold. It is less easy to explain why companies that were rumored to have perfected potato-borne immunizations against diseases that were themselves mere rumors should have benefited to an even greater extent. The money to feed these momentary fads had to come from somewhere, and it wasn't only the buyers who risked impoverishment. All kinds of other enterprises vital to the economic health of the nation and continental Europe found themselves starved of capital, and all kinds of biotechnological enterprises with a far greater hope of producing something useful were denuded even of labor, as the salaries available to plantigen engineers soared to unmatchable heights.

The advent of the spring thaw was eagerly awaited by everyone, because that was when planting would become possible again and all the potential stored in the nation's potatoes and carrots would be actualized. The process of actualization would, of course, take an entire growing-season, but in agriculture, as in the stock market, anticipation is all; the initiation of movement is more significant, psychologically speaking, than any ultimate result.

THE TREE OF LIFE, BY BRIAN STABLEFORD

I knew, therefore, that prices would continue to rise at least until the end of March and probably well into April—but I also knew that I had to be increasingly wary once the vernal equinox was past, lest the mood began to change. Collapses are far more abrupt than escalations; they can happen in minutes.

Martha continued to urge me to play safe and get out "now." She had said as much in December, January, and February, and her pleas increased their urgency at exactly the same rate as the value of my holdings.

"At least take *our* money out," she begged me, on the first official day of spring. "Your clients have far more money than we have, and fewer responsibilities; they can afford to gamble. They don't have Frances' home schooling fees or your mobility expenses to deal with, let alone the prospect of huge medical bills if more effective treatments are ever developed for either or both of you."

"I can't do that," I told her. "I can't do one thing on behalf of my clients and another on my own behalf. It would be professional suicide to admit that I daren't follow my own advice."

"So pull it all out," she said.

"I can't do that either," I lamented. "Even if my timing is spot on, I'll still miss the published peak prices. The clients never understand why it's impossible to sell out at the absolute top, and every percentage point below the published peak increases their dissatisfaction. If any of my competitors gets closer than I do, my clients are likely to jump ship. Loyalty counts for something when everything's just bumping along, but it counts for nothing in times as crazy as these. I have to get this right, Martha, or I'll lose at least half my business."

I had to compromise in the end, by cashing just enough of everyone's holdings to make certain that nobody could actually lose—but I knew that if I didn't manage to hang on to the rest until the day before the crash, if not the hour before, then those sales records would come back to haunt me. The clients would see every one as an unnecessary loss rather than a prudent protective move.

THE TREE OF LIFE, BY BRIAN STABLEFORD

****

As the last day of March arrived I could see no sign of the boom ending. Every day brought new rumors speaking of horrid devices being cooked up in the labs of terrorist-friendly governments and clever countermeasures developed in our own. The pattern established in January was still in place, and the drying of the ground following the big thaw was proceeding on schedule, increasing the anticipatory enthusiasm of professional and amateur planters alike.

Everybody knew that prices could not continue to rise indefinitely, but no one had any reason yet to suppose that they would not do so for another month, or a fortnight at least. There was even talk of a "soft landing," or a "leveling off," instead of a collapse.

To increase optimism even further, the plantigen manufacturers were beginning to increase the rate at which they released actual products. Forty new strains of potatoes and six new strains of carrots had been released in the month of March, and there was hardly a household in the country that did not place each and every one of them on the menu, even though the great majority of the diseases against which they offered protection had not registered a single case in Europe.

I understood that this kind of news was not entirely good, because few of the new strains would generate much in the way of repeat business, and people would realize that fact when they actually used them—but the short term psychological effect of the new releases seemed wholly positive.

There was no reason at all to expect trouble, and April fool's day passed without any substantial incident in spite of the usual crop of preposterous postings. April the second went the same way—but the fact that spring was so abundantly in the air had other consequences for a family like ours.

Even now, people think of spring as a time when "nature" begins to bloom, but that's because we like to forget the extent to which nature has been overtaken by artifice—a process that began with the dawn of civilization and has accelerated ever since. The exotic organic compounds to which Frances was so prone to form allergies were not confined to household goods; they were used with even greater profligacy in the fields of the countryside, and with blithe abandon in the gardens of suburbia.

I had hoped that '30 might be one of Frances' better years, on the grounds that few people with land available would be planting ornamental flowers while they still had their pathetic potato collections. Alas, the possession of alleged plantigens actually made more people anxious to prepare their ground as fully as possible, and much of the preparation they did involved the new season's crop of exotic organic compounds.

We kept the windows tightly shut, and we controlled Petra's excursions as best we could, but it was all to no avail. On the third of April, at approximately 11:30 A.M., Frances' breathing became severely restricted.

Frances was in her own room when the attack began, in attendance at her web-based school. She did nothing wrong. She logged off immediately and called for Martha. Martha responded instantly, and followed the standard procedure to the letter.

When its became obvious, at 11:50 or thereabouts, that the Ventolin and the antihistamines were not inhibiting the closure of her windpipe, and that insufficient oxygen was getting through from the cylinder to our little girl's lungs, Martha dialed 911 and called for an ambulance. She was in constant touch thereafter with the ambulance station, which told her exactly where the ambulance was.

The traffic was not unusually heavy, but it was bad, and by noon Martha knew that it would not arrive in time for the last few emergency medical procedures to be carried out by the paramedics.

She had already told me what was happening, and I had told her to call me if the situation became critical. She would, of course, have called me anyway, and I would have responded.

Strictly speaking, I had no need to leave my computer. Martha had undergone exactly the same training as I had, and the fact that she had legs and I did not made her the person capable of carrying out the procedure with the least difficulty. To say that, however, is to neglect the psychological factors that govern such situations.

If I had hesitated, Martha would have carried out the emergency tracheotomy immediately, but I did not hesitate. I *could* not hesitate, in a situation of that kind. I had always taken it for granted that if anyone had to cut my daughter's throat in order to give her a chance to live, it ought to be me. I maneuvered my wheelchair to the side of Frances' bed, took the necessary equipment out of the emergency medical kit that lay open on her bedside table, and proceeded with what needed to be done. Martha could and would have done it, but the psychological factors said that it was my job, if it were humanly possible for me to do it.

It was, and I did.

The ambulance arrived at 12:37 precisely. The paramedics took over, and Martha accompanied Frances to the hospital. I could not go, because the ambulance was not a model that could take wheelchairs as bulky as mine. I returned to my computer instead, arriving at 12:40.

I had been away for no more than forty-five minutes, but I had missed the collapse. Shares in plantigen producers were already in free fall.

I had missed the last realistic selling opportunity by sixteen minutes.

Would I have been able to grasp that opportunity had I been at my station? I am almost certain that I would have been able to bale out at least part of my holdings, but I cannot know for sure. The only thing of which I can be certain is that I missed the chance. I missed the vital twenty minutes before the bubble burst, when all kinds of signs must have become evident that the end was nigh.

With the aid of hindsight, it is easy to understand how the collapse happened so quickly, on the basis of a mere rumor. When a rumor's time is ripe, it is unstoppable, even if it is absurd. The rumor that killed off the great plantigen panic was quite absurd, but it had a psychological timeliness that made it irresistible.

One of the most widely touted—but as yet undeployed—weapons of the imaginary war was what everyone had grown used to calling "human mosaic virus." There is, in fact, no such thing as a human mosaic virus and there never was. The real and hypothetical entities to which the name had been attached bore only the slightest analogy to the tobacco mosaic virus after which they had been named. Tobacco mosaic virus was not merely a disease but a favorite tool of experimental genetic engineers. Strictly speaking, that had no relevance to neurotoxic HMV or any of its imagined cousins, but the language of rumor is utterly devoid of strictness, and extremely prone to confusion.

There is and was such a thing as potato mosaic virus, which also doubled as a disease and a tool of genetic engineering. The rumor which swept the world on the third of April '30 was that terrorists had developed and deployed a new weapon of plague war, aimed in the first instance not at humans but at potatoes: a virus that would transform benign plantigens into real diseases: HMVs that could and would infect any human beings who ate plantigen-rich potatoes in the hope of protecting themselves.

Scientifically, technologically and epidemiologically speaking it was complete nonsense, but all the psychological factors were in place to make it plausible nonsense—plausible enough, at any rate, to knock the bottom right out of the market in plantigen shares.

I wasn't ruined. None of my clients were ruined. Compared to the base from which the bubble had begun, six months earlier, we had all made a small profit—considerably more than one could have made in interest had the money been on deposit in a bank. But no one—not even me—was disposed to compare the value of his holdings with their value on last October the first, let alone July the first. Every eye was firmly fixed on the published peak, weeping for lost opportunity.

And that, my dear young friends, is what it was really like to be on the home front during the First Plague War.

* * * * * * *

Frances recovered from the allergy attack. She recovered again the following year, and again the year after that. Then new treatments became available, and the necessity of administering emergency tracheotomies evaporated. They were expensive, but we managed in spite of everything to meet the expense. By '36 she was able to leave the house again, and she went on to attend a real university rather than a virtual one. She was never completely cured of her tendency to form violent allergies to every new organic molecule that made its debut on the stage of domestic technology, but her reactions ceased to be life-threatening. They became an ordinary discomfort, a relatively mild inconvenience.

By then, alas, Petra was dead. She was an early casualty, in July '34, of one of the diseases that the ill-informed still insist on calling HMVs. She died because she was too much a part of the world, far too open to social contacts and influences. Of the four of us, she had always been the most likely casualty of a plague war, because she was the only one of us who did not think of her home as a place of confinement. Petra always thought of herself as a free agent, a free spirit, an everyday entrepreneur.

We were grief-stricken, of course, because we had always loved her. We miss her still, even after all this time. But if I am honest, I must confess that we would have suffered more had it been Frances that we lost—not because we loved Petra any less, but because Frances always seemed more tightly bound to the nucleus of our little atom of community.

Unlike Petra, Frances was never free.

Nor am I.

Thanks to the march of biotechnology, I have a new pair of legs to replace the ones I lost in '19. They were costly, but we managed to meet the cost. I still have a loving wife, and a lovely daughter. I have everything I need, and I can go anywhere I want, but I feel less free today than I did on April the Second '30, because that was the day before the day on which a prison of circumstance formed around me that I have never been able to escape. Although neither my family nor my business was completely ruined by my failure to get out of plantigens in time to avoid the crash, it was the last opportunity I ever had to become seriously rich or seriously successful. The slightly-constrained circumstances in which we three survivors of the First Plague War have lived the rest of our lives always seemed, albeit in a purely theoretical sense, to be both unnecessary and blameworthy. If they were not quite the traditional wages of sin—with the exception of the price paid by poor Petra—they were surely the commission fees of sin.

The prison in question is, of course, purely psychological; I have not yet given up the hope of release. In much the same way, I continue stubbornly to hope that we poor and pitiful humans will one day contrive a world in which psychological factors will no longer create cruel chaos where there ought to be moral order.

HIDDEN AGENDAS

As soon as the sound of the Sloth's wake-up call speared its way into my ever-so-pleasant dream, before I was even awake, I knew that the Dead Cat Squad had come to call again—and I was instantly afraid, not for myself but for Cade.

Carol-Anne woke up too, and forced her eyes open while I was hauling myself from the sheets and groping for a deadgown to hide my sexsuit.

"Who can that be?" she asked—or words to that effect.

"I'll take care of it," I said. "Go back to sleep." She must have heard the anxiety in my voice because her eyes didn't close again. She didn't get up until I'd left the bedroom, but as soon as the door closed behind me I heard the bed creak as she levered herself off the mattress into an eavesdropping stance.

I had to rub my eyes before I could bring the pasty face on the screen into focus. I'd never seen the man before, but I knew the type. Neat and bland, with a face shaped to stereotype: an individual molded to look like a clone. He probably thought that his bland exterior allowed him to keep the unique truth of himself hidden, but his hidden self was surely indistinguishable in any significant respect from millions of other hidden selves. I turned on the intercom and said: "Who are you and what do you want?" Or words to that effect.

He wasn't in the least upset by the curses. "I'm Alexander Chesterton, Mr. Maclaine," he said. "I'm an executive officer in the Scientific Civil Service. I need to talk to you about Cade Maclaine Senior." He inserted his card into the slot beneath the door-camera and his image on the screen was replaced by the usual cataract of unreadable print. The gist of it was that he had been authorized by some duly-appointed committee or other to conduct an interview and that I was required to affirm that I would answer his questions truthfully.

The Sloth let him in, as it was legally obliged to do. I knew from past experience that it would take him between ninety seconds and two minutes to get from the street-door to the apartment-door, depending on the starting-position of the elevator. I had just enough time to get rid of my sexsuit and select an appropriate dayskin—but I had to go back into the bedroom to do that.

"Who is it, Carly?" Carol-Anne asked, fretfully. She'd switched on the bedside screen and the ever-dutiful Sloth had shown her the warrant, but she'd never seen one before and she didn't have a clue what was going on. I'd introduced her to Mum but I hadn't mentioned Cade—not because I was ashamed of him, or of who and what I was, but because I didn't want the bright glow of our burgeoning relationship clouded by ancient shadows.

"Just routine harassment," I told her. "If you want to know what it's about, check the library for information on my namesake and clone-brother, Cade Carlyle Maclaine. According to a generation-count, he's my adoptive great-great-great-grandfather. According to what Cade always refers to as PEST Control, I'm his other self."

She looked puzzled. She hadn't known that my first name was Cade because I never used it. I didn't have time to explain. I went to talk to the government man, who had taken up position at the centre of the pattern on the deadrug.

"I'm afraid that I have some bad news. Mr. Maclaine," he said.

The knot in my stomach had begun to form in anticipation the moment the Sloth had hauled me out of my dream, but it had formed a dozen times before; this time, it tightened.

I had a line ready. "You mean the old bastard croaked overnight and nobody even bothered to tell me?"

He wasn't surprised or disturbed by my contrived callousness. "I think you'll find when you check your mail that you have been notified of the change in Cade Senior's condition," he assured me, smugly. "The change wasn't sufficiently drastic to trigger an immediate alarm-call. He has, however, had to be placed on an external life-support system, thus activating his Last Rights contract. Death is currently scheduled for Thursday the Twenty-Second at twenty-one hundred hours GMT."

I sat down on my armchair without bothering to offer the guest armchair to my visitor. Chesterton despaired of the unoffered invitation and sat down on the guest chair anyway, pausing momentarily to judge the quality of its reflexive adaptation. "I need to talk to you about the terms of Cade Maclaine's will, and the substance of your inheritance," he said. "You're required to give the standard affirmation."

I rattled it off in fifteen seconds flat through gritted teeth, promising to tell the truth, the whole truth and nothing but the truth.

"Cade Carlyle Maclaine Junior," Chesterton said, savoring the formality of it. "Have you, since you last gave testimony, received from Cade Carlyle Maclaine Senior any information related to the researches which Cade Carlyle Maclaine Senior carried out in and around the city of Geneva between 2034 and 2074?"

"No," I said.

"Do you know where any records of that research are kept?"

"No."

"In that case, I hereby give you notice that if, in the course of the next twenty-one days, you receive any such information, or make any such discovery, you must immediately communicate that information to an authorized officer of the Scientific Civil Service. If you fail to do so, you will be committing an offence under the provisions of Act 3593 of the reconstituted Parliament of the British Commonwealth."

"This is unnecessary," I said.

"My superiors thought it politic to remind you that they take this matter very seriously," he informed me, solemnly, "and to point out that your own interests would be best served by co-operation. Cade Maclaine Senior is one of the oldest men in the world; he's always known he wouldn't have to face the challenges of the twenty-fifth century—but you're one of the youngest people in the world, and you have every reason to expect that you might have to face the challenges of the twenty-ninth and thirtieth centuries. Do you keep up with the news, Mr. Maclaine?"

"The election news? No. I know there's been an earthquake in the Ottoman Republic, though—and that the resettlement of the former Australian State of Tasmania by the United States of the Pacific Rim had finally been authorized by the UN."

"Two hundred and thirty new species of insects have been identified since the beginning of the year within the boundaries of the British Commonwealth. Plus ninety-two arachnids, and various other oddments."

"That's hardly surprising," I said, "given the number of new ecological niches opening up as ap-systems extend their shadow from pole to pole. Cade will be pleased—especially if the new boys can make significant inroads into the dread empire of ap, but I can't really believe that *you* care."

"Our calculations suggest that the biodiversity index should have peaked a hundred years ago," he said. "The spread of artificial photosynthesis systems should not have been a significant selective force, given that the systems were designed to be immune to infiltration and exploitation by DNA-based organisms."

"But they're not immune, are they?"

"That's why we need the records, Mr. Maclaine. We need to know the exact designs of the various superstrings with which Cade Senior stocked his so-called omnispores. We need to know how many individuals he implanted to serve as vectors, and exactly what range of species he employed. We do understand and sympathize with his desire—his need—to keep his early work concealed from his twenty-first century paymasters, but there is no comparison to be made between the governments of that period and the governments of today. Cade Maclaine's refusal to understand that is pure paranoia."

"If he'd kept records of exactly how many cockroaches and woodlice he'd made pregnant," I said, tiredly, "and exactly how many different kinds of spiders he interfered with, he really would have been mad. If he had any records at all you'd have found them. You've put enough effort into the search."

Generations of Chesterton's ancestors had gone through the hardware and software of Elba House with a fine toothcomb, and searched every inch of the estate. Anything left behind in Switzerland or Stornoway would certainly have come to light. Sometimes, even I was inclined to believe that Cade's dark hints about there being more things in Heaven and Earth than PEST Control were capable of dreaming of, and more places to hide them than they could ever think of looking, was mere bluster—just one more game, designed for the purpose of making an unprecedentedly long life seem a little more interesting than it really was.

"Your clone-brother was a clever man," Chesterton said, not bothering to stress the *was*. "He had the best access of anyone now alive to pre-Spasm technology, and once his original paymasters had perished he had a hundred years to work, with no one looking over his shoulder. He had time and space to bury a thousand treasures where no one would ever find them. We're supposed to have recovered everything that was lost in the Spasm—all the theory, all the equipment, all the imagination—but we only have the outlines, not the detail. We have technologies the people of the twenty-first century only dreamed of—but we can only guess how much *they* had that we haven't yet recovered...."

He stopped to draw breath, then continued on a slightly different tack. "We really do have problems, Mr. Maclaine. All kinds of undesirable traits are returning. Toxins, parasites, blights—every evil known to Nature is coming back in a headlong rush, and it isn't just the ap-systems that are suffering. The cost is rising year on year, and if we can't regain control we can't begin to estimate the burden that the Commonwealth will have to carry in ten or twenty years time."

He meant the economic cost of course, and the tax burden. He wasn't counting the toll of human misery and mortality—but he could have done. Toxins, parasites and blights all cause discomfort, and they all put a strain on the resources of human internal technology. If the evils continued to multiply, people could and would begin to die a little bit sooner than they would have in more hospitable natural surroundings.

"If you found one of the orbital spore-banks...." I began.

"Don't be obtuse, Mr. Maclaine," he said. "There are no orbital spore-banks. There never were. The only omnispores that ever existed were the ones manufactured in the twenty-first century, and we're almost certain that the only place their archetypes were manufactured was the European Bioresearch Complex in Switzerland. Apart from Cade Carlyle Maclaine, everyone actively involved in their manufacture and subsequent distribution is dead. If any records of the project still exist, or any information at all that would help us understand the sustained increase in invertebrate biodiversity, it is in your interests as well as ours to find it and give it to us."

"Fuck off and leave me alone, you whey-faced ghoul," I said, in exactly those words. "I need to pack—I have a wake to go to."

He'd obviously hoped that our conversation might end on a brighter note, but he hadn't really expected it to. He was just going through the motions, to make sure that his superiors could never accuse him of leaving a vital stone unturned. He did as he was asked—but I knew that I'd be seeing him again.

* * * * * * *

Carol-Anne had been doing her homework. If any other boyfriend she'd known for as short a time as she'd known me had told her that he had to go to Kirkcaldy for a family wake she'd have been out the door like a flash, telling him to call her as soon as he got back, but the first thing she said to me when I went back into the bedroom was: "Can I come with you?"

"Sure," I said, hauling a traveling-case from under the bed and throwing it open. "I'll even introduce you to the old man. But you'll have to make allowances for PEST Control and the relatives."

"What's PEST Control?" she demanded.

"It's what Cade calls people like Alexander Chesterton. During the Repopulation, way back when the Commonwealth was re-formed there was a government department that was called that by its detractors. It was supposed to be shorthand for Political and Environmental Security, Transfiguration and Control. It was never a real title, of course, but the newstapes took it up and it stuck for a while. Cade still uses it—and if I thought for a moment that they were the kind of people who enjoyed a joke, I'd assume that their ostensible avid interest in controlling the pests that have begun to feed on their precious ap-systems was a witty riposte rather than a stupid cover story." I fed the bag with skins and gadgets, not bothering to make a careful selection.

Carol-Anne retreated to matters of more intimate interest "What allowances will I have to make for your relatives? Won't they like me?"

"Oh, they'll like *you*. It's me they don't like."

"Why?"

"Because they think I was custom-designed to be the old man's favorite, and that I'll get uniquely favorable treatment in his will, thus depriving every one of them of some microscopic fraction of his or her already-meager share of the loot. Bad enough that the cake has to be cut more than two hundred ways, without some twenty-one-year-old upstart claiming more than his measly due just because he's a clone."

"Aren't any of the others clones?"

"Not one. The big clone explosion was back in the twenty-third, when it was practically a social duty to produce children by the truckload. That was before what Cade calls the Peasant's Revolt—the people who ran the world in those days were almost all old enough to have lived through the Spasm, and they remembered the war. The idea of cloning Cade Carlyle Maclaine when there were so many *innocent* people around would have been controversial bordering on horrific. Even now, when the war is ancient history to all but a few ancients—all of whom seem equally venerable simply because they *are* so ancient—the family wouldn't have consented to the cloning if it hadn't been for the subtle encouragement of PEST control. Effectively, I was the result of a conspiracy by my clone-brother and his enemies, in which the relatives—including my foster-parents—were rather reluctant participants."

"You didn't have to be fostered within the family," Carol-Anne pointed out.

"Lesser of two evils, from the viewpoint of the Big Uncles," I said, closing the bag and thumbing the seal. "I presume you want to call at your place, pick up a bag? Your parents won't mind, will they?" The second question was rhetorical. Carol-Anne's foster-parents were both in their nineties and it was a third bond-contract for both of them; they were very relaxed. An only child must have seemed like next-to-nothing to people who'd probably had eight or ten each during their first bondings and another six apiece during their second.

Before leaving the apartment I downloaded the night's messages from the Sloth. There were more than fifty, of which half would be junk and most of the rest empty condolences. I figured that I'd scroll through them in the car. I knew from experience that Kirkcaldy was a two hour drive, whether I took the direct route through the Uplands or the motorway dogleg via Glasgow. Skipping north along the coast to pick up Carol-Anne's luggage would add another twenty minutes in either case, so there was plenty of time to fill.

"Ever been to a wake before?" I asked, as the elevator took us down to the garage.

"Once," she said. "Great-great-aunt Clare. Can't remember much about it—I was only six. It was very crowded."

"This one will be pretty crowded too. Every rentable room from Dunfermline to Cupar will be full of Maclaines, MacDonalds, and McAllisters. All fake, of course. Cade was born in Manchester, educated in Paris and held pan-European citizenship before the Spasm. At least a quarter of his genes had come from Africa via Jamaica. He still laughs every time someone reminds him that Stornoway was once reckoned to be the only secure refuge of civilization west of the Alps and east of Yucatán."

"According to the Library," Carol-Anne observed, tentatively, "that was partly his fault."

"He tells it differently," I informed her, dryly.

I threw my traveling-bag into the rear seat-space of the car and got into the front. Carol-Anne threw the plastic pouch containing her crumpled sexsuit on top of the bag and got in with me. I let her program the driver.

It wasn't until she'd plotted a way home that she said: "How differently?"

"According to him," I said, "the war didn't make any difference whatsoever. It was the Spasm that wiped out ninety-nine per cent of the human population and ninety-nine per cent of our cousin species. The billion and a half people killed in the war would have died anyway, just as nastily—and they might well have taken additional casualties with them, human and unhuman. Cade says that the war actually saved the world, because if it hadn't been for the funding he and others like him got to carry out war-related biotech programs, they wouldn't have been able to carry out the parallel lines of research that paved the way for the emortalization of the survivors and the Repopulation. Cade says that calling him a war criminal was just scapegoating, and that redesigning a few viruses to kill a few million people was a small price to pay for all the lives—human and unhuman—that his work eventually saved."

The car picked up speed as it hit the coast road. The morning dew hadn't yet risen and there was mist on the grassy embankments to either side of the causeway. Beads of moisture clung to the multitudinous spider-webs which dressed the neatly-pruned bushes. I wondered how many of those webs had been spun by spiders descended from Cade's omnispores. There was no way of knowing; nobody knew how many arachnid species had come through the Spasm, and nobody knew what contribution the mutation and selection of archaic stocks was making to the figures quoted by Alexander Chesterton.

"The digest I read didn't say anything about Cade Maclaine's research saving lives, or about secrets," Carol-Anne told me, a little hesitantly. She'd only done a few minutes' research. "We did emortality, ectogenesis, and cloning at school, and I don't remember ever coming across his name there."

THE TREE OF LIFE, BY BRIAN STABLEFORD

"Omnispores were his biggest contribution to the future of the planet," I said, "but if you touched on them at school, it was probably under the derisory heading of the Trojan Cockroach Plan."

"I never heard of that," she said, although she didn't seem certain. "Maybe when I go to uni—the foundation year has a compulsory bioscience component."

Carol-Anne was due to go up to Edinburgh in January for training in Pragmatic Archaeology. She was sensible enough to know that all the real treasure-troves had already been exhumed, but also sensible enough to know that reclamation work would provide safe and continuous employment at least until she turned a hundred and fifty—by which time she'd presumably be desperate to try something new. I was half way through a course in Elementary Ectogenesis at Stirling, but that was only one small step in my Life Plan. Cade had advised me that omnispores are useless unless you have somewhere to put them where they'll do some good—and he didn't mean an orbital spore-bank, or the ovaries of cockroaches.

"Don't expect too much," I warned her. "Cade might not have any secrets to pass on at all—it could all be just a game. You don't get many laughs once your body is eighty-percent synthetic. One day, cyborgs will be able to feel things as deeply and as subtly as the fleshy few, but it's been a long time since poor Cade had the whole hormonal orchestra to feed his heart. I only hope that I still feel like giving people the runaround when I'm four hundred years old."

"I thought people as old as that couldn't possibly remember any secrets they might once have had."

"It's not as simple as that. Memory isn't like a tank that has to be drained periodically in order to take in new information. It's because the various technologies of repair that have been added to our repertoire during their lifetimes have worked far better on the brain's wetware than the software. Once lost, memories stay lost—and a lot of people who lived through the Spasm were severely damaged by it. Nobody really knows how much memory people of Cade's age *can* hang on to, because the sample is so small and so various. He might remember a lot more than he lets on, or a lot less than he pretends—but if his memories *have* survived, his habits must have survived too. He spent the greater part of his first century cultivating the habit of obsessive secrecy, and the whole of the second being reviled as a war criminal. If he had any secrets left, it would have taken a lot more than wild horses to drag them out of him these last hundred years, even if he had no particular reason for keeping them to himself except plain and simple stubbornness."

She didn't understand, but she wanted to. She lingered in the car as it drew up in front of her building. "I suppose designing viruses for the Plague War isn't the sort of thing you'd want to tell people about," she said.

"That's not the point," I told her. "That was only what he was supposed to be doing. He and his fellow conspirators kept their consciences clean by telling one another that their real work was entirely virtuous, and reveling in the paradox of having a noble cause that they could only serve by stealth in a deeply sick world. Go on—get your stuff."

She consented to be waved away.

While Carol-Anne busy explaining to her parents—probably via the household Sloth—that she had been invited to the wake of the last living war criminal by his fresh-faced clone, I took the opportunity to call Mum. Even on the tiny dashboard screen her image seemed to radiate world-weariness.

"I got the message," I told her. "I'm on my way. I'm bringing Carol-Anne." I figured that it was safer to make the bald declaration. If I'd asked for permission, it might have started an argument. "How's Cade?"

"Better, actually," she said, sounding mildly surprised. In fact, there were perfectly good reasons why he should feel better now that his heavily-cyborgized body had finally given up on him. The life-support machine had better oxygenators, a more powerful blood-pump and more sophisticated waste-disposal systems than any patched-up lungs, heart and kidneys. The costs of their involvement would be subjective rather than objective; his hormonal orchestra would be strictly player-piano now, and he wouldn't have time to learn how to use a new pair of artificial hands. In theory, Cade's brain might be capable of remaining operational for another hundred years, but what he thought of as his *essential self* had crossed the last boundary. Everyone knew by now what happened to people who hung around too long; all sane people made contracts voluntarily disposing of their Last Rights.

"Is he going to try to see everybody?" I asked.

"As many as he can," Mum said, passing a hand across her brow with reflexive theatricality. "It's a matter of form. Some won't be able to come, of course, and some simply won't, but there'll be nearly two hundred. It'll be five or ten minutes each, and he'll need an earpiece to remind him who most of them are. He wants to make a speech to a full assembly, of course. I'm not at all sure it's wise, given that the newstapes are bound to rake up all that war criminal nonsense, but there's no way he'll consent to go quietly. He'll want a proper talk with you, of course. He'll probably save it up for the final evening, although he'll be utterly exhausted by then. I've already had *calls*, of course. Some say they're academic historians, but they're all newstape people really—all scum, Cade says, especially the ones who work for the government. It's going to be difficult. I can't remember the last flurry of scandal, of course, but...."

Mum was only a hundred and two. She was a second-generation product of the Repopulation, one of the vast majority of humankind for whom all other eras were items of bizarre history.

"Carol-Anne's coming back," I said. "We'll be there by eleven, probably. See you soon."

She didn't try to keep me on the line; she had plenty to do.

"Was that your Mum?" Carol-Anne said, as she threw her bag into the back. "Is she upset?"

"As upset as might be expected," I said, knowing that Carol-Anne hadn't the least notion of what might be expected. Mum had been living under Cade's roof for a long time, and it would be a major break in her life to have the obligation of his primary care removed. She would never find another burden remotely like it, no matter how hard she tried. Cade's death would release her, just as it would release me—and she must be just as frightened and confused by that prospect as I was.

****

I took the motorway rather than the direct route. The motorway ran through the valleys and didn't offer the same panoramic views as the Uplands A-road, but the sky hadn't brightened up and the thought of seeing all the jet black corrugated ap-layouts following the contours of the hillsides to the distant horizons wasn't appealing.

Cade hated ap-tech even more ferociously than those survivors of his own generation who harbored more general resentments against biological inventions. Artificial photosynthesis was far more efficient than Nature's chlorophyll-based technology, and its supportive apparatus was reportedly cleverer than the basic ACGT finger-exercises, but Cade loved *real life*. Ap-systems are black because they absorb and use all the solar energy that fall upon their surfaces, wasting nothing. Cade's refusal to admire that cut deeper than aesthetically superficial arguments about the joy of color; he was the only man I knew who could wax lyrical about the essential propriety of waste. "If PEST Control has its way," he was fond of saying, "the whole world will end up clothed in black: black oceans, black continents. It will be the funeral of the ecosphere. Everything Gaia ever did will be done by machine, with no hint of excess, nothing to *spare*, no margin for creativity. They're trying to cut out a whole section of the wheel of existence, simply because it seems to them to be *dirty* and *messy*. They call it hygiene but it's really a kind of neurosis. Anal retentiveness, Freud would have called it."

Cade was no Gaian mystic, of course, and certainly no Freudian, but he wasn't overly particular about the sources from which he borrowed his inspiration. I wasn't sure how far to go in agreeing with him about the evils of ap. I retained the usual Romantic regard for all the subtle variants of natural greenery, but I understood that human aesthetic sensibilities are only geared to color and growth because we haven't yet got around to retuning the relevant genes. I knew, too, that even the world's Alexander Chestertons wanted to preserve life, in all its myriad wild and domestic states. The real debate wasn't a matter of either/or—it was about striking the right balance. According to Cade, however, there was no myth so ridiculous and pernicious as the myth of the *balance of Nature*—not, at least, since we had contrived to rid ourselves of the myth of God. I usually sat on the fence when we talked about such matters, although he always said that I'd be better off playing Devil's Advocate. To accept that there had never been any balance in Nature was one thing; to infer that what we were putting in nature's place ought not to embrace balance as a goal seemed to me to be a step beyond the bounds of logic, into the unknown.

The motorway was flanked by embankments every bit as green as those dressing the western coast-road, and much steeper—but the greenery was just as carefully-disciplined as the coast-road's single rank of bushes. Now that the dew had risen, I couldn't see spider-webs any more. The tiny predators were still there, growing fat on the liquidized flesh of even tinier plant-parasites, but from the vantage-point of the car I had to take that on trust. Everything I could actually *see* in the full glare of daylight was the product of elaborate landscape-gardening.

"What's an omnispore?" Carol-Anne asked, jutting her chin out to signify that she wouldn't be at all impressed by the suggestion that she should connect the car's Sloth to the Library and research the matter herself.

"It's a means of taking out insurance against the effects of a mass-extinction," I told her. "Opinions differ as to whether it's ever been one of Nature's ways. Cade first got interested in the idea because he thought that it would be the logical means for intelligent species to use in beginning the colonization of other worlds—what used to be called Terraformation. He still thinks that Earth's ecosphere may have been kick-started by a cargo of omnispores delivered by a space-probe, and he thinks that it might have been re-booted the same way, at least twice in the last few hundred million years. Way back before the Plague War, when Cade was just starting out on his career and rockets were carrying clever machines into space on a regular basis, he wanted to mount a search for spore-banks hidden in the asteroid-belt. He thought there might be hundreds of them there, each one waiting patiently for the chaotic effects of gravity to shift it into a collision course with Earth. No such dedicated mission was ever mounted, of course, but when Cade went to work for the Plague Warriors they sweetened the deal by offering him the chance to add a little extra programming to the Chaos Patrol."

"Chaos Patrol?" she queried.

"A ring of probes between Mars and the asteroids, set up to monitor the orbits of asteroids. The orbits are slightly unstable even at the best of times because of the immeasurably intricate play of gravitational forces exerted by the planets, and they become vulnerable to more profound disruption every time a big comet passes through. The Chaos Patrol was put in place as an early-warning system designed to anticipate possible collisions with Earth. They're still out there. Cade has his own tracking system built into Napoleon—that's the family Silver—dutifully collecting the data that falls like the gentle rain from Heaven."

"Your family has its own Silver?"

"We didn't buy it—Cade built it bit by bit. Napoleon's a quirky beast, but we all love him, even Dad. I suspect that Cade's been waiting for centuries for him to make the leap to self-consciousness, the way Silvers were always supposed to do, but if he ever did he's had the sense to keep quiet about it. Various PEST Control hackers have been through his files looking for Cade's secret records, but they've never been certain whether their failure to find anything proves that there's nothing to find."

Carol-Anne was having trouble prioritizing all the questions that she wanted to ask. I could see that she was vaguely annoyed with me because I'd never seen fit to explain any of this before. My failure to mention Cade now seemed to her to be a major deception, whose magnitude and complexity was just beginning to become apparent. It seemed to be a good idea to keep talking.

"The dinosaurs are everybody's favorite example of a mass-extinction," I rattled on, "but it wasn't just the dinosaurs. They were just the tip of the iceberg. The attrition rate was just as bad among the invertebrate phyla—the insects were devastated. Marine life fared better than land-based life and plants better than animals but relationships within an ecosphere are so complicated, and chains of influence so far-reaching, that the whole system collapsed, just as it did in the Spasm. Cade told me that the wave of extinctions really started some time before the famous asteroid hit, just as the Spasm really started long before the Plague War—but according to Cade, the real question wasn't so much *what did the killing?* as *how did the ecosphere recover so quickly?*

"That question must often have been on his mind while he and his colleagues sat inside that Swiss mountain making germs more virulent than any that natural selection had ever contrived. They made agents to blight crops and devastate stocks of domestic animals as well as people—and they engineered insect vectors to carry nasty bacteria and bacterial vectors to carry deadly viruses. Cade's paymasters didn't understand what had already been done to the ecosphere by two hundred years of heavy-duty pollution, and they probably didn't understand or care what their new campaigns were likely to do to the ailing ecosystems of which they were a part. The scientists, of course, saw things a little differently.

"What fascinated Cade wasn't so much the species that disappeared in the extinction-events of the remote past as the ones that didn't. The dinosaurs perished, except for a handful of species that turned into birds—but frogs came through. How? What frogs had, Cade says, was *genetic resilience.* A frog's egg has more DNA than a human's, because it has several distinct suites of genes which can carry out certain basic tasks in embryo-development. That means that a frog's eggs can develop in different ways, according to the environment in which the eggs find themselves. The frogs that were around in the early phases of the Spasm weren't very versatile, and Cade felt reasonably certain that they weren't going it make it this time—but that only convinced him that the alternative sets of genes that modern frogs had must be a vestigial relic of something much more complicated. And that made him wonder whether the highly-specialized gene-sets of all modern species might be fragmentary relics of sets that were once much more complicated and much more versatile."

"Omnispores," said Carol, to prove that she was following the argument.

"Sort of," I agreed. "Once the Plague War began, Cade stopped worrying about whether he'd come up with a correct explanation of what happened in the past. The question of whether the original omnispores might still exist out in the asteroid belt, having been carefully sown by cosmic gardeners while the sun was young, seemed far less important than the possibility of building artificial omnispores that would get evolution kick-started again after the impending ecocatastrophe. And who better to figure that out, and get the production-line moving, than scientists working with the most sophisticated gene-splicing machinery that had ever been manufactured?

"That was the beginning of the Trojan Cockroach Plan. It wasn't just cockroaches, of course—but Cade figured that if the cockroaches didn't make it through the Spasm, nothing would. He used woodlice, beetles, flies, and spiders—but in every instance, the principle was the same. He implanted packages of DNA into their reproductive organs: massive supplies of genes gathered from hundreds of different species, all locked into self-replicating megachromosomal structures he called superstrings. He fixed it so that the omnispores could hitch a ride in the eggs of the vector species, multiplying as their hosts multiplied—and he also fixed it so that they would be able to feed fragmentary packets of their own DNA into a tiny minority of the eggs, so that those eggs might hatch into something that wasn't a cockroach at all. The idea was that the cockroaches would carry the genes of hundreds of other species through the worst years of the Spasm, when virtually everything else died—and would then begin to make those genes available again, to kick start the evolutionary process and re-boot the whole ecosphere back to something like its former complexity within the space of a few hundred generations. That's roach generations, not human generations—thirty days or less.

"The passenger DNA was mostly taken from other insects and arachnids. *Forget what they say about poets, Carly,*

Cade says. *The true legislators of the world are flies and mites. They make all the flowers grow and they mop up all the shit. Without flies and mites, the world would have gone straight to hell. They'll teach you in school that it was men who saved the ecosystem after the Spasm, but the so-called Noahs and their so-called Arks would have had a lot harder time of it if it hadn't been for my guys. Whenever they ask you who really saved the world, Carly, tell them that it was Mister Cockroach, with a little help from Mister Spider and Mister Fly.* He exaggerates, of course. The men from PEST Control think that the business of pollinating flowers is far better handled by careful gardeners armed with airbrushes, and that modern sewage-systems are as far ahead of maggots as ap-systems are of pondweed. Anything arthropods and DNA can do, humans and nanotech can supposedly do better: even evolution. Natural selection is messy and very wasteful by comparison with computer-aided design. That's in theory. In practice, PEST Control's computers can't figure out why so many new species are appearing with every year that passes. According to their models, Cade's omnispores should have run out of innovative steam a hundred years ago. Chaos should have shot its bolt, and Order should be well and truly enthroned as the Way of the World—but it isn't. Not yet."

"And the man who came to see you this morning wants to know the reason why?" said Carol-Anne.

"So he says. He might even be telling the truth. On the other hand, he might *want* me to think that all he's interested in is how to keep the roaches out of his precious ap-systems so that I'll meekly hand over Cade's secret files—whereas the thing he's *really* interested in is something *else* that's buried there."

"Like what?" said Carol, resentful of the implication that everything I'd been explaining so carefully might be little more than a smoke screen.

"Who knows? Maybe even *he* doesn't know. Maybe he just can't stand the thought that there *might* be something Cade's been holding back since the day the world went *splat!*"

"But he thinks that your clone-brother's dying gift to you will be a password that will let you into some hidden corner of the family Silver?"

"So it seems. I suppose I ought to hope that he's right, so that I can finally get the Dead Cat Squad off my back—but even if I give them whatever I get, they'll never be sure whether there might be something else even more interesting that I've managed to keep back. In a world of near-emortals, suspicions and obsessions can last forever. That's why Cade is the way he is."

We were just crossing the Forth, by way of the Replica Bridge. The busy grey waters of the river provided a sharp contrast to the sculpted slopes of the embankments, but the green corridor soon swallowed us up again. It wasn't until we approached the spangled towers of Kincardine that we would leave the motorway for good. I felt a little guilty because, when I'd got into the car, I'd automatically taken the right-hand seat, so I'd have the river on my side while Carol-Anne would only have ap-farms on hers. Until we passed Crossford and emerged into the so-called wildland I'd be able to look out over the placid waves while she'd have the matt-black shadow looming up to her left. The interceptors were carefully shaped, of course, but they were so very accomplished at soaking up the light that it was almost impossible to make out the individual cones and fans. Sometimes, driving home along the Kincardine Road, I would stare intently at the black wall, searching for some hint of decay—some firm evidence that Cade's tiny *protégés* were making inroads into PEST Control's pride and joy. Unfortunately, black is a good color for concealment and if you stare at an ap-ribbon long enough you begin to feel that it's sucking you into oblivion. The side nearer the water was the better side to be, especially on a day like today, when the sky and the sea would be radiating more than their fair share of gloom.

* * * * * * *

I'd have liked it better if the wildland—however fake its wildness might be—had extended all the way from Crossford to Elba House, but it didn't. Kirkcaldy's population had doubled since I was born, and its supportive ap-farms had more than doubled their size in response. North of Burntisland the black ribbon reasserted its grip on the north side of the road, and only slackened it slightly as we skirted Kinghorn.

Mercifully, Elba House itself was set on a green headland to the north-west of the town, and the family land extended for at least a kilometer in every direction. The estate was wilder than wild—as wild, in fact, as the patient bureaucrats of PEST Control would allow. None of our neighbors appreciated the visitations they received from our mites, wasps and centipedes, but they did like the butterflies and dragonflies, so their attempts to maintain a strict no-fly zone around the estate were always half-hearted. Elba wasn't an ecological island—but no island ever really is.

The traffic had decreased markedly in volume once we'd passed Kirkcaldy by, but I knew that the lonely road would soon be busy, by virtue of the extra traffic attracted by news of Cade's imminent demise. The clan was already gathering, and the gathering would drag in its fair share of hangers-on and parasites. News of the invocation of Cade's Last Rights hadn't yet been broadcast, but the information would be making its leisurely way through the Net, triggering responses in hundreds, or even thousands, of Sloths. Much that had long been forgotten was about to be remembered as countless soft triggers were pulled. The last war criminal in the world was about to be switched off, and millions of young people who had not yet discovered that there were such things as war criminals were about to get a cautionary dose of education.

As soon as I began to think about it, I realized that Cade's last address to the assembled family would undoubtedly be broadcast live, perhaps to an audience of millions. It would be taped for posterity too. It would be the only chance he had ever had actually to plead his case; despite the label applied to him, he'd never actually been tried in an open court. In the days when there had been enough hatred left to fuel a show-trial, there'd also been enough desperation left to let him get on with the serious business of saving the world. Now, if he took the opportunity, he would be able to set his defense before the world. The world would listen—but would it understand? Could anyone understand, after all this time, all that Cade had done, and why? Could anyone ever have understood, whether in the war-torn twenty-first century, the Spasm-devastated twenty-second, or the rapidly-Repopulated twenty-third?

"It's beautiful," Carol-Anne said, as we drive through the estate—but she didn't mean it. She had been reared to find beauty in gardens, and showcase wilderness. To her, the family land looked scruffy.

"Beauty isn't everything," I told her—but that made her frown, because she took it entirely the wrong way. *She* was beautiful, and wanted that to be everything because she wasn't yet confident enough to think that she had much else to offer, especially now that she knew what a rare and exotic bird I was.

Mum came out to meet us before the car had slowed to a stop. Everybody else would have had to make their own way in, but I was special. She looked even more tired and fretful in the flesh than she had on screen. A hundred voices must have been clamoring for her attention since the small hours, and they weren't going to let up for a week. She couldn't expect Napoleon and his legion of Sloths to keep her safe. Sloths are no good at anything that can't be routinized and even Silvers, for all their superhuman cleverness, can't cope with the unprecedented any better than mere humans. As for the Big Uncles—nothing short of cosmic disaster could cope with *them* when they found an excuse to carp and criticize.

"I'm glad you're here, Carly," Mum said, as soon as she'd hugged me and said a dutiful hello to Carol-Anne. She meant that she hoped that I could take my full share of her burden. "He wants to see you now, but only for a few minutes. He says he has a million trivial things to do before he gets to the important stuff. It's all nonsense of course—there's nothing at all he *has* to do—but that's the way the formalities work. The others will feel slighted if they don't get their chance to say goodbye *properly*. It's going to be *so* difficult, Carly."

I kept my arm around my foster-mother's shoulder as we walked into the mazy corridors of the house, and she took what comfort she could from the gesture. Carol-Anne followed us, carrying her own bag. Although Carol-Anne had met Mum before, it had always been at my place or in Glasgow; she'd never had the opportunity to see us in our native habitat. She looked around in every direction as we went upstairs, but when we got to my old room she fixed her eyes on Mum and me, as if seeing us properly framed for the first time. It wasn't until Mum had gone that Carol-Anne let her eyes travel studiously around the room, taking note of the bed, the curtains, the chairs and the desk.

"Is this really *you*?" she finally enquired, having contrasted its antiquity and dilapidation with the careful modernity of my apartment in Ayr.

"Not really," I said. "Everything here is Cade. He's been here so long he's seeped into the walls and the foundations, the dust and the soft furnishings. It's all reflective of the same genes, but it's not *me*."

"Who was the guy who gave you a filthy look?"

"Which one? The one on the stairs is Cousin Harry; the one who stuck his head out of the room along the corridor is Uncle Jack. He's only a Little Uncle, though—Mum's generation. The Big Uncles will arrive soon, trailing stormclouds, especially the three Sons. Please don't expect me to recognize everyone who gives me a filthy look, or even the ones who are too polite. I can't even begin to sort out the various degrees of relatedness. Far better to take refuge in kiddy-speak and think of them all as uncles, aunts and cousins, little or big according to antiquity. They, of course, have no such trouble regarding me; every one of them knows *my* name and exactly how his or her position on the family tree relates to mine."

Carol-Anne nodded her head yet again, this time with genuine sympathy. The difficulty of keeping the generations of one's ancestors straight was something she did understand. People our age had by far the worst of it, of course, because the Repopulation had imposed such a powerful demand that the intermediate generations separating us from our several-times-great-grandparents should be fruitful and multiply, by whatever means that came to hand. We were more likely to be subject to the opposite kind of pressure.

THE TREE OF LIFE, BY BRIAN STABLEFORD

Our lives would be dominated by the question of how many people the world could and ought to contain, and the question of how to keep that number fixed once it was attained.

I left Carol-Anne to settle in while I went to see Cade. Mum had already moved half a dozen chairs into the corridor outside his room, anticipating the queues that were bound to form—but the vast majority of his descendants had to come from much further afield than Ayr. Uncle Jack had nipped in ahead of me, but as soon as the door-Sloth notified Cade that I was there Jack was summarily dismissed.

The mechanical cocoon that had taken over the burden of Cade's exhausted Internal Technology covered his entire body apart from his head, arms and shoulders. All its complexity was packed into the inner surface; from the outside it looked like a shiny plastic sack. No artificial limbs had been fitted to it to compensate for the nearly-useless ones that rested on the bed. The tubes and leads connecting the cocoon to the house were neatly tucked way under the bed.

"So you finally decided to die, you old bastard," I said, with all the fake acidity I could muster. "About bloody time, isn't it?"

He laughed. The last time I'd seen him, he hadn't had breath enough to muster anything more than a hoarse cackle, but this was a full-throated laugh seemingly redolent with amusement. His face was flushed; the surge of new blood had broken numerous capillaries but it had also put some turgor back into his flesh, lightening the ruggedness of his wrinkles.

I went to pick up his right hand, intending to clasp it to my chest, but he shook his head slightly. I knew immediately what he meant and let the hand lie where it was.

"Somehow," Cade said, "it just doesn't feel as if it's mine any more. Where's Carol-Anne?"

I raised an eyebrow. I had assumed that he'd want to see me on my own.

"I want to look her over," he told me. "I can't die happy unless I know that you've got taste at least as good as mine, can I? Bring her along after the big show. We'll have a real talk, when the crap's run its course. Everything that needed settling is settled, but you have to go through the motions.

Everybody that has a right to be seen has to be seen, every 'I' that has to be dotted and 'T' that has to be crossed. How are *you* feeling?"

"Grief-stricken," I told him, making the effort to sound sarcastic.

He laughed again. "You can't kid me," he said. "You're overjoyed at the thought of being the one and only."

"Sure," I said, dryly. "Overjoyed." I touched him lightly on the cheek, and suppressed a sudden tear. Until that moment, I'd managed to keep the extent and complexity of my feelings submerged, but I couldn't hide from him.

The panel beside the bedhead was already showing three amber lights: calls for his attention that dear old Napoleon had been forced to let through.

"Have to watch your back, Carly," Cade said, soberly. "PEST Control will be on to you, eager to rifle through anything and everything I give you."

"They already paid me a call," I told him. "They knew before I did—serves you right for losing your lungs while I was fast asleep."

He was startled by that, and slightly offended too. "The bastards," he murmured. "After all these years, the hate still lingers. I wish I could believe that there was more to their crusade than petty vindictiveness."

"Perhaps there is," I said. "I think they're genuinely worried abut something. Bugs in the ap-systems, I think—*literal* bugs."

"The best kind. But there's nothing in that to disturb them—not really. Ap may not be DNA-based but it still produces the same old foodstuffs. *Of course* the roaches and the weevils are getting stuck in and having a ball. Always have, always will."

"You have a broader vision than they do," I pointed out. "They're obsessive about control, paranoid about anything they can't quite force into line. They really are worried about the rate of speciation, because it informs them that they aren't yet the emperors of the ecosphere—you're a court jester, murmuring reminders in their ear to the effect that their power isn't godlike."

"That's not it," he said. "They're bursting to know exactly what I did and how because they can't stand *not knowing*. They can't abide the thought that I've kept a secret from them all this time, and that I might be able to deliver it into your safe keeping without it passing through their sticky hands."

I smiled, probably unconvincingly. "We'll keep them guessing for a while yet," I said.

"You'll do a lot better than me, Carly," he said, signifying by his tone that he was no longer talking about PEST Control. "I'd already done a lot of dying before I was kitted out for longevity. With luck, you might live to be a thousand. But you won't have to go through all of this family gathering shit. Before you're much older, courtesy and the law will require people to postpone the business of reproduction until after they're dead."

"We're not quite there yet, Cade," I said. "They've only just authorized the repopulation of Tasmania. Now that Greenland's green again, there's a lot of empty territory in the far north—and the Continental Engineers are talking about raising a thousand new islands in Oceania. The Weather Control people are actually backing them, on the grounds that it will help them fine-tune Greenhouse Compensation."

"All crap," he said, predictably. "I wish I could be around to see it come unstuck. You'll have to say it for me, Carly. The day it all falls apart, I want you to be there to say: *Cade Maclaine told you so.* You'll do that for me, won't you?"

"Depend on it," I assured him. There were now ten amber lights demanding his response. He was pretending not to have noticed them, but I could see that he was getting fidgety—or would have been, if he'd had sufficient control of his fingertips to fidget. Finally, he surrendered to the pressure of inevitability and looked at the bedscreen keyboard.

"After the big show," he said, "Everything will be blocked. *Everything*. We'll have as much peace and quiet then as we need, Carly. Bring Carol-Anne, so that I can take a good look at her—then we can take care of our own business."

"Sure," I said. "If there's anything you need...."

"Shit, Carly—I have everything I need and plenty more, except for time. No power on Earth can give me more of that. If I hadn't signed on the dotted line, I'd have rotted just the same. Best to go while I can still string a sentence together."

I nodded, to show that I understood. Then I kissed his forehead, aiming for the mind within the failing flesh.

"Thursday afternoon," he said. "As soon as the show's over."

"It's a date," I told him, as I moved towards the door. "Best of luck with the valedictory."

"Luck," he assured me, sardonically, "has absolutely nothing to do with it. If a man can't deliver an appropriately hypocritical suicide note, he's got no business dying at all."

* * * * * * *

I helped as much as I could with the logistics of the family gathering, but it wasn't the kind of task at which I excelled, and once the Sons began arriving they began to make a big song and dance about taking care of their responsibilities. The process of sorting out who was going to stay where, and how we were going to accommodate the audience for Cade's final address, was simple enough—Napoleon had no difficulty at all in coming up with optimal distributions—but the real problem was dealing with the backlash of grumbles and complaints. No Son or Silver in the world had genius enough to calm the seething cauldron of real and imagined slights, or patrol the chaotic traffic in hypocritical condolences and inexpertly-veiled insults. I didn't want my share of that—all the more so, given the resentment that my face generated. None of the Big Uncles really remembered what Cade had looked like when he was young, but they only had to look at me to convince themselves that they did, and to resent my imagined sacrilege.

There was, of course, a countervailing flow of honest condolences and polite conversations, sincere expressions of grief and genuine gestures of friendship, but pain never has the slightest difficulty eclipsing pleasure during a wake. No matter how hard you try, the bad things always demand more attention than the good, at least until the whole thing's over. Then the clever sieve of memory can get to work in filtering out the best and consigning the worst to oblivion.

Whenever I could get away, I got as far away as possible. While the weather lasted, I took Carol-Anne on long walks to show her the remotest corners of the estate. I proudly showed her all the local wildlife, no matter how ugly or insignificant. Unfortunately, I also made her stand idly by while I scanned the surfaces of the ap-systems beyond the southern border for tiny signs of dilapidation and infestation. I tried to make it up to her by taking her to the shore of the firth, but Greenhouse Compensation had moved the waterline so markedly during the last half-century that there was nothing at the margin of land and water but a slowly-settling morass. It would be another hundred years before we got the beach back. We sat on a rock above the muddy shore and skimmed stones in the shallows of the firth. The water was still retreating to the second millennium levels presently considered to be optimal, but it hadn't far to go. The estate had just about reached the limit of its acreage.

Unfortunately, the rain that held off on Saturday and Sunday began to fall with grim determination of Monday, and didn't let up for thirty-six hours. Even if the weather hadn't made further outdoor excursions impossible, the local population pressure would have had the same effect. The number of aunts, uncles and cousins taking turns around the perimeter to "get away from it all" would have increased to saturation point by Tuesday morning. The population density indoors was ten or twenty times as great, of course, but indoors has the advantage of being liberally equipped with walls. Indoors, you can always hide—and if you switch off the neighborhood Sloths, you can protect your privacy from everyone except discreet electronic eavesdroppers.

So hide we did. Sometimes, Carol-Anne and I took the opportunity to enjoy one another's close company, but we mostly did what everyone else was doing—including Cade, alongside his petty valedictory duties. We watched TV.

TV was the panacea that kept everybody's woes and worries at bay, because it offered us a delicately-curved mirror in which all our private concerns were reflected and distorted. Now that he was dying, the world had briefly rediscovered Cade Carlyle Maclaine, and all his long-forgotten but never-forgiven sins were taken down from the shelf and dusted off for reconsideration. The exercise of his Last Rights became the hook on which to hang a orgy of remembrance; for a few dark days the Plague War was hot news, or at least hot history.

So far as I could tell, from an admittedly patchy sample, four-fifths of the TV coverage was about the Plague War and the Spasm, and four-fifths of the remainder was about Cade's informal judgment and not-so-informal penance. Only a tiny fraction of the family-related TV time was devoted to his work on omnispores, and most of that was straightforwardly historical. Nothing was said about the possible contribution that Cade's omnispores might be making to the continuing emergence of new invertebrate species, let alone the hypothesis that there might be banks of natural omnispores waiting patiently in the Asteroid Belt to reboot the ecosphere if it were ever disrupted so severely that no human Arkwrights would be around to oversee the job.

Carol-Anne watched the Cade-inspired documentaries with as much fascination as I did, not because she was passionately interested in history's official verdict on the life and works of Cade Maclaine, but because she wanted to be able to understand as fully as possible what my mysterious legacy might amount to.

"The omnispores that Cade Maclaine devised," one dutiful voice explained, in that curious purring tone which documentary voices always assume, "were awkward and unstable, even by the normal standards of natural biological material. There is an understandable temptation to think of omnispores simply as massive eggs crammed with the chromosomal packs of dozens of different species, but that analogy is misleading. Maclaine's DNA superstrings were much longer than the chromosomes of any existing species; they were chromosomal libraries of the genes possessed by what he deemed to be *archetype species*—species closest to the root stocks of whole genera or families.

"These superstrings were capable of reproducing themselves *in toto*, exactly as ordinary chromosomes do in mitosis, but they were also capable of fragmenting into thousands of randomly-formulated subunits, any group of which could isolate itself from the protoplasmic mass within a nuclear membrane. These isolated sets of chromosomes would test their own viability as potential egg-cells by attempting to divide into two, then four and then eight associated cellules. Those which succeeded would then borrow oval surrounds from the reproductive apparatus of their host species—most famously, the American cockroach.

"The anomalous omnispore-carrying eggs would be laid by the host along with clutches of ordinary eggs; any organisms they produced would be capable of parthenogenetic reproduction as well as sexual reproduction, and the archetypal species thus regenerated would be ripe for rapid evolution and diversification in response to whatever conditions they might find and set forth to modify...."

"It's too superficial," Carol-Anne complained, in disgust. "The explanations don't have sufficient depth or detail."

"It's still too complicated to hold its audience," I said, pointing to the indicator gauge, which had registered low to begin with and was now descending into abyssal depths. "Anyone who really cares will use the Library. This junk is just to reassure the people who are watching the summary obituaries that they really don't want or need to know exactly what it was that Cade *ought* to be famous for. It's so much simpler to understand how he and his co-conspirators played along with the generals, making hardier strains of smallpox and AIDS and devising cleverer ways of distributing them to a target population while leaving everyone on the side of the angels untouched."

We watched the program to the end anyway, helping to keep a little light shining on the indicator gauge.

"How many calls from TV people have the Sloths intercepted now?" Carol-Anne asked—meaning calls to me rather than to the family entire.

"A couple of hundred," I said.

"Are you ever going to talk to any of them?"

"No. I've got a dozen Big Uncles who are only too happy to feed their appetite; they only want me because I'm the kid with Cade Maclaine's very own face. Once the switch is thrown it'll all die away—except, of course, for the Dead Cat Squad. *They*'ll still want to keep track of me."

She went to consult the register of her own messages; requests from various journalists to talk to her were mounting up. I could see that she was tempted, but while I was keeping quiet she felt obliged to stay in step.

"Strange that they should be called Sloths when they're so hard-working," she observed.

"The name has nothing to do with the deadly sin," I said, unable to resist the temptation to show off my erudition. "In the early days, systems of that general kind were called AIs. In the beginning that stood for Artificial Intelligence, but when the first Silvers were developed it was necessary to make a distinction. Common parlance began to discriminate between Artificial Geniuses on the one hand and Artificial Idiots and Imbeciles on the other. Silvers got their nickname from the chemical symbol for silver, Ag, and the dictionary obligingly revealed to people who'd never before had occasion to look that *ai* was the Tupi name for the three-toed sloth. It started as a joke."

"Your great-great-great-great-grandfather must be very proud of you, Carly," she observed, proving that there's many a true word spoken in jest.

"I had a lot of expectation to live up to," I told her, not jesting in the least.

Evening mealtimes were the hardest of all because protocol demanded that all those members of the family who still called Elba House "home" should actually gather together—except, of course, for those requiring non-portable life-support systems. My presence was obligatory, but Carol-Anne was in the invidious position of taking up a place at the fourteen-seater table which might otherwise have been available to a Big Uncle or Aunt. Everyone was terribly polite to her, but she sometimes felt—understandably—that she was under bombardment.

The conversation at dinner was invariably as boring and as stodgy as the food, and wine was not served. Nobody in the British Isles had contrived to shake off the dread legacy of the fact that it had been Stornoway, not Bordeaux, that had kept the flickering candle of civilization alight through the Spasm's generation-long Dark Age. Because their misappropriated names all began with "Mac," most of my older aunts and uncles thought that the new British Commonwealth really ought to be called the Scottish Empire.

Mum had by now been joined by my official foster-father, Stephen Harding Maclaine, who had always filled that position rather grudgingly, knowing full well that Cade was my *real* foster-father. Fortunately, the title carried with it certain responsibilities in respect of Mum, the house and me, so Dad was obliged to pull his weight both organizationally and conversationally.

As the main-course dishes were being cleared away on the evening before Cade's farewell address, my foster-father leaned towards me and said: "Carly, do you know a man called Chesterton? Alexander Chesterton?"

"We've met," I said.

"Same crew that keeps searching the house and grounds, I suppose?"

"The name of the Department changes periodically," I agreed, dolefully, "but the mission remains the same."

Dad nodded, philosophically. "Do you think they'll stop now?" he asked.

"With luck," I said, guardedly, having belatedly realized that he was trying to pump me.

"Nothing in it, I suppose? There isn't actually any secret to pass on, is there?"

I was suddenly aware that all the other dialogues-in-progress had lapsed, and that a profound and pregnant silence had descended. I realized, with a slight shock, that some of Cade's authority had already passed to me. It wasn't just that Dad expected me to know the answer; *everyone* expected me to know. The power was delicious; so was the temptation to dissemble.

"If there is," I said, judiciously, "you can rely on me to keep it in the family. We all owe Cade that much, don't we?"

The Tree of Life, by Brian Stableford

For the first time, I realized that there is a unique joy to be found in filthy looks—but when I turned to Carol-Anne with a beaming smile, she didn't smile back.

"Has the old man told you what his big speech is going to be about?" Dad asked, trying to sound condescending.

"No," I said, "I think he wants it to be a surprise."

"Judging by the TV coverage," Dad pressed on, knowing that the eyes and ears of all the diners were still firmly fixed on the pair of us, "it would be a very wise move not to talk about the war. If he tries to justify what he did...."

"He's not a man to do the obvious thing," I said, reassuringly. "If he were, the world might still be a desert, and civilization might have been lost forever, even in Stornoway."

* * * * * * *

Mercifully, the weather brightened up considerably once the deluge had exhausted itself. I say "mercifully" because Cade wanted the family to gather outdoors to hear his final address. It would have to be relayed by video, of course, because his cocoon was immobile, but he had ordered a giant screen from Edinburgh, which was to be erected beside the house, facing outwards to the south-east. He wanted the family distributed in a great semi-circle with the headland and the firth at their backs, surrounded by the wildland—or, to be strictly accurate, the insects and spiders infesting the wildland. The world could watch from its myriad couches, surrounded by walls, but the family had to be knee-deep in Cade's pride and joy, however uncomfortable it became.

By the time his final address began he had seen everyone individually, if only for a matter of minutes, and the elaborate terms of his will had already been made public, but there are different kinds of farewell and different kinds of legacy. I heard half a hundred bitter complaints about being required to stand in a field, but I knew that no one had dared to stay indoors watching on TV. I was positioned between Mum and Carol-Anne, with an arm round each of them.

When Cade's face appeared on the screen I was surprised how hollow it looked. His eyes seemed to have shrunk back into their orbits, and his cheeks had lost the pressurized bloom they had worn when I'd seen him in the flesh. He was obviously and conspicuously tired: a dying man putting on a show of dying.

It was, as he had promised, a big show—but it was not at all what I'd expected.

He began by thanking everyone for coming, keeping his voice low although there was no physiological necessity. He told them how pleased he was to have become the patriarch of such a vast and multi-talented family, and how proud he was of all their myriad accomplishments. He told them how enormously privileged he felt, all the more so because he had spent his formative years in a world in which large families were frowned upon, because of the strain they put on the ecosphere. He did not mention that the "strain" in question had precipitated the Spasm.

He claimed to be equally proud, pleased and privileged because of the work he had been able to do in the aftermath of the ecocatastrophe that had all-but-destroyed the world. He made no mention whatsoever of the war that had preceded that catastrophe.

He was, he said, extremely glad that he had been able to play a part, however small, in the salvation of civilization from the direst threat it had ever faced. He made no mention of the fact that civilization had brought that disaster upon itself, and had failed to recognize that it was happening until it was far too late.

Because he had been a working biotechnologist during the Dark Age, he said, he was now able to think of himself as a foster-parent to *all* of the people of the new world, and to love them as much as he loved the members of his actual foster-family and all of *their* foster-children. He was able to take a delight in all their achievements, all their accomplishments, all their ambitions.

And so it went on.

Although he had warned me, during our brief interview, I hadn't taken the warning seriously. I had never imagined that there might be so much hypocrisy in the old man, nor that he was capable of pouring out such an astonishing cataract of treacle.

THE TREE OF LIFE, BY BRIAN STABLEFORD

He went on to talk about his hopes for the future of the world. He said that he had every faith in the ability of his foster-children, and their foster-children, and all the multitudes he thought of as his foster-children, to keep the new world safe—to make sure that the ecosphere would never suffer another Spasm. He complimented the ingenuity of the new generation of biotechnologists, who had devised such marvelous systems of artificial photosynthesis, and he complimented the ingenuity of Nature, which was generating new species at such a phenomenal rate. He apologized—actually *apologized*—for the special sentimental interest which he had always taken in insects and arachnids, and expressed the hope that the people of the future would be more appreciative of the wonderful work they did in sustaining the complexity of the ecosphere. There was no obvious *wit* in what he said, no contrived cleverness; it was all cliché, all banality.

I could not help but wonder whether he meant the insincerity of his words to be more obvious than it was. The people actually standing in the field on every side of me knew full well, of course, that he did not mean a word of it, but how could the millions watching him on TV have known it? Perhaps, I thought, he was taking it for granted that everything he said would be construed as sarcasm—and perhaps he was wrong to do so. No sooner had I thought that, however, than I was forced to wonder whether he might know perfectly well that the vast majority of those who were listening to him would simply take him at his word, not knowing enough about him to penetrate the levels of hidden meaning. Then again, I had to wonder how deep those layers of hidden meaning actually went. Did he intend the members of his immediate family—especially me—to be able to read between the lines of his speech in a way that others could not? Was he actually trying to say something to me and others like me that was not apparent on the surface—and, if so, what?

I could not tell. I could not, for the life of me, figure out why he was piling one sanctimonious vapidity on another, and another on top of that, instead of simply saying what he really thought...always assuming that I actually knew what he *really thought*.

So I stood, uncomprehending, as Cade Carlyle Maclaine Senior told the people of the world what a privilege it had been to have lived so long among them, and how much he had enjoyed their company, and how glad he was to be able to say goodbye in this ordered and dignified fashion, and how much he loved life: *real life*, in all of its magical richness and strangeness and loveliness.

Towards the end, I found myself railing silently against him, saying: *Tell them about the Plague War! Tell them how you had to fight to save the world in secret, because you dared not let your masters know that you weren't laboring full-time on ways of killing people! Tell them what it felt like to be hounded and harassed during and after the Spasm, always under threat of being charged as a war criminal but never actually granted the privilege of a trial at which you could have set your defense on record! Tell them how monstrously unjust it is that your greatest triumph—the technological miracle that repopulated the ecosphere so that the world of men could be repopulated in its wake—should have been derided and dismissed as the Trojan Cockroach Plan! Tell them that the vast new family of man is reaching the limit of its expansion, and that if it can't find a broader and better consensus than the one that exists within the ranks of your foster-descendants, then the next Plague War will be upon us soon enough, and the next Spasm too!*

But he said none of that. It was sugar and spice and all things nice. It was nothing remotely like the Cade Maclaine I knew—the Cade Maclaine whose clone I was.

As his oration wound down, he addressed himself again to the people actually gathered in and around Elba House. He thanked us all for listening, and for coming to mourn his passing. He told us that he hoped with all his heart that we would be able to live happy and creative lives, no matter what challenges we would have to meet in the course of our long existence. He said goodbye, over and over again—and almost wept.

Almost, but not quite; of that hypocrisy, at least, he was incapable.

When the screen went blank, the crowd moved back towards the house, dispersing as it went. I moved with a better sense of purpose than anyone, dragging Carol-Anne behind me.

* * * * * * *

"All this must be very boring for you, Carol-Anne," Cade said, when we had taken up our positions by his bedside. "Family business is always tedious, always impenetrable to outsiders. I'm sorry. Carly should have brought you to see me before."

"It's all right," she replied, valiantly. "I wish I'd met you before, but I'm glad to have met you now." She'd obviously caught the mood of his valedictory speech.

"I'm glad too," he said. "Unfortunately, the family business isn't quite done. I'll have to ask you to leave us alone for a while."

"No problem," she said. She touched the old man's cheek before she left, and slightly increased the flush that sat upon it. Cade's eyes were no longer feverish, and his artificially-assisted voice was strong and level as he bade her a fond farewell.

As soon as the door closed behind her the lights flickered, and the temporary silence became strangely profound.

"It's okay," Cade said. "Napoleon's closed everything down. He's killed the bugs the eavesdroppers planted, inside and out. We have privacy, at least for a little while."

"You're sure they're all out of commission?" I said, warily.

"Of course I'm sure. Chesterton's cronies may think they're professionals, but not one of them has ever employed or endured the kind of surveillance that was routine in Geneva. I know more about the business of keeping secrets than they'll ever learn, and they know it."

"Well, you certainly don't believe in letting people know what you really think," I said, trying to keep a tight rein on the resentment I couldn't help but feel, "and you certainly haven't lost the art of surprising your nearest and dearest."

"Don't be angry, Carly," he said. "I didn't give them the truth because they haven't *earned* the truth. I've always saved the truth for the people who were entitled to it."

"Your other self," I said, dryly. "They were right, weren't they? The Uncles, even that bastard Chesterton. You wouldn't trust your secrets to anyone but yourself—but because you had to die, you had to go for the next best thing."

He looked at me sharply. "You don't sound too pleased about it," he observed.

I took a deep breath. "I'm not you, Cade," I said. "I may look like you—or like you used to look in your glorious heyday—but I'm not *you*. I haven't been formed by the kind of world that formed you. I don't have your paranoia. I'm not at all sure that I want to live the next few centuries the way you've lived the last few, guarding secrets and playing games—and I'm *very* sure that I never want to subject anyone to the kind of contempt that you've just poured all over your immediate family and everyone else who cared to listen. I've been a part of your game for a while now, and I won't say that it hasn't been fun, but I'm not sure that I can see any good reason for carrying on with it."

Cade looked up at me, with less hurt in his expression than I had feared to see.

"You're right," he said. "You weren't formed by the world that formed me. You didn't live through the war, desperately glad for the protection that came with being an expert designer of cunning weapons. They *were* cunning, Carly—not just because of the work that went into their design, but by their very nature. Plague War isn't like other kinds of war, you know—it's war by stealth, with betrayal built into it at every level. If you want to wipe out your declared and recognized enemies, you use bullets and nukes. Plague War is for your neighbors, for the people you want to wipe out without their ever suspecting that you want them dead. You didn't live through the Spasm, either, having lost all hope for humankind. You'll never know what it is to have nothing left to pray for but the possibility that the cockroaches might make it, and might carry the seeds of something better through the worst of the worst. Even *you*, Carly, can't even begin to imagine the experiences that shaped me—so don't you get pissy with me because I didn't try to explain it to the world at large."

That stung—but I could see a glimmer of justice in it, and he *was* dying.

"I'm not getting pissy with you," I lied. "I just don't know whether I can keep your precious secrets, if they even exist. I'm not sure that I can keep Chesterton and the Inquisition at bay, and I'm not sure that I even want to."

"Fair enough," he said. "But don't make up your mind until you know what they are—and they most certainly do exist. It wasn't just the habit of keeping my true feelings secret from anyone I didn't trust that I acquired in the bad old days. I also got the habit of keeping *very* meticulous records. I was *extremely* paranoid—but in those days, anyone who wasn't paranoid was off his fucking head. Do you really think that the world's changed? Do you really think that it doesn't make sense to be paranoid any more?"

"I think it's at least *possible* that PEST Control really are worried about problems of pest control," I admitted, uncomfortably. "I even think that the kind of control they want to exercise over the ecosphere isn't entirely a bad thing. I'm not your double, Cade. I don't want you handing me any secrets under the assumption that I'll look after them the way you have, for the same reasons. You have to understand that whatever you give me will become mine. I don't want to be permanently in trouble, Cade. I don't want Chesterton on my back for the next ten years, let alone the next hundred. I don't know how you've managed to hide your secret files for so long, and I admire the fact that you've been able to do it in spite of all the searches, but I'm not sure that I'll want to continue the game once I'm the only player on my side."

He didn't seem disappointed. In fact, he seemed ever so slightly *amused*. I realized that he must have anticipated the possibility that I'd react this way—and that he still thought that he had the last trump in his hand.

"Would you rather I didn't tell you?" he asked. "Would you rather leave now, and never know where I put the files?"

"It wouldn't do any good," I pointed out. "If Napoleon really has killed all the bugs, Chesterton will assume that I know even if I don't. If I really *don't* know, I'll *never* be able to get him off my back. If I do, at least I have the choice."

Cade knew that, of course. "You really haven't worked out where I put the files?" he said, challenging me one last time.

"No," I admitted, "I haven't. But I don't know how clever Napoleon really is, and I don't know the family estate like the back of my hand. There might be a hundred hidey-holes I couldn't know about."

He sighed, but time was getting short. "No place on Earth would be safe," he said. "I had to put the files where people couldn't get at them, even if they knew where to look. I uploaded them to the Chaos Patrol. Everything I ever wanted to hide is in orbit on the far side of Mars. You and Napoleon will have to work together to release it. No one else can do it without the full co-operation of both parties—unless, of course, they have some way of getting hold of the actual hardware. You can tell Chesterton that, if you want—but you might not want to."

"Why not?" I asked, knowing that there had to be a reason, even if it reeked of paranoia.

"Because he's a liar, like all of his kind. I'm sure he'd like to get hold of the omnispore records if he could, but concentrating his and your attention exclusively on them is a ploy. It's the other records he *really* wants to find."

"What *other records*?" I asked, although I thought I had it figured out.

"Don't be naive, Carly. As I said, I got into the habit of keeping *very* meticulous records. When they closed Geneva down, the bosses got all the official records of the work we were supposed to be doing, but we were the people doing the work and we were just as anxious to cover our arses as our careful superiors were to cover theirs. The Chaos Patrol has all the documents the bosses didn't want to leave lying around for posterity, and it has all the documents the bosses didn't even know we had. Come on, Carly, did you *really* think that I was never prosecuted because the world was prepared to forgive and forget? I always knew *too much*, not just about the way the ecosphere was saved, but about the way it was damned in the first place. If you give Alexander

Chesterton everything that's locked up safe and sound in the memory-banks of those satellites, you'd better pray that you won't have to be an innocent bystander in the next Plague War. I know more about security than he does, because I've had more practice—and I also know a hell of a lot more about the art, science and downright dirtiness of plague warfare than he ever will. I've spent the last three hundred years trying to make sure that it stays that way."

"You could have wiped the files," I pointed out.

"So I could," he said. "But the real artistry of plague warfare is in the defense, not the attack. Anyone who has the data will be better equipped to launch a plague war because they'll be better equipped to make sure they survive it—but anyone who *hasn't* got the data is going to be left flat-footed if anyone else launches one. I'm paranoid, Carly—I never throw anything away, just in case the day comes when I need it. I don't want to hand it over to PEST Control, in case they start using it to clear out the wrong pests, but I don't want it destroyed, because there might come a day when the pests really do get out of hand. That includes flies and mites—but it's not the flies and mites that cause the worst problems."

"And you always thought that you were the only one capable of making that decision?" I said, knowing that he very probably did. "You've always thought that you were the only one who could be trusted with the responsibility—except, of course, for your faithful clone-brother."

"I had it," Cade said, stubbornly. "Nobody else did, once my co-workers had been swept away. I never felt like giving it to anyone else, but as you pointed out, I can't hang on to it forever. It's you or them, Carly, and I prefer you. Once I give you the codes, it'll be your decision, your responsibility. You can give it away if you want to, or you can keep it. You're not me, because you haven't grown up in a paranoid world—but what you have to ask yourself, Carly, is what kind of a world you're going to be living in when you get older, and older, and older. Just how confident are you of the new order, the black world? You can get Alexander Chesterton off your back, if you want to, for ten or a hundred years—but what you have to ask yourself is whether *anything* you do can keep people like him off your back forever, and whether they're the kind of people who can be trusted to run the world for the next *thousand* years. If you're even a little bit like me, and I think you are, you'll decide that there's no rush—that maybe you'll come clean tomorrow, or the next day, but for now you'll hang on to what you've got, just in case."

I looked down at him, remembering that he probably knew certain aspects of me better than I knew myself.

Finally, I said: "Are you *sure* that Napoleon has killed all the bugs?"

"Oh yes," he said. "Of that I'm sure. He's not really a he, of course. He's just a machine—but you and he will be able to have a lot of fun together, when you get to know one another a little bit better. He's very good at games."

* * * * * * *

Carol-Anne and I hadn't been back at my apartment for half an hour before Alexander Chesterton turned up, cramming the inevitable warrant into the Sloth's slack mouth. This time, Carol-Anne wasn't content to eavesdrop; she stayed in the room while the government man took up his position in the guest armchair, eyeing the pair of us speculatively.

"Don't tell me," I said. "You need to talk to me about the terms of Cade Maclaine's will, and the substance of my inheritance."

"We've seen the will," he said, dismissively. "What we need to talk to you about it what passed between you and Cade Maclaine Senior in the hour immediately preceding his death. I'll have to ask for your affirmation, of course."

For once, as I promised to tell the truth, the whole truth and nothing but the truth, I wasn't able to take refuge in the fact that I could do exactly as promised and not give anything away.

"Cade Carlyle Maclaine Junior," Chesterton said, sonorously. "Have you, since you last gave testimony, received from Cade Carlyle Maclaine Senior any information related to the researches which Cade Carlyle Maclaine Senior carried out in and around the city of Geneva between 2034 and 2074?"

"Yes," I said.

"Do you know where any records of that research are kept?"

"I know where certain records *were* kept," I admitted.

"Where were they kept?" Chesterton was looking at me with keen interest, avid to find out what my next move would be, but my scrupulously pedantic shift of tense had brought a slight frown to his face.

"They were uploaded by Cade Maclaine into the guidance computers installed in a ring of artificial satellites set up in the twenty-first century to track comets and monitor fluctuations in the orbits of asteroids."

I was glad that I'd told him, because it would have been a pity to have missed the expression of shock and slight disgust which crossed his face. Like me, he hadn't been able to guess, and like me he'd immediately started kicking himself because he figured that he *ought* to have guessed. He had to pause for a moment or two in order to formulate the next question.

"Do you know the codes which would give an earthbound observer access to those records?" he asked.

"No," I said.

"I suggest that you think very carefully about that answer, Mr. Maclaine," he said.

"I have," I assured him, truthfully. "And I suggest that you think very carefully too, about the question. To the best of my knowledge and belief, there are no longer any such codes—because, to the best of my knowledge and belief, the records in question no longer exist."

"And what reason do you have to think so?" he asked, sharply.

"Because, with the assistance of the Silver at Elba House and with Cade Maclaine Senior's consent, some fifteen minutes before Cade's life was terminated, I transmitted an instruction to the satellite-computers which shredded all the records he had placed there. There's nothing left in the repositories but random numbers."

That brought Alexander Chesterton bounding out of his seat.

"You did *what*?" he demanded.

"I believe," I said, coldly, "that I have already answered that question." I looked at Carol-Anne, who was regarding me with as much amazement as the civil servant—but her eyes were already clouded with doubt, because she couldn't quite believe that it was true. Chesterton had to wait until his alarm had faded before it could be replaced with a similar skepticism.

"Are you aware," he said, when he had recovered his composure, "that if what you say is true you then have committed an offence under the terms of Act...?"

"No," I said, not waiting to hear which Act I had allegedly violated. "To the best of my knowledge and belief, those records were private, relating entirely to research which Cade Maclaine carried out on his own initiative, and to which no present government has any justifiable claim. To the best of my knowledge and belief, the records were also irrelevant to any contemporary concerns, given that the omnispores whose design was catalogued therein no longer exist."

"You were warned...," Chesterton began.

I cut him off again. "I heard the warning, Mr. Chesterton. If you want to charge me, charge me. Then we can discuss in open court the exact nature and extent of the information you've been trying to recover, and your probable motives for attempting to recover it. I shall be perfectly happy to explain my reasons for destroying the information, and to have those reasons placed on the official record."

"Maclaine would never have let you do it," he said, not bothering to formulate the judgment as a question.

"He needed his secrets to keep him alive and interested," I retorted. "I don't. I don't have his frailties, or his history. I'm not him. He understood that. He *always* understood it. He gave me the option, but when I made my decision, he was perfectly happy to carry his secrets to the grave, where they belong."

"You're lying," he said.

"It's the truth," I assured him. "It's the *whole* truth, and nothing but the truth. If you don't believe me, you can interrogate the satellite computers—and if and when you revive the space program, and send someone who can check the hardware, you'll have the final proof. I fully intend to be around when that day comes, so I certainly wouldn't take the risk of lying about it. I'd like you to leave now, if you don't mind. The founder of my family is dead, as is my one and only clone-brother. I'm still trying to come to terms with that. I don't think we have anything further to say to one another—now or ever."

For a moment, I thought that he might sit down again, out of sheer stubbornness, but he didn't. After a moment's hesitation, he nodded his head. As he left, though, he took care to say: "This isn't the end of the matter, Mr. Maclaine. We *will* check the satellite computers—and we'll certainly keep a very close watch on any traffic between the satellites and the Elba House Silver. If you ever attempt to access those files...."

"There are no files," I told him. "Not any more."

He didn't believe me. Nor would his superiors.

I sat down, but Carol-Anne remained standing. We'd been in the car for over two hours, and she had become used to he fact that there was no point in asking questions which caution and pragmatism forbade me to answer. She had to use her eyes to say the words that she couldn't speak.

Are you lying? her eyes asked. *Are you taking up where Cade left of, ready to play the game forever?*

"I'm starving," I said, as affably as I could. "It's a bit late, but shall we get something to eat?"

I knew then that she would never be able to take my word for it. She would never be able to rest content with the notion that I had done what I said I had done. She would never be able to accept that, although I was Cade's clone, I wasn't his shadow, his heir, his second self. It was one thing for Alexander Chesterton to take that view, because he was professionally obliged to, but Carol-Anne was different. I wondered whether I ought to like her less or more because she couldn't take my word for what I said. It wasn't a failure of trust. In a way, it was a special kind of trust—a trust that took it for granted that I would never yield to external pressure, and that I would always find a way of staying one step ahead of any game I decided to play.

I suddenly realized that I could change my name now, if I wanted to. Now that I was the one and only, I could be Cade *or* Carly—or maybe even both.

"Are you really that hungry?" she asked, lightly. Alexander Chesterton could never have contrived such a deft question.

"Yes," I said. "I wasn't earlier, but I am now. It's been a long, hard day at the end of a long, hard week, and I've really built up an appetite."

"In that case," she said, "I'll see if the cockroaches have left you anything that's fit to eat."

"Don't disparage the cockroaches," I told her. "They might not look like much, but their great-great-great-great grandparents were hosts to multitudes. Even now, there may be a few left who have hidden agendas."

"Even now," she agreed, in a manner which suggested that she really had been glad to have had the opportunity to meet Cade Carlyle Maclaine before he said goodbye.

ABOUT THE AUTHOR

BRIAN STABLEFORD was born in Yorkshire in 1948. He taught at the University of Reading for several years, but is now a full-time writer. He has written many science fiction and fantasy novels, including *The Empire of Fear, The Werewolves of London, Year Zero, The Curse of the oral Bride* and *The Stones of Camelot.* Collections of his short stories include *Sexual Chemistry: Sardonic Tales of the Genetic Revolution, Designer Genes: Tales of the Biotech Revolution*, and *Sheena and Other Gothic Tales.* He has written numerous non-fiction books, including *Scientific Romance in Britain, 1890-1950, Glorious Perversity: The Decline and Fall of Literary Decadence* and *Science Fact and Science Fiction: An Encyclopedia.* He has contributed hundreds of biographical and critical entries to reference books, including both editions of *The Encyclopedia of Science Fiction* and several editions of the library guide *Anatomy of Wonder.* He has also translated numerous novels from the French language, including several by the feuilletonist Paul Féval.

CPSIA information can be obtained at www.ICGtesting.com
Printed in the USA
LVOW08s2143261113

362919LV00002B/369/A